THE SIMPLE TRUTH

www.penguin.co.uk

Also by James Buckler

LAST STOP TOKYO

THE SIMPLE TRUTH

James Buckler

doubleday

TRANSWORLD PUBLISHERS
Penguin Random House, One Embassy Gardens,
8 Viaduct Gardens, London SW11 7BW
www.penguin.co.uk

Transworld is part of the Penguin Random House group of companies
whose addresses can be found at global.penguinrandomhouse.com

Penguin
Random House
UK

First published in Great Britain in 2022 by Doubleday
an imprint of Transworld Publishers

A CIP catalogue record for this book
is available from the British Library.

ISBNs 9781787636064 (hb)
9781787636071 (tpb)

Typeset in 11.5/16pt Sabon by Jouve (UK), Milton Keynes
Printed and bound in Great Britain by Clays Ltd, Elcograf S.p.A.

The authorized representative in the EEA is Penguin Random House Ireland,
Morrison Chambers, 32 Nassau Street, Dublin D02 YH68.

Penguin Random House is committed to a sustainable future
for our business, our readers and our planet. This book is made
from Forest Stewardship Council® certified paper.

For Jane

Prologue

MIST DRIFTED OVER the frozen ground. Dawn was breaking. A low winter sun skirted the treetops. The marshland lay still, the reed beds dusted with frost. To the south, the Thames curled through the landscape, rippling over the mudflats where its flow met the incoming tide. Beyond the horizon, London began to stir as the city woke to a new day.

The dogs were out in front, their owner following behind, still warm from his bed, shattering ice in the puddles with his heavy boots. Beyond the entrance to the nature reserve, a car was parked in the lane, two wheels in the drainage ditch, listing like a shipwreck under the bare branches of the sycamores. At first the dog walker thought the car was abandoned, by joyriders perhaps, or a drunk driver. Seeing there was no damage, no broken glass or dented panels, his second guess was an early morning tryst. It wasn't unusual for this part of Coldharbour Marshes. Either way, it was none of his business. He intended to give the car a wide berth as he passed.

The dogs had other intentions. They sniffed the wet ground

around the tyres, growling furiously as if they had cornered some prey. The walker slowed his pace, expecting a frightened rabbit to burst free and dart across the lane to the safety of the undergrowth. The lead dog, a golden Labrador, dark with mud to its haunches, began to sniff at the driver's door, standing on its hind legs to gain a better vantage. 'What have you found there, boy?' his owner called.

Wary of disturbing a moment of passion, the walker peered cautiously through the driver's window. The glass was misted with frozen condensation. He wiped the ice crystals from the surface with his sleeve but still couldn't make out anything inside. Squinting hard, his hands cupped against his face, he could just about see a blurred shape lying across the front seats. He tapped on the glass and looked again but there was no movement or sound. Maybe it was a blanket or coat that someone had left inside? He couldn't be sure. He walked around to the front of the car, scanning the vehicle for clues. A note was tucked beneath one of the wiper blades. It was handwritten on a single sheet of waterlogged paper, the ink running in spidery patterns, the words deformed. Craning forward he could just make out the text.

BEWARE. DO NOT OPEN. CALL POLICE.

He stood back for a moment, the dogs circling him excitedly, and pushed his hands deeper into his pockets. Should he carry on walking? This wasn't any of his concern, after all. But what if someone was hurt? What if his intervention was a matter of life and death? It was in his nature to help in circumstances like this. A Good Samaritan streak, his friends called it.

He took the dogs further along the lane to a safe distance and told them to sit. When they heard the grave note in his voice, they squatted side by side on the wet gravel, panting. Returning to the car, he took one last look through the fogged glass. It was still all a blur. Reaching for the handle, he pulled the door open.

That was when he saw her. It was only a glimpse. A shutter-stop image. She was lying on her side, knees huddled to her chest, still and cold. Her mouth was slightly open, her lips pursed in a tight circle, eyes wide like she was caught in the beam of a strong spotlight. Her blonde hair hung over her face in damp strands, skin as pale as milk under lines of black mascara.

Then he felt it in his nostrils. A caustic bite that made him instinctively twist away and take a faltering step backwards towards the tangled hedgerow. As he breathed in, a burning hit his throat and lungs, scouring soft tissue and flecking his lips with blood and foam. He fell to his knees, spluttering, his eyes wild.

He lay there an hour or more, rotting leaves disintegrating on the sodden ground around him, shadows falling over his prone figure as the bodywork of the car rattled in the wind. Crows settled on the high branches, staring down, beady-eyed. Over the horizon, the sound of traffic rumbled on. At the end of the lane, the dogs waited, tongues lolling, sitting obediently under a rain-heavy sky.

1

THE NEGOTIATION WAS nearly over. The lawyers had been working through the night, haggling over the smallest of details. The conference room was scattered with coffee cups and takeaway boxes containing the remnants of half-eaten meals. Pale sunlight caught the motes of dust hanging in the stale air. At around four that afternoon, a German merchant bank would be purchased by a British conglomerate. There would be handshakes and practised smiles and empty promises to meet later for drinks. Lewis Miller was fighting the drag of fatigue, willing the clock to wind faster. Lean and solemn with sandy hair and an air of thoughtful concentration, he tracked his pen across the text of the contract as the speaker droned from the head of the room. Around the conference table, other lawyers representing different parties, all in various states of dishevelment, steeled themselves to reach the finish line.

Lewis was focused on the page before him when his phone rattled on the mahogany tabletop. It lay face down, light pulsing from its edges as a message came through. Disapproving eyes looked up from paperwork. The speaker gave a low grunt of irritation. Lewis grabbed the phone, cursing himself. He was sure he'd switched it off. As the junior member of the team, he was supposed to stay in the background, unheard, ready when called upon to supply a statistic or point of law. For the majority of the night he had followed the proceedings in silence. The lack of influence was hard to bear. It wasn't in his nature to remain on the sidelines.

Lewis glanced at the screen like a poker player protecting his hand. He frowned momentarily as he saw the name of the sender. The skin on the back of his neck turned cold. The message was ruthlessly brief.

Outside. Five minutes. It's urgent.

He leaned into the ear of the senior negotiator seated beside him.

'I have to go,' he whispered.

'Who is it?'

Lewis breathed the name. 'Charlie King.'

As head of the Commercial Division, Charlie King was someone Lewis had only heard speak from behind a lectern when giving his standard motivational address at the quarterly team meetings. He wasn't the kind of man to fire off random text messages to junior employees.

The negotiator turned to him in surprise. 'What does Charlie King want with you?' he asked.

'I have no idea,' Lewis whispered.

The negotiator's expression darkened. 'What have you done?' he growled.

Lewis ran a mental recap of his previous week's work. He couldn't recall any mistakes that were sacking offences.

He shrugged. 'Nothing. As far as I know.'

Offering a weak smile to the room, Lewis stood and pushed his chair back into place. The meeting continued without pause, the speaker paying no attention to his exit. Lewis closed the door gently behind him as he stepped out into the corridor.

We are what we repeatedly do, he thought as he descended in the lift. It was a mantra he used often, one his father had taught him as a child. Lately what Lewis did repeatedly was bite his tongue and hold the muscles in his face still as he was condescended to and snapped at by privileged superiors. Ordinarily he was confident and assertive, quick to snap back when provoked, but it was a tactical necessity to conceal these attributes at work. He wasn't one of 'them', that much was made plain to him every day. He hadn't attended the right schools and wasn't part of the same network of old family connections as his colleagues. He was a cuckoo in the nest and, until he could prove himself, he was determined not to get ejected. To play along quietly and do nothing to jeopardize his precarious place on the career ladder. He was biding his time and needed to be patient. Lewis knew his professional future depended on it.

Outside, the rain was humming down. The towers of the financial district, Canada Square and West India Quay, loomed high above the streets, the vast plain of London sprawling hazily beyond Docklands. A black taxi flashed its lights as Lewis scanned the line of parked cars. Spotting a gap in the traffic, he ran across the busy road. He was tall and long-limbed with a runner's gait, light on his feet as he moved, his shoulders hunched against the weather.

The rear door of the cab opened as he approached. Lewis buttoned his jacket and straightened his tie. He had never spoken alone with one of the firm's senior partners before.

'You wanted to see me, Mr King?' he asked, peering inside.

'You're Miller?'

'Yes. Lewis Miller.'

'Get in.'

Charlie King was immaculately dressed in a charcoal worsted suit, his silver hair combed back from a deeply lined face. A formidable lawyer, he had built Renfrew and Hall into one of the City's elite firms. A select few had ascended to exalted heights in his slipstream. Lewis was planning on following them.

King nodded to the flip seat. Lewis shook the rain from his hair as he stepped inside and folded the seat down.

'I need to send you on an errand,' King said. 'It's straightforward but it's urgent.'

Lewis was hesitant. 'You want me to go now? We're still negotiating the bank merger. It's going to take a few more hours at least.'

'This is more important. I'm pulling you out immediately.'

There was no point in protesting. Anyway, being entrusted with a task by Charlie King was the opportunity Lewis had been waiting for.

'What do you want me to do?' he asked.

A stack of document files stood on the rear seat. King took a Manila envelope from the top of the pile and handed it to Lewis.

'It's a non-disclosure agreement. Completely standard. Nothing you haven't seen before. The terms are all agreed. I need you to take it over to a firm in East London and witness the signature.'

Lewis waited for more but King seemed to have finished. 'That's all? You want me to deliver a contract?'

King softened his tone reassuringly. 'That's all.'

'Where in East London?'

'Whitechapel. You're from there, aren't you?'

There was something in King's cut-glass accent that made the question sound like an accusation.

'I'm from Stepney,' Lewis said. 'It's not far.'

'The place you're going to is a small local firm. Ask for a lawyer called Martin Sobel. He and I have already discussed the details. The address is written on the envelope. It's near Cable Street.'

Lewis began to guess why he had been chosen. A last-minute errand to Whitechapel would be a hard sell to the posh boys he worked with. Most of them hated travelling east of Chelsea.

'Who's the client?' Lewis asked.

King paused before answering. 'Robert Carlson,' he said.

It was a name spoken in the office with a respect bordering on reverence. Robert Carlson was one of the firm's most prestigious clients, a tech entrepreneur, specializing in green energy. His company, Ever Sine, was spearheading a clean power revolution. Some counted him among the select few who could save the planet. A very modern kind of saviour. Looking at the envelope in his hands, Lewis was too curious to remain silent.

'Can I ask what the purpose of the NDA is?'

Ruffling through the stack of documents beside him, King

pulled out a newspaper, a copy of that morning's *Metro*. He opened it and handed it to Lewis, pointing to an article below the fold on page six. Lewis skimmed it quickly.

'A death in Coldharbour Marshes? Why is Robert Carlson interested in this?'

'The unfortunate woman was called Maria Brennan,' King said. 'She worked as a climate scientist at his company. Carlson wants to make sure no adverse publicity washes his way. You can imagine the scrutiny the press like to keep him under. They haven't connected him to this yet but it's only a matter of time.'

Lewis looked at the photo, a blurred thumbnail in soft newsprint. She looked young and bright and striking. He read the headline out loud.

'*Bizarre Blonde Suicide in Local Beauty Spot.*'

King huffed in distaste. 'Disgraceful, isn't it? The standard of journalism in this country is lamentable.'

'The police think she killed herself?' Lewis asked.

'Yes. There was no doubt about it.'

'Why?'

'Why does anyone do something so drastic? She was only twenty-eight. It's the method she used that's garnering all the unwanted attention.'

Lewis scanned the paragraph again. 'She suffocated herself?'

'By breathing in chemicals. Apparently a few cups of domestic bleach mixed with some solvents and other household products is all it takes. Together they form a toxic mixture. It's deadly within seconds. It seems the instructions are readily available on the internet. Maria Brennan had viewed some of

10

these sites on the night she died. The dog walker who found her was lucky it didn't kill him too.'

'This all sounds very strange,' Lewis said.

'Which is exactly what Carlson is concerned about. He wants to avoid any blowback over this. If the press want to drag him into the story, they'll go to Maria Brennan's family and try to stir them up. Anything to sell newspapers. The NDA is to encourage the family not to speak out. The terms are very generous – a hundred thousand pounds, payable immediately. A cashier's cheque is attached to the contract.'

The amount cast the errand in a different light. It was a lot of money to keep a bereaved family away from the media, Lewis thought. This was starting to look like a classic gagging order. There had to be something more scandalous that Carlson was trying to conceal.

Charlie King saw the doubt in his eyes. 'I know it's a high price,' he said, 'but we don't need to question why. That's not our concern. It's best to consider this a sympathetic gesture from an ex-employer.'

'I understand,' Lewis said.

'I've heard good things about you, Lewis. You're keen, eager to learn and progress. Your qualification scores were impressive. How long have you been with us now?'

'Nearly three years.'

'Then it's time for you to step up a gear. Get this signed and we'll discuss finding you more responsibility in the department.'

Lewis was flattered to hear that his work had been noticed. 'Leave this with me. I'll get it done today.'

A rare smile broadened Charlie King's face. 'Thank you, Lewis. I appreciate it.'

'If you're in the office later, I'll bring the signed copies of the NDA up to you.'

King pointed to the small travel case at his feet. 'Unfortunately not. I'm in New York until Saturday. My flight leaves in a few hours. I'm trusting this to you while I'm gone, Lewis. Let me know when it's all done and dusted.'

Lewis nodded and stepped out on to the pavement. He slipped the envelope inside his jacket to protect it from the rain as the cab sped away. Treading lightly, he ran back across the street, dodging through the afternoon traffic.

He had always wanted to be lawyer, ever since he could remember. He had never thought of doing anything else, even though the profession seemed reserved for others, far removed from people like him. Being a lawyer was the ticket that would get him out of the dead end he had grown up in. He had worked hard at university, kept his head down and studied while everyone around him was partying. It had paid off. His grades were high enough for Renfrew and Hall to accept him on to their trainee scheme fresh from graduation. Since starting there, Lewis had found he was good at the job. The logic and fastidiousness suited him. But the salary had failed to live up to expectations. Competition among junior lawyers was too fierce. Like the rest of the city, he was struggling to keep his head above water. Lewis needed a chance to prove himself, to get noticed and climb the ladder. Maybe this was it.

Riding up in the lift, Lewis considered what Charlie King had told him about Maria Brennan. She had taken her own life, alone in a car out at Coldharbour Marshes. It seemed a tragic, senseless choice for such a young woman to make. Now he was tasked with trying to buy the silence of her family to protect the rich entrepreneur she had worked for. Something about it left a sour taste in his mouth. It was a grubby assignment, Lewis thought. But if it got him on to Charlie King's radar, it would be worth it.

2

ROBERT CARLSON TOLD his driver to stop on the patch of waste ground at the entrance to the nature reserve. Behind the tinted windows of the Mercedes, he peered along the lane. Finding it deserted, he opened the door and stepped out into the drizzling rain. A large bouquet of white roses and Oriental lilies was cradled in his arms.

The driver took an umbrella from the boot and began to walk alongside him. Carlson stopped. He thought it best to do this alone, away from prying eyes.

'Wait for me in the car,' he said.

The driver looked sceptical. The empty wetlands of Coldharbour Marshes seemed to make him nervous.

'Are you sure, sir?'

'Perfectly.'

Carlson took the umbrella and strode on alone, holding the flowers close to his chest. They were for a memorial, he had told the florist in Belgravia. For a young woman who had died in tragic circumstances. The florist had been adamant that white roses and lilies were fitting and he had accepted the advice humbly, his head bowed as if the weight of emotion made conversation difficult. Now, carrying the cellophane-wrapped flowers, he felt a growing sense of unease. It was an alien feeling but one that had become worryingly familiar in recent weeks.

At the start of his fifties, he was still youthful – a picture of corporate endeavour and high achievement. His hair was flecked with grey but his expression bore an undiminished severity that he used to his advantage when necessary. There were deep creases around his eyes but the gaze behind them was pin-sharp blue. Clutching the outsized bouquet awkwardly in one arm, he looked a long way from his natural habitat as he trudged along the track.

At the end of the lane, tangles of police tape criss-crossed the path. The muddy ground had been churned by tyres where Maria's car had driven. A small cluster of floral tributes had already been arranged nearby. A bunch of supermarket carnations propped up against a rain-soaked teddy bear. A few cards with handwritten messages inside. Carlson set his flowers down beside them. The bouquet looked gaudy and out of place. Too melodramatic for a tribute left by an ex-employer. Silently he cursed the florist for her extravagant taste.

It was strange, Carlson thought. The modern obsession with shrines and tributes. He saw them everywhere. Brief glimpses of flowers tied to lamp posts and railings as he passed by in the Mercedes. They seemed pointless and sentimental, trying to bestow poignancy on a futile event. He solved problems the way an engineer would, his training so engrained it was inescapable to him now. Quantify, assess, analyse. He

15

could only comprehend the world in this way. Through the purity of numbers and algorithms. He had filed his first patent at twenty-two. Reinvented the energy industry by thirty. Most problems collapsed before him, defenceless against the application of his will. It was frustrating that this situation had proved immune to his methods. So far, nothing in the chain of events had played out as predicted.

Pinned to a single red rose was a snapshot of a child, blonde and gap-toothed with long yellow braids. Carlson bent low to look closer. The resemblance to the vivacious young woman who had worked for him was unmistakable. She had the same modest smile, the same serious intensity. A rush of emotion hit him, strong enough to make his stomach turn.

Carlson could hardly believe she was really gone. He stood back, his breath quickening. The cold penetrated everything with an insidious chill. It was a sad place for anyone to meet their end. It wasn't where he would have chosen. But these thoughts would gain him nothing now, Carlson told himself. Events had taken their course.

He turned his collar to the wind and looked around. The nature reserve was empty and still, an unspoiled landscape so close to London. No buildings, no roads. All around him, the scrubby marshland was peaceful except for the calls of nesting waterfowl and the rustle of voles in the reed beds. Lapwings and redshanks whirled in the winter sky. The Thames lay close to the south, the marshes draining steadily out into its flow. The hazy outlines of passing boats were visible through the river mist. How long would it be until all this was gone? How long until everything changed? As Carlson looked around at the pristine view, he could picture the structures growing out of the untouched land. Loading docks. Smokestacks. Money.

Footsteps on the loose gravel snapped him back and he turned around. A couple were approaching. From their tearful expressions, the woman's puffy eyes, he guessed they were there to lay flowers at Maria's memorial. Carlson felt like an intruder on private grief. Lowering his head beneath the protection of his umbrella, he began to walk back along the lane. He passed them on the way to the waiting Mercedes and the woman gave a brief smile, a pained look of solidarity.

'Were you a friend of Maria's?' she asked tentatively.

Carlson nodded silently.

'It's so sad, isn't it?' she said. 'Maria was my cousin. We grew up together. I never thought she could do something like this.'

Tears welled up in her eyes. Her companion hugged her close.

Carlson began to move as if to walk on.

'Did you work with Maria?' the woman asked.

He paused. 'I used to.'

'At the energy company? What was it called?'

'Ever Sine,' he said flatly.

'That's it. Are you a research scientist as well?'

'Not exactly,' Carlson said.

The woman looked at him, taking him in, reading the signals in his air of affluence, his technocratic manner, his self-possessed body language. She began to scowl as a realization hit her.

'Are you Robert Carlson?' she said, her voice filling with anger.

For a moment he considered lying but he could see it was futile. She had already figured it out.

'That's right,' he said.

The woman slipped from her partner's embrace and took a step towards him, her fists clenched in anger. He thought she was going to strike him but he stood his ground and his sense of inviolability seemed to deflect her. Instead she strode to the pile of flowers on the verge and grabbed the spray of roses and lilies he had placed with the others. She swung them at him in disgust and a shower of creamy petals burst on his chest. They fluttered down to the wet ground at his feet.

'How dare you come here,' the woman spat, tossing the remnants of the bouquet at him.

Carlson caught the broken flowers. He wanted to speak up but could tell it was pointless. He turned and carried on walking. The couple watched him leave in disgrace. At least he could be certain of one thing now. It was obvious that Maria hadn't been discreet about their history together.

3

LEWIS TOOK AN Uber from Docklands to Whitechapel. It was a while since he had been back to the depths of East London. More than a year at least. He still had friends who lived in the area but seldom saw them now. There were too many bad memories in this part of town. Whitechapel was only a few miles from the financial district but the journey transported him into a different world. The great bluffs and cliffs of steel and glass gave way to rust and decay. A pale daylight hung over the streets, washed out and colourless. Everything was ragged and worn.

Watching the passers-by outside the window, Lewis knew he'd been lucky. He'd broken out, made his escape to the safety of the professional classes. He had some security now, even if he only had one foot inside the door. He'd recently turned twenty-six so there was plenty of time still to establish himself properly, as long as he played his hand well. Patience was the key. He'd worked hard to get this far, making sacrifices, taking on debt. Lewis was sure his efforts would be worth it in the long run. They had to be. Failing wasn't an option for someone without a safety net.

The driver stopped in a run-down street behind the bus station. The solicitor's office had a sign so faded Lewis could barely make it out. *The Whitechapel Law Centre.* Behind a steel grille, the window advertised the firm's expertise. Crime, Divorce, Immigration. They were open twenty-four hours a day. He double-checked the address again. It wasn't the kind of venue he associated with a man like Robert Carlson.

Certain it was the right place, Lewis walked into the lobby and announced himself at the desk. The receptionist looked him up and down.

'You're from Renfrew and Hall?' she said sceptically.

'Charlie King sent me.'

'You're not who we were expecting,' she said, and pursed her lips at him. 'We thought they'd send someone a bit more . . . experienced.'

Lewis let a glint of bite shine through his calm demeanour. 'How experienced do you need to be to deliver an envelope?' he asked.

Stepping out from behind the desk, the receptionist led him back through the tight warren of the building. The walls were hung with drug prevention and anti-gang posters. Coloured bins were lined up for the disposal of sharp objects. Yellow for syringes, blue for knives. In the background, a rattle of typing drifted from the doorways. Filing cabinets opening and closing. The receptionist stopped at an office at the end of the corridor. The door was already open.

'This is Lewis Miller,' she called out brusquely. 'He's here about the Brennan case.'

She ushered Lewis inside and closed the door behind him.

There was a tension in the room, a strained atmosphere that was obvious as soon as he entered. Martin Sobel was gaunt and bearded, his eyes radiating distrust from behind his wire-framed glasses. He had the look of an activist, a community campaigner. Sobel offered Lewis a seat with a wave of his hand.

Two others were in the room. A middle-aged woman, pale and shell-shocked, and a young man in his early twenties, standing behind her, his arms folded defensively across his chest. They eyed Lewis suspiciously as he took out the envelope containing the copies of the non-disclosure agreement and set it on the desk.

'Would you like anything to drink?' Sobel asked.

Lewis shook his head. 'I'd prefer to get started if that's OK with you.'

Sobel gestured to the woman seated opposite. 'This is Maria Brennan's mother,' he said. 'I'm representing her today.'

'I'm sorry to hear of your daughter's death, Mrs Brennan,' Lewis said. 'This must be a difficult time.'

'My name is Irina Koval,' she replied coldly. 'My daughter used her father's name. It was easier that way.'

Her English was fluent but her accent was East European. She was small and delicate with an upright posture and a direct, steady gaze. Her hands were clasped in her lap, her fingers knotted tightly together.

'I'm sorry, Mrs Koval. I didn't know.'

She glowered at him. 'What you know is of no interest to me.'

Lewis accepted her hostility without reaction. It wasn't his place to complain. He removed the copies of the contract from the envelope and began to hand them over.

21

'I understand that you're here to sign this non-disclosure agreement,' he said. 'The cheque is ready to be cashed, so—'

Irina looked outraged as she interrupted him. She was gripping her hands together, knuckles gleaming white in her lap.

'I don't want your money. I want answers. I want to know what happened to my daughter.'

Lewis looked at Martin Sobel, rocking gently in his office chair. 'I thought this had all been agreed?' he said.

Sobel shook his head. 'I think you've been sent here under false pretences. The last conversation I had with Charlie King was three hours ago. I told him exactly what the family want in order to get this finished. And it isn't money.'

Lewis sensed a trapdoor opening up beneath him. 'Then what is it?'

Sobel leaned forward. 'Robert Carlson,' he said. 'We want him to come and explain himself. I know he thinks his money makes him untouchable, but he's wrong. If he doesn't agree to meet with my client in person, we have no other choice.'

'Than to do what?'

Sobel shrugged. 'To go to the press. The fact that my client has a different surname to her daughter is the only reason they haven't tracked her down yet. But I can assure you it's only a matter of time. If Carlson wants to prevent his actions from becoming public, he'll do as we ask.'

They stared at each other over the paper-strewn desk. If Sobel was playing an angle, Lewis thought, he was doing so convincingly.

'What do you mean by "his actions"?' he asked.

Sobel's voice grew stern. 'Robert Carlson deliberately ruined the career of my client's daughter. He dismissed her from his

22

company without notice or warning. He waged a campaign to blacklist her. Then he began stalking her, calling her repeatedly, even confronting her at home. He drove her to an act of desperation that cost her her life. I think the least Mrs Koval deserves is an explanation from him in person.'

Lewis struggled to keep the surprise from his face. Surely this was a bluff? Sobel was grandstanding in an attempt to leverage a higher fee. 'Mr Carlson has made a generous offer,' he said.

'A derisory offer,' Sobel scoffed.

Lewis blinked. 'A hundred thousand pounds is derisory?'

'It is to a man like Carlson.'

Irina cried out to stop the meeting descending into a squabble. 'Enough!' she shouted. 'I don't care how much you think my daughter's life is worth. All I want to know is what really happened to her.'

Lewis turned to face her. 'I've seen the news reports, Mrs Koval. They all said that your daughter committed suicide.'

The young man behind Irina took a threatening step towards him. 'You need to shut your mouth with that talk,' he said. He was resolute, menacing, his nose flattened. He was wearing white trainers and a down jacket zipped up to his chin. He stared at Lewis defiantly, his fists clenched at his sides.

'I'm only repeating what was written in the newspapers,' Lewis told him.

'Say it again and I'll make you sorry,' the young man said.

'Excuse me?'

'You heard me.'

'I don't actually know who you are,' Lewis said.

The young man made no attempt to reply. The temperature in the room was rising quickly.

Finally Sobel spoke up. 'This is Drew Brennan. Mrs Koval's son. He's here to support his mother.'

Drew and Lewis stared at each other fiercely, each holding their ground. Lewis knew the type. He had grown up around men who were quick to intimidate and throw their weight around when it suited them. He hated to back down but had no choice.

'I'm not here to make trouble,' Lewis said. 'My only job is to deliver this contract and the cheque that goes with it.'

Drew's scowl remained frozen on his face. 'My sister is dead. We want to know why.'

'I understand. But I don't have any information to help you with that.'

'Robert Carlson does,' Drew said. 'Tell him to come here. I'll make him talk.'

Lewis shook his head slowly. 'All I can offer you is his money.'

Drew looked at his mother and waited for her response.

'I don't want a single penny from that man,' Irina said. 'All I want are answers.'

Reluctantly Lewis said, 'Then I'm afraid I can't help you.'

Irina reached out and took the copies of the NDA and the cheque from the desktop. 'This is what I think of your blood money,' she said, and ripped the pages into pieces. She let the fragments fall from her hands as she stood and began to gather her coat and bag.

'The last two days have been hell,' she said angrily. 'The

police came to my house to tell me my daughter was dead. They made me identify her body. Now you come here and try to buy me off. I won't take your money. I won't let that man get away with what he's done to Maria.'

Lewis tried to answer but he was cut off.

'Stay away from us,' Drew said. 'I don't want to see your face again.'

He opened the door and led his mother out of the room. Lewis watched them go, his career prospects disappearing with them. The weight of failure on his shoulders was overwhelming. He'd been given a simple task, a chance to prove himself, and now he had blown it.

When they were alone, Lewis bent down and picked up the torn pieces of the contract and the ripped cheque from the floor. It took a moment for his heart rate to settle. Martin Sobel swung gently in his chair. Framed photos of his wife and children stood on the windowsill. He watched Lewis with a benevolent smile.

'Charlie King sent you here on a fool's errand,' he said. 'Don't blame yourself.'

Lewis nodded in agreement. It was becoming clear that King had gambled on the sight of the cheque persuading the family to abandon their principles. He'd used Lewis as cannon fodder in an attempt to close an impossible deal. Lewis kicked himself. He wanted to get out of there quickly to save what face he had left.

Sensing his embarrassment, Sobel said, 'Look, for what it's worth, you did a good job.'

'Thanks,' Lewis said. 'But I'm in a lot of trouble now.'

Sobel looked at him sagely. 'You're thinking of ways to salvage the situation?'

Lewis held up the torn pages in his hands. 'If I don't get a signature on this contract, I'm finished.'

'There's only one way,' Sobel said. 'Arrange a meeting with Robert Carlson. The family aren't going to settle for less.'

'That's impossible.'

'Then Carlson had better get ready to see his name in the papers.'

'If anything libellous is printed about him, you know Carlson will sue.'

Sobel shrugged. 'It's only libellous if it's not true.'

Lewis thought for a moment. 'Do you really think he's involved in this?'

'Carlson was following Maria like a shadow. Calling her. Harassing her. Now she's dead and he's trying to distance himself from the fallout. That's what the rich always do – try to buy their way out of trouble.'

'Do you have any evidence for this? Or are you taking the family's word for it?'

Sobel looked cautious, weighing up whether to answer.

'Maria Brennan came to me,' he said. 'About two weeks ago. She told me everything. The phone calls. The visits to her house. She wanted my help to begin legal action.'

'So Carlson had some kind of vendetta against her?'

'It certainly seemed that way.'

'But he's a powerful man. Why would he risk everything over an employee dispute?'

'That's what he needs to account for. Otherwise there's a big question mark hanging over him.'

'You can't really be suggesting he had a hand in Maria's death?'

'How else would you explain it?'

Lewis looked at him hopefully. 'Coincidence?'

'One piece of advice I can give you,' Sobel said. 'If you want a long legal career, stop believing in coincidence.'

4

IRINA KOVAL STEPPED out into the darkening street. Litter was skittering along the pavement in the frozen wind, twisting in circles around her ankles, whipping her fine blonde hair into her eyes. She gathered her coat and scarf tightly around her and began to walk down towards the high street where she could catch a bus to take her home. She looked so weary and drained that even carrying the weight of her clothes seemed an ordeal. Her son followed two paces behind, his hands shoved deep in his pockets. The solidarity they had shown in the lawyer's office seemed to evaporate in the piercing cold.

'Happy now?' Drew called out to her as she walked away.

Irina turned to face him. Her mouth was drawn tight, her lips thin and straight. 'Happy? *Zvychayno, ni.*'

Drew knew his mother was angry if she was answering in Ukrainian. 'What do you mean, "of course not"?' he said. 'You just ripped up a cheque for a hundred grand. At least tell me you got a kick out of it.'

'That cheque was a bribe to keep us quiet,' Irina said. 'If we take it, it's over. Carlson will never tell us what was really going on with him and Maria. We'll never find out the truth.'

'How do you know anything was going on?'

'Because I overheard the phone calls. The arguments.'

'There could be a thousand explanations.'

'Then let Robert Carlson come and tell us what they are.'

Drew lifted his arms to the sky as if in despair. 'Maria is dead. She did it to herself. The only person who thinks differently is you.'

'I'm her mother. I know she wouldn't hurt herself like that.'

'I hope you're right. You've just torn up a cheque that could have changed our lives.'

'We can't accept blood money.'

'It's easy money.'

Irina shook her head at her son's priorities. 'Easy money? Is that all you ever think about? You should try working for a change.'

Drew puffed his chest out at the accusation. 'I work hard every night.'

'I know what you do,' Irina said contemptuously. 'And I know the kind of people you work with. Maria would never stoop so low.'

The look of disgust on his mother's face was painful for Drew to see. He knew how proud she was of Maria, the favoured child. The daughter whose brilliant progress over the years she had recounted to neighbours and shopkeepers and every random stranger who cared to listen. The epitome of the immigrant success story. A part of him had always hated Maria for making it impossible for him to measure up to her. Now she was gone, he knew he was going to have to compete with her ghost.

'I'm all you've got left now,' Drew said. 'You better start getting used to it.'

Irina's eyes began to well with tears. 'You don't know how much that saddens me,' she said.

She turned her back and strode away. Drew didn't bother trying to stop her. There was no point. He knew how much of a disappointment he was. It was made plain to him daily. All around him, people went about their business, walking with their heads lowered. No curious eyes were cast in his direction. The locals knew better than to pry into the lives of others, especially with the aura that Drew Brennan projected. Hostility seemed to emanate from him in waves.

He held his chin high as he stalked away into the pitiless wind, dark thoughts passing like daggers behind his eyes.

5

IT WAS TOO late to go back to the office so Lewis walked to the Overground station and took the train home. He wanted to sleep, the rocking of the carriage making his eyelids heavy, but he had to stay focused if he was going to find a way out of this mess. There had to be a way to persuade Irina Koval to sign the NDA. Lewis had three days until Charlie King was back from New York. In that time he had to come up with a plan to close the deal. His future depended on it.

If there was a secret reason for Maria Brennan's suicide, Lewis needed to find it quickly. As the train trundled onwards, he took out his phone and searched for media reports about her. She wasn't exactly headline news. The few articles he found focused on the grisly details of her death, the strange method she had used, rather than portraying her with any sensitivity or dignity. But all of the reports were clear that her death was a suicide. There wasn't even a glimmer of doubt. The articles described how she had visited suicide sites to research mixing household chemicals on her phone before she died. The names and brands and amounts that were necessary. It was bizarre, Lewis thought. He had never come across anything like this before.

It only took a cursory search to find the kind of websites that Maria Brennan had visited. Lewis selected one from the search list and clicked on it with trepidation. It was a twisted information page, with chat rooms and discussion groups, all dedicated to suicide methods. He read entry after entry, his heart sinking. So much desperation, so much misery. He shielded his phone as he read, protecting his screen from the passengers seated beside him.

After a few minutes, Lewis closed the site down. It was too grisly. Nothing he found there was of any value anyway. He wanted to understand Maria. To build a picture of her. Who was she? Why would she do something so drastic?

He searched various social media pages but couldn't find any accounts under Maria's name. Changing tack, Lewis found the Ever Sine corporate web page. He clicked on the personnel listings and scrolled through. Her employee bio was still online.

Reading it, Lewis was impressed. Maria Brennan had been a high achiever. She had won awards for climate campaigning as a teenager and been granted a scholarship for underprivileged students to attend a top university. Robert Carlson had recruited her when she completed her master's degree. Within a few years, she had risen to the top of the company. Carlson had appointed her Senior Climatologist when she was still only twenty-eight. It was a meteoric rise.

The bio included a photo. Maria was white blonde with a reticent smile that showed her straight white teeth. Looking at the photo, Lewis wondered if something personal had been going on between Maria and Robert Carlson. An affair of some kind or even just a one-night stand? That would explain why Carlson had been turning up at her house unannounced. Lewis could picture it – they had had a relationship and it had ended badly. When it finished, Maria had been heartbroken and taken her own life. Or maybe Carlson had wanted it to continue so pursued her but Maria rejected him? There were myriad plausible explanations.

Lewis thought of her family. Irina Koval seemed like a decent woman of honour and integrity. Those were rare qualities in the people he encountered professionally. But her hothead son was a different matter. The way he was so eager to throw his weight around wasn't a good sign. Sitting in the rolling carriage, Lewis mulled over the size of the cheque Irina had torn up. A hundred grand. Who walks away from so much money?

He left the train station and walked up to Highbury Fields in the dark. Beyond the wrought-iron fence, the park was shrouded in mist and shadow. His flat was in a Victorian conversion in a terraced street. It was small and cramped, the rent punishing. He unlocked the front door and climbed the steps, lost in thought. In the gloom of the stairwell, he caught sight of a figure sitting outside his door. It was his neighbour, Rachael, who lived in the flat upstairs. She looked at him sheepishly.

'I was waiting for you to come home,' she said. 'I've locked myself out.'

'Again?'

'I don't know what happens to my keys. It's a mystery. They seem to have a life of their own.'

Rachael was a science teacher at the local school. She was disorganized, scatty in an endearing way. There were notes to herself written in red biro on the backs of her hands. Her coat was folded into a pillow to rest against the wall while she waited. She seemed to lock herself out regularly, always ending up staying for dinner after retrieving the spare keys she kept in Lewis's flat. Over time, one thing had led to another and now they were drifting into a relationship. Lewis liked her. She had a calm, carefree style. There was an honesty about her, a directness. Spending time with Rachael was an antidote to the stress of his working days.

'Have you eaten?' he asked.

'Not since breakfast.'

Lewis held out a hand to help her up. He sensed his plan to carry on working through the evening had just changed.

'I'm making pasta,' he said. 'There's plenty for two.'

Rachael smiled at him as she rose to her feet. 'That's the first good thing that's happened to me all day,' she said.

6

THE LIGHTS WERE dimmed in Robert Carlson's office. He was reaching the end of the video presentation he'd been preparing for weeks. A slick promotional film played out on the screen before him. The audience of civil servants from the Department of Energy, their attentive faces arranged in a neat grid of squares on the screen, watched in rapt silence as Carlson talked. The detail in the animated model of the hydrogen plant was astonishing. The huge chambers housing the water electrolysis units with their exoskeleton of pipework. The banks of pressurized storage containers. The vast turbine halls where the electricity to power the facility would be generated. Carlson kept his voice low as he described the workings of the plant. The path that its raw material – water – would take as it was pumped through the system. Simple liquid becoming zero-carbon, combustible hydrogen gas.

'As you can see,' Carlson said, 'this plant is of a radical new design. It will produce totally clean energy, enough to power an entire city.'

The civil servants blinked into their webcams. The model of the hydrogen facility spun and zoomed on the screen.

'Hydrogen is the future,' Carlson continued. 'Cheap, clean, efficient energy produced from water. It can power our modern lifestyles without the need for fossil fuels or the corrupt regimes that supply them. We can have a different future. A green future. Only this can save London.'

Carlson allowed his words to hang in the electronic ether for a few seconds as the final wide shot of the giant production plant was displayed on the screen. As it faded out, the house lights in his office brightened.

Seated in an oak-panelled room somewhere in Whitehall, the Minister for Energy led his advisers in a round of applause. Behind him hung a crisp Union flag. He fiddled with the signet ring on his little finger as he spoke. 'Thank you, Robert. That was truly magnificent.'

'Thank you, Minister,' Carlson said.

'I believe I speak for us all when I say that we intend to strain every sinew to assist you in this marvellous new project.'

Carlson cast his eyes down humbly. 'I'm honoured.'

'We've taken up enough of your time today. All you require from us now are the necessary permits and licences to get this hydrogen plant underway.'

Carlson indicated the smartly dressed woman seated beside him. Her hair was a fierce shade of red, cut in a severe bob. She was wearing a double-breasted jacket with gold buttons. It gave her a commanding, military air.

'This is Olivia Ward,' he said. 'Olivia heads up the legal department here at Ever Sine. She will be the point person for any contractual queries.'

Olivia Ward gave a quick nod to camera. In their video boxes, a few civil servants nodded back in acknowledgement.

'Oh, and one last thing,' the Minister added. 'I've taken the precaution of not placing any technical restrictions or covenants on the land rights we're granting you. I hope this meets with your approval?'

Carlson was thrown off temporarily. 'If you think that's necessary, Minister,' he said.

'I do, Robert, I do. And thank you once more for your marvellous presentation today. Good luck with the first stage of the build.'

With this, the Minister's webcam switched off and, one by one, his advisers followed.

Carlson ended the meeting. When he was sure the line was dead, he turned to Olivia Ward. 'What was that?' he asked. 'No restrictions or covenants? Why?'

Olivia Ward shuffled the paperwork on her lap. She gave a non-committal shrug. 'I don't know, Robert. It's probably to make life easy for the pen-pushers in Whitehall. Save them having to do everything by the book. You know what civil servants are like.'

She stood from her chair and tucked the sheaf of documents under her arm. 'I've got a mountain of paperwork that I need to get started or I'll be here all night. You don't need me for anything further, do you?'

Carlson was lost in thought. He didn't look up as he answered. 'No. That's all for now, Olivia. Thank you.'

The Ever Sine offices were housed in a decommissioned iron foundry on the banks of the Thames. A Victorian edifice of rust-red brick and towering chimneys. Carlson's suite was on the top floor, all polished concrete and stone pillars, devoid of any decoration or personal touches. An internal gallery window looked down eight storeys into the atrium of the building, the heart of the foundry where the furnaces had been built. The blackened steel casings of the smelting ovens were still in place. The giant overhead pulleys that had transported the iron ore to the furnaces were suspended from the roof beams. It felt strangely appropriate for a green energy company to be head-quartered in such a place. The new high-tech world of the twenty-first century meshed into a redundant industrial shell, ancient soot and grime still baked into the walls.

Alone, Carlson slumped in his seat. He was spent. The pressure of the past few days had taken a heavy toll on him. He needed this new project to succeed. The future of the company was depending on it. He was hearing all the right noises from the government, but he knew better than to trust the word of a politician, no matter how obliging. He had learned that lesson the hard way in the past.

His phone had been muted for the video conference and Carlson took it out to check his messages. There were two from the construction company working on the hydrogen plant, chasing him for money. One from his wife, Susannah. He remembered that she was taking their daughter for her appointment that afternoon. He knew he should really check in. Susannah would need his support. As hard as he tried, Carlson failed to muster the necessary energy. It would all have to wait.

On a side table in his office, the broken bouquet of white roses and Oriental lilies stood in a crystal vase. Carlson could see the flowers from the corner of his eye. No matter how hard he tried to resist, his gaze kept wandering to the battered and torn blooms. It was a sentimental gesture to have brought them back to the office. He should have left them out at Coldharbour Marshes. They were rejects, tainted by their association with him. All they symbolized now was the fact that Maria was dead.

Carlson tried to push the thought away. If only Maria had trusted him. After the years they had spent together, it was the least he could have expected. He had made her career. Lifted her from obscurity and given her a voice. Why should he allow that voice to be turned against him?

Going to her flat that night had been a mistake. Carlson could admit that much to himself. Recklessly asking his driver to chauffeur him out to the dreary estate in East London on impulse. He should have realized that if Maria had refused to take his calls, she was never going to welcome him into her home. When she had opened the front door to him, her family had seen them arguing. They had seen how distressed Maria had been in his presence. He never should have allowed that to happen. It was a strategic mistake, one he was going to pay for now.

Carlson scrolled through his emails on the screen before him. Message after message remained unopened in his inbox. He knew he should be drumming up investment for the new hydrogen project but his mind was too raw to concentrate. He switched off his computer and stared at his reflection, his face distorted in the black surface of the monitor. No matter how hard he tried, his thoughts were consumed by a constant image, one he couldn't shake.

In his mind's eye, all he could see was Maria's face, gagging and choking as she suffocated in a locked car.

7

ON THE FOURTEENTH floor of Crowmoor House, Irina Koval was sitting alone in the dark. Through the thin walls she could hear her neighbours arguing and slamming doors. The moonlight seeping through the blinds cast cold shadows on the living-room wall. She was practically a recluse these days. It was impossible to experience as much heartbreak as she had and still want to face the world.

Spread out on the low table in the middle of the room were copies of the newspaper reports she had found on Maria's death. Irina couldn't bring herself to look at them any more. The lies and falsehoods they contained. When the truth was revealed, she was going to make each of these journalists apologize in person for what they had written. It was still impossible for her to comprehend that Maria was gone. The finality of it all was too distressing. It had always been her son that she feared would end this way. Dead before his life had really begun. Irina knew how hard she was on Drew but it was for his own good. Without a father, he needed discipline. Trouble had always followed him and he seemed to thrive on its turbulence. Drew was like a moth to a flame. It was a miracle his wings hadn't been torched already.

Maria was different. She had been such an easy child, wise even before she was old enough to leave school. The world seemed to lie wide open for her. In many ways, she had held the family together through the difficult years. Growing up in this part of London in a single-parent family hadn't been easy, but Maria had turned adversity to her advantage. She had worked hard and prospered. Now it was all gone.

Irina pictured Maria's face as she left the flat on the night she died, gaunt and tired. Maria had been depressed ever since she'd lost her job at Ever Sine two months earlier. In that final week, her mood had swung between rage and fatigue. Irina had been worried about her daughter's appearance. The amount of weight she had lost. The manic tremor in her voice. Maria had refused to say where she was going as she left the flat that night. Only that after she was done, the world would finally see who Robert Carlson really was.

When the police came to the flat to deliver the news, knocking on the door in their heavy-handed way, Irina had at first believed what they told her. Maria had taken her own life, they said, and Irina had been too stunned to argue. But then, as the shock wore off, she realized that Maria would never do such a thing. There hadn't been a single struggle in Maria's life that she hadn't fought head-on. She was half Ukrainian. She simply wouldn't have given up like that.

Sitting there in the silent room, Irina began to rake it all over in her head again, the emotion weighing on her like stone. She walked out into the hallway, opened the door to Maria's room and turned on the light. Everything was tidy and neat. Her books were standing in straight lines on the shelves. Her single bed was carefully made, the pillows stacked against the headboard. Irina walked to the wardrobe, opened the door and took out the large green plastic sack that lay inside.

The sack was similar to the kind Irina had used in her job as a cleaner on the hospital wards, working the night shift until her arthritis forced her to stop. This one had just as little ceremony or glamour to it. It was full of the clothes and personal effects found in Maria's car. Irina supposed that the police had no budget for anything grander. They had handed these personal items back only hours after Maria's death. It was a clear sign of how quickly the police had wanted to close the investigation. They had pressed for the coroner to reach a verdict of suicide, almost desperate in their haste, Irina thought. Whether this was a sign of incompetence or corruption, she didn't know.

Irina lifted the pieces out of the bag one by one and laid them on the chenille bedspread. A black pleated skirt and cashmere sweater. Flesh-coloured tights and flat shoes. Irina stared at the clothes her daughter had died in. It was like Maria had gone out dressed for an interview. She had taken a laptop and a folder of paperwork with her that night. Forms and printouts that Irina didn't understand. Those kinds of documents were a part of Maria's working life. She always had such things in her possession. But why had Maria gone out that night as if she was attending a business meeting? That wasn't the behaviour of someone suicidal.

Taken alone, this didn't amount to any kind of proof. Irina knew that. But it was the piece of loose paper folded up in the bottom of the plastic sack that made her certain. Irina took it out and read it again. She felt heartsick at the sight of the washed-out paper, the blotted ink.

BEWARE. DO NOT OPEN. CALL POLICE.

Irina placed the note carefully on the bed and stood back. She knew this piece of paper meant that her daughter's death was no suicide. The police had told her it was common for people who killed themselves in this way to leave a note. It was to prevent anyone inadvertently breathing in the poisonous fumes in the car, they had said. Irina had kept silent when she first saw it, but she knew what the note meant straight away. No matter what the police might believe, there had been other people with Maria out at Coldharbour Marshes on the night she died. Who they were exactly, Irina didn't know. But Robert Carlson had been among them. She was certain of that.

8

RAIN WAS SLUICING down the taxi window. Susannah Carlson could barely see across the street and into the lobby of the Harley Street clinic. She wiped the glass and pressed her face to the window. The lobby was empty. There was no sign of Emilia waiting where they had agreed. With a nervous voice, Susannah asked the driver to go around the block once more. She didn't want to be seen outside the clinic. That would be a scandal she would never live down.

Susannah checked the time as the taxi drove on. She was a few minutes early, that was all. She willed herself to relax. Of course Emilia had attended her appointment, just as she had promised. After everything that had happened in recent weeks, even a wayward girl like Emilia knew she had to change her ways.

Looking at her messages, Susannah saw there was still no reply from her husband. His presentation to the Department of Energy was that afternoon, she remembered. He'd been rehearsing into the small hours every night for weeks. Robert didn't need her chasing him when he had such an important meeting to take care of. All of their futures were dependent on his proposal being a success. But she needed his support to help her through these desperate family problems. It was too much for her to cope with alone.

Susannah thought of the conversation she'd had earlier with the florist on Sloane Street, the hushed tone in which the woman told her that Robert had bought an expensive bouquet that morning. White roses and lilies for a funeral, she had whispered mockingly, as if it were the most clichéd of cover stories. At first Susannah had been shocked. Robert had never set foot in a florist's shop in his life. But then it began to fall into place. The way he'd been acting recently. The problems he'd had at work. He really should know better. This was the kind of gossip that could lead them all to disaster.

As the taxi completed its circuit and turned back on to Harley Street, Susannah saw her daughter standing outside the clinic entrance beneath an umbrella, her face illuminated by the screen of her phone. She was wearing dark sunglasses despite the foul weather, the fur collar of her designer coat pulled tightly about her face. Her hair was long, hanging down to obscure her features, but Susannah could see how painfully thin her daughter had become, her skin pallid and her cheeks sunken. She was nearly overwhelmed with worry every time she saw Emilia these days. Emilia had been emotionally fragile ever since she was a child, socially awkward, a sensitive girl who struggled to fit in. Having such a high-profile father hadn't helped, especially when Emilia decided she wanted to follow in Robert's footsteps. In order to learn the intricacies of the business, she had interned at her father's company, only for a short while, but she had been sullen and depressed ever since.

Susannah opened the taxi door and waved quickly to catch Emilia's attention. Her daughter looked sour and irritated as she walked down the steps of the clinic and climbed in.

'How was it, darling?' Susannah asked.

Emilia shrugged. 'I did what you wanted. That's all.'

'It must have helped?'

'I don't need any help.'

'We both know that's not true.'

Emilia flashed her a withering look, cutting the conversation dead. 'Look, I don't want to talk about it, all right?'

Susannah touched a soothing hand to her daughter's arm. 'Then I won't mention it again. I promise.'

Pressing her would only make it worse, Susannah told herself. She couldn't force Emilia to communicate. She was a closed book at the best of times.

'I'm having some people over later,' Emilia said. She made the announcement as if it were a final decree.

'Again?' Susannah said despairingly.

'It's just a few friends. Nothing for you to worry about.'

'Are you sure that's a good idea?'

Susannah asked the question gently but Emilia snapped.

'I'm doing everything you asked,' she barked. 'I'm seeing the therapist. I signed in under the stupid false name you told me to use. The least you can do is treat me like an adult.'

Susannah watched as her daughter turned her face away in disgust. Treat her like an adult? If only Emilia knew how to behave that way, so much heartache could already have been avoided.

9

FIVE MILES AWAY, Drew Brennan was in a stolen BMW in Hampstead, watching the driveway of a mock-Tudor mansion. Beyond the wrought-iron gates, a party was taking place, the windows of the house lit up, bodies silhouetted against the glass. He could hear the sound of voices mixing with the soft music floating from the walled garden.

'Who lives here?' Drew asked.

'Probably best if you don't know that.'

Drew shrugged. It was good advice, considering what they were planning to do. Seated beside him in the driver's seat, Glenn Egan began assembling everything they would need. A long screwdriver, some wire coat hangers and a packet of cotton wool balls.

Glenn had been in Drew's class at school, had played on the same football team, had chased the same girls. Now Drew worked for him on a freelance basis, had done so for over a year. The Egan family ran a construction business, one of the biggest in London. They had built skyscrapers and airport terminals and sports stadiums. In the world of major infrastructure projects, they were at the very top. But the family also had interests and ventures of an illegitimate nature, the unconventional management techniques of one line of business sometimes bleeding over into the other.

'You ready?' Glenn asked.

Drew nodded towards the house. 'What if anyone else arrives? Don't you think we should give it another few minutes?'

Glenn looked at him in disbelief. 'Are you joking? Do you want to listen to this shitty music any longer?'

Opening his door, Glenn stepped out on to the street. He was heavyset and thick-necked. Drew followed, taut and stealthy. Both were dressed in black – hoodies, jeans, trainers, even their gloves. Around them, beneath the soft glow of the street lights, the road was quiet and still. The other houses were silent, their curtains drawn. That was good, Drew thought. It was better not to have anyone wandering around. No prying eyes.

They crossed the street and stood at the foot of the perimeter wall, scanning the surroundings. When he was sure it was safe, Drew hoisted himself up, checked there was no broken glass embedded in the top of the wall and then rolled his body over the top and slid down on to the flower bed on the other side.

'Throw it over,' he whispered.

Glenn tossed the bag with the equipment over the wall. It fell on to the grass nearby with a dull thud and Drew scampered over to retrieve it. He crept along the lawn towards the house. A line of expensive cars snaked up the driveway, bumper to bumper. A Porsche Carrera. A Maserati Ghibli. A brand-new Range Rover. At the head of the line was a silver Bentley Continental, parked in pride of place facing the stone staircase leading to the grand entrance doors. He bent down by the rear offside wheel and took the long screwdriver out of the bag. Jamming the flat head into the hinges of the fuel compartment door, he wrenched it open. The Bentley was solidly built and took three strong heaves before the door popped out. The sound of buckling bodywork and shearing bolts was too loud for comfort. He glanced up at the house. All clear. Everyone inside was too busy drinking champagne and eating canapés to notice.

Unscrewing the petrol cap, Drew took a handful of cotton wool and wadded the balls together in his fist. When he had made a solid lump, he untwisted the wire coat hanger and stretched it out lengthways. He pressed the cotton wool on to the hook and made it secure. Using the screwdriver, he jammed open the safety latch leading down to the fuel tank and dropped the hanger inside. He left it there for a few seconds, letting the cotton wool soak.

Looking up at the windows, Drew could see the shadows of people standing and talking in groups. The music was playing, the sound of clinking glasses ringing out over the bright chatter of the guests. The owner of the house was probably a cement contractor or haulage operator who owed money to the Egans, Drew guessed. A wide boy made good. People had the mistaken notion that it was only bankers and stockbrokers making fortunes in London these days. The real money was flowing into the pockets of men in construction, blue-collar people in heavy trades with dirt under their fingernails. People who found it difficult to part with cash when it was owed. Drew assumed the Egans had asked politely for their money several times before sending him in. He knew his services were used only as a last resort.

When it was ready, he pulled the hanger out of the fuel tank and turned it around in his hands. The cotton at the end of the hook was sodden, the heady smell of high-octane petrol drifting off it in clouds. Drew pushed the free end of the hanger back into the tank, leaving the soaked cotton suspended a few inches clear of the car. He jammed the screwdriver down into the fuel pipe to keep it open. Taking a lighter out of his pocket, he lit the cotton wool, sprinted back to the garden wall and hauled himself over. Glenn was waiting, his arms outstretched to catch him as he dropped to the pavement on the other side.

They jogged across the road and jumped back into the BMW. The engine was running by the time they heard the first soft pop as the gases in the Bentley's tank caught fire. Then Drew saw a bright flash of amber and gold as the petrol ignited. Moments later there was a second pop and then another. Finally a mushroom cloud fireball ascended, illuminating the house, the carved stone lions and hanging baskets, the fake half-timbered façade. The cloud of flame rose like a vision of Hades, plumes of black smoke tumbling upwards into the night sky. A scattering of broken glass showered out into the street.

Glenn turned to Drew in the passenger seat. His eyes were wide with amazement.

'You torched all of them?' he said.

Drew shook his head. 'Just the Bentley. But they're parked so close together that they've all gone up.'

'Fantastic,' Glenn laughed. 'My uncle will love this.'

Drew watched the inferno rage as they sped away. He couldn't take his eyes off it. The colours were always so beautiful.

10

WHEN THEY HAD finished eating, Lewis gathered the plates from the table and stacked them in the sink. He poured Rachael another glass of red. She was trying to stop him but her protests were half-hearted. Constellations of vivid freckles patterned her cheeks and forehead. Her hair was thick and dark, hanging in loose curls over her shoulders, her grey eyes bright from the wine. It was warm and steamy in the kitchen, the window cracked open to let out the heat from the stove.

'That was delicious,' Rachael said.

Lewis smiled at the compliment. 'My sister taught me to cook when I was a teenager, when it was just the two of us growing up together. She took care of me almost single-handed.'

Rachael sipped her wine. 'You know, every time you mention your sister, you always talk with real admiration.'

Lewis nodded. 'Without Angela I don't know what would have happened to me. She's great. You'll have to meet her one day.'

'I'd like that.'

'Be prepared for a grilling, though. My sister's a Stepney girl. She doesn't mince her words.'

Rachael looked at him mischievously. 'Maybe she'll tell me what you used to be like when you were younger, before you got all polished and lawyerly.'

Lewis laughed. 'I had to stop dropping my aitches once I began working in the City. I had no choice. The clients have to take me seriously if I'm going to climb the ladder. I can go back to talking like a Cockney barrow boy just for tonight if you want?'

'No thanks,' Rachael said. 'I get enough of that from the kids at school. Although with them it's the other way around. Most of them have second homes in Suffolk but talk like they're running with the local gangs. Most of the time I can't follow a word they say. It makes teaching the Periodic Table a real challenge.'

Lewis finished his wine. He stared at the empty glass for a moment. He didn't let it show but he often felt a fraud for softening his accent to improve his career chances. It had been a tactical necessity but it left him feeling inauthentic. Now he was an outsider in the neighbourhood where he had grown up, but was still kept at arm's length by the people he worked with. It was like existing in a kind of No Man's Land.

Rachael sensed his attention had drifted off. She reached across the table and gently touched her fingertips to his.

'Still with us?'

'I'm just tired,' Lewis said. 'It was a long night.'

'So what's your company got you working on now?' Rachael asked. 'More tax dodges for the one per cent?'

She was teasing but there was more than an element of truth in the jibe.

'You don't want to hear about my job,' Lewis said. 'It's boring.'

Rachael laughed. 'You're always so evasive about work.'

'I don't like to talk about being a lawyer. It's not that interesting.'

'You must enjoy something about it or you wouldn't keep doing it.'

Lewis sipped his wine. 'It pays the rent. That's enough.'

'Tell me the latest case you're working on.'

'I can't.'

'Why?'

'It's top secret. It involves a young woman who committed suicide.'

Rachael's eyes lit up with interest. 'I thought you said your work was boring?'

'I can tell you about the background to the case,' Lewis said. 'I just can't discuss my client. That part's privileged.'

'This sounds a lot more exciting than being a science teacher.'

Lewis took out his phone and found a news report on Maria Brennan. He passed it across the table and waited while Rachael read it. He could see her leaning into the screen, engrossed.

When she had finished, she looked up at him inquisitively. 'Are you sure this woman killed herself?'

'That's what the police decided. No one found anything suspicious about her death.'

Rachael shook her head. 'It doesn't look like a suicide to me.'

The playful tone had left her voice. Lewis could see how serious she was.

'Why?' he asked.

'The article says that this woman mixed up a batch of household chemicals in her car, then inhaled the toxic fumes.'

'That's right.'

'Do you know how difficult that would be? The report makes it seem like an easy thing to do. It doesn't work like that. It would have looked like a chemistry lab in her car.'

Lewis could see the sense in what she was saying, but he didn't want to go down that path. Getting Maria Brennan's family to sign the NDA was going to be hard enough. He didn't need the case becoming any more complicated than it was already.

'Maria wasn't the only person to die this way,' Lewis said. 'There's been a whole wave of teenagers using the same method. Maria viewed a couple of suicide sites on her phone on the night she died. She followed their instructions to mix the chemicals. The police searched her internet history and found everything. The investigation was closed on the day they discovered her body. They're just waiting for the coroner's verdict to confirm it officially.'

Rachael considered this for a moment. 'I bet your client's a rich man,' she said. 'Maybe he pressured the police into jumping to a quick conclusion?'

It wasn't an impossible suggestion. Robert Carlson was a powerful individual. Lewis thought of the other accusations that had been made against him. Wrongful dismissal. Harassment. Stalking. None of those charges had stuck. Maybe he had exerted some influence over the police investigation into Maria's death. It was a sobering idea. If true, it would change the nature of the whole case, Lewis thought. He knew his career was already hanging in the balance. He didn't need any further headaches.

'My job is to protect my client,' Lewis said, cutting off this line of thinking. 'I can't start suggesting he's involved in foul play or police corruption. That's not a smart direction for me to take.'

Rachael put her glass down heavily. 'Don't you want to find out what actually happened to this poor woman?'

'I want to keep my job.'

'You're a lawyer. Don't you want to know the truth?'

'You know what I want? To get a pay rise. To pay off my student debt. To buy a house one day. Not get caught up with someone who killed herself because she was having an affair with her boss.'

Rachael raised her eyebrows. 'So you see an attractive, successful woman and you assume she was sleeping her way to the top?'

'That's not what I'm saying.'

'It sounds like you are.'

Lewis knew Rachael was right. He had jumped to the conclusion without giving it much thought. Deep down, he knew it was a way to justify what he had been asked to do. He had become a lawyer to *help* people, not protect the wealthy.

'Maybe you're right,' Lewis admitted reluctantly. 'There is something strange about this case. But my job is to get a signature on an NDA, not investigate a woman's death.'

Rachael pursed her lips. 'It's late now. I'm going home.' She stood and began to gather her things.

Lewis knew he'd acted brashly. He made an attempt to salvage the situation. 'Don't go now,' he said. 'Have another drink.'

'I've had enough already.'

'You know I want you to stay.'

Rachael was refusing to meet his eye, rummaging in her bag like she was looking for something important. 'Not while you're acting like this,' she said.

Lewis looked up at the ceiling. Her flat was only the other side of the greying plaster. 'It's such a long way to go,' he said with a smile. 'Stay. Please.'

Rachael put her bag down on the table. He could see she was changing her mind.

'Only if you promise me one thing.'

'What?'

'That you'll keep looking into this case,' Rachael said. 'This poor woman needs someone to fight her corner and it looks like that's going to be you. The only question is whether you're up to it or not.'

11

GLENN PARKED BY the graffiti-sprayed entrance to the tower block where Drew lived. It was lit up in the night like a beacon, the grid of illuminated windows blinking on and off like Morse code. Late trains thundered past on their way out of Liverpool Street, flashing by in the gloom. The windscreen of the car was drenched with drizzling rain. Whoever had built the estate had taken the meaning of 'high-density housing' too literally, Drew thought. Everything was solid and austere. Towering walls of hard-faced brick and unfinished concrete. It was like living in a bunker complex.

A group of boys stood at the foot of the block. Dealers protecting their turf. They stared out into the dark, narrow-eyed, warding off passers-by. Recognizing Drew, they nodded, turning their backs and looking away. Drew had lived there his whole life. His reputation kept him free from hassles with the local gangs. With a member of the Egan family seated beside him, he was untouchable.

In the safety of the car, Glenn lit a joint. The blue-grey

smoke twisted off the end in thick curls. He puffed on it greedily and passed it to Drew.

'Come to the site tomorrow and I'll pay what I owe you,' Glenn said. 'I don't have the cash with me tonight.'

'What time?'

'Before lunch. I've got somewhere I have to be later.'

'Fine,' Drew said. 'But do me a favour. When I come by tomorrow, introduce me to your uncle. It's time I met him in person.'

'Why?'

'Because I want to do more than torch cars for the rest of my life.'

Glenn slapped him playfully on the shoulder. 'You looking for promotion?'

'You know what I mean. If I meet your uncle, I can ask him for a job. Something more permanent.'

'Like what?'

'Anything legit. Punching a clock. Paying taxes. Becoming a productive member of society.'

Glenn smirked. 'You'd last a day or two at most.'

'You manage to deal with it,' Drew said.

'I'm only working for the construction side of the business until I can prove myself. I don't want to be getting my hands dirty for ever. I want to make some real money.'

Drew took a thoughtful drag on the joint. 'You've got a good thing going and you don't even know it,' he said. 'You've got a proper job. A chance to have a future.'

Glenn waved the idea away. 'I wish I was like you. Free to come and go when I please. No responsibilities, just like when we were kids.'

'That's the point,' Drew said. 'We're not kids any more. Responsibilities come along whether you want them or not. Look at me. I've got a funeral to pay for now.'

Glenn glanced at him apologetically. 'I heard about your sister,' he said. 'I'm sorry.'

Drew was surprised at the sentiment. They never really shared any personal details about their families despite the years they'd been friends. Sensitive subjects were off-topic. In their world it was dangerous to ever reveal weakness.

'Maria and I weren't that close,' Drew said with a shrug. 'She couldn't stand me and I felt the same about her. Maria thought she was better than everyone just because she'd passed a few exams.'

'Still, she was your sister.'

The rain was falling steadily outside. Drew thought of the meeting earlier that day in the lawyer's office. The cheque that had been dangled in front of them like bait. His mother's refusal to accept it.

'The company that Maria worked for offered to pay compensation,' he said. 'There was something going on with her boss. I don't know what exactly. He offered us money to keep quiet.'

'How much?'

'A lot. Six figures. Enough to leave here for good.'

Glenn gave a low whistle. 'That's like winning the lottery. I hope you remember me when you're counting the cash.'

'Don't start getting excited. My mum refused to accept it.'

Glenn looked at him in disbelief. 'She walked away from a big pay-off like that?'

'She thinks there's something strange about the way Maria

killed herself. She won't let it go. She can't recognize good luck when it stares her in the face.'

'Are you going to try to convince her to take it?' Glenn asked.

'I already have. She won't listen.'

Glenn opened the window. It slid down with a buzz. A dense cloud of weed smoke filtered out.

'Time for me to go,' he said. 'I've got an early start in the morning.'

He fired up the engine and Drew stepped outside into the cold.

'I'll see you tomorrow,' he said.

'Listen, I have a meeting with my uncle at eleven,' Glenn said. 'Come around and I'll introduce you. You can ask him if there's any job vacancies on the project we've got coming up. I'll set it up for you but I can't promise anything.'

12

IT WAS THE night of his daughter's twelfth birthday and Martin Sobel had promised to be home in time to kiss her goodnight. He had already missed the party his wife had organized earlier that evening. Yet another one he had failed to attend. He hated that his kids were becoming used to him not being there on big occasions, had practically come to expect it. He was determined not to let his daughter down this time.

He wheeled his bicycle out on to the street and locked up the office behind him. Fastening the straps on his helmet, Sobel rode down to the main road heading east, his high-vis jacket flashing brightly in the headlamps of passing cars. He kept pace with the traffic as it filtered along the high road, his breath billowing in great clouds before him. It was a journey he made so often that he couldn't help but let his mind wander as he pedalled steadily into the dark. The world was full of injustices that the rich forced upon the poor. Hunger, homelessness, neglect. All aided and abetted by unscrupulous lawyers. It was a mark of shame how his fellow professionals sold themselves to the highest bidder. There were very few like him, willing to forgo the lure of money to serve the common good. Surely that was the purpose of their trade, Sobel thought.

He'd been disappointed to see another decent young lawyer lost to the corporate world, corrupted by the sharks at Renfrew and Hall. What was his name? Miller, that was it. Lewis Miller. He'd seemed capable and straightforward – smart, but with a touch of humility. It was a shame such a promising young lawyer had been dragged into the Maria Brennan affair. It would be a lesson to him, Sobel mused, to see how far the wealthy will go to protect themselves.

Cycling over the railway bridge at Limehouse, Sobel manoeuvred himself into the right-hand lane to pass a waiting bus. A car horn sounded angrily. Sobel ignored it. As usual, the speeding drivers were inconsiderate of the needs of others. Turning back into the left lane, he had to assert himself to avoid colliding with a taxi. Another impatient horn blast. London had always been a tough city but now it was becoming a cold, heartless place. Sobel was proud he had maintained his high personal standards in the face of this onslaught. He encouraged his children to do the same.

He was thinking of this when he heard a large truck rumbling close behind, the heavy engine thudding through the back of his chest. He increased his pedal speed to get some distance, his pulse quickening as he pumped his legs.

To his right, Sobel noticed a black car, sleek and shiny, its windows darkly tinted. As it slipped alongside him, he changed gears and began to pedal faster, lifting himself from the saddle. The car tracked him. He peered into the black glass. His reflection stared back, lean and bearded, red-cheeked from exertion.

A sudden movement in front caught Sobel's attention. A pedestrian was hesitating on the pavement, trying to judge if it was safe to cross. He stepped out and Sobel clutched the handlebars and swerved right, barely missing a pothole, turning into the path of the black car beside him. Seeing this, the man stepped back to the safety of the pavement and Sobel decreased the angle. As he did so, he heard a shout.

'Sobel!'

Instinctively he turned towards the call of his own name. The window of the black car had rolled down enough for him to see the profile of a figure, silhouetted by the lights of the dashboard. Sobel stared into the car's interior for a split second, mesmerized. Who was this person? How did he know his name? In that critical moment his focus was lost.

An undulation in the road jolted through the frame of the bicycle. The handlebars shuddered in his fists. Sobel felt the tyres losing grip, his momentum becoming a liability. Another deep pothole loomed in his path. As he hit it, his front tyre buckled and he began to fall. In that weightless moment, the bicycle twisted out of his grip and his body lurched forward. The frame flipped out from beneath him and he hit the surface of the road hard, skin peeling away from his hands and knees on the rough tarmac. With a smooth burst of acceleration, the black car pulled away.

Martin Sobel thought again of his daughter's birthday. The promise he had made to see her before she slept. The look of inevitable disappointment on her face was bright in his mind as the truck, its brakes squealing, careered over him, crushing the frame of the bicycle under its heavy tyres.

13

THE MERCEDES STOPPED in front of an elegant five-storey mansion in Lowndes Square. The driver hurried back to open the rear door. He stood aside as Robert Carlson stepped out on to the pavement.

'Will you need me again tonight, sir?' the driver asked.

Carlson seemed surprised. 'Need you?'

'To drive you, sir?'

Carlson gave a shake of his head as he recovered himself. 'No. That will be all.'

The car sped away, its brake lights flashing in the dark. Carlson looked up at the tall façade of the house. The grand portico. The grey slated mansard roof and arched pediments. The gleamingly polished front door. The windows of the neighbouring houses were mostly dark, the owners away in their primary residences in Shanghai and Moscow, the shutters closed.

As he mounted the steps to the door, he thought of the presentation he had made earlier to the Department of Energy.

The project had to succeed. If he could establish the first hydrogen production facility in the city, others were bound to follow. It would transform the fortunes of his company, potentially the whole economy. The government would see how simple it was, how lucrative, then more facilities would be licensed in its wake. It had to work, he told himself. The future of the energy industry was depending on it.

Inside the marble hallway, Carlson removed his coat and hung it in the cloakroom. The crystal chandelier sparkled above him. He could hear the sound of laughter rising up from the swimming pool in the basement. It sounded like a party was taking place down there. A heavy electronic bass line rumbled through the stairwell. The echo of youthful voices. The slap of water on tiles. Emilia must have invited friends over again, he thought. It was becoming far too frequent for his liking. It was strangely unsettling to hear young people having fun while he was mired in so much stress. Carlson pushed it from his mind as he climbed the grand staircase to the first floor.

He found Susannah in the living room. She was on the phone discussing her plans to redecorate the house. Swatches of material lay on the floor at her feet. She acknowledged his entrance with a light kiss on her fingers, waving them breezily in his direction.

In the kitchen, Carlson poured himself a glass of Chablis and stood at the long quartz worktop. He tried to force his face into a visage of calmness. When Susannah came in, she tutted at the glass of wine in his hand.

'You told the doctor you would only drink on weekends, Robert,' she said. 'You promised.'

'It's only one glass.'

'How was your presentation to the Minister?'

'So so. I think I just about managed to pull it off.'

She looked at him with a soft smile. 'You're too hard on yourself. I'm sure it was perfect.'

'It sounds like a nightclub down there,' Carlson said, nodding down at the floor where a rhythmic tremor of music could be felt.

'Emilia asked if she could have a few friends over. I said yes.'

'That's the third time this week.'

Susannah looked at him like he was making a fuss. 'Emilia needs to unwind. She's had a stressful time.'

Carlson was incredulous. '*She's* had a stressful time?'

'Her appointment at Harley Street was earlier this afternoon.'

He took a deep breath and relented. It was a rebuke, no matter how gently delivered. 'Of course. I'm sorry,' he said. 'How did it go?'

Susannah's eyes moistened. 'I think it was very traumatic for her, actually.'

Carlson put his wine glass down and walked over to his wife. He took her in his arms and hugged her close.

'I'm sorry I couldn't be there. I'll make more time in future, I promise.'

'I know you're busy, Robert. But it would mean a lot. For all of us.'

'I'll make time to talk to Emilia. I know how much she's trying.'

'Oh, by the way,' Susannah said innocently, 'I was at the florist this morning. They told me you bought a bouquet of white roses and lilies. For a funeral, they said.'

The words left Carlson struggling to think of a plausible excuse, his mouth dry.

'It wasn't a funeral,' he said weakly. 'It was a memorial.'

'For whom?'

'Someone at the office.'

'Anyone I know?'

Susannah asked the question with a lightness of tone that sounded forced. Carlson paused. He thought of the countless times his wife had met Maria. The social functions and evening visits Maria had made to the house. The suspicious, searching look that had crossed Susannah's face every time their paths had crossed. Listening to her, there was something in his wife's voice that made him think she knew exactly who the flowers were for.

'No,' Carlson lied. 'No one you know.'

14

EMAILS WERE PINGING relentlessly into his inbox, the grind beginning before he reached the Tube station. Lewis scrolled through the messages as they appeared on his phone, his heart sinking at the workload building up. It would be impossible to finish these cases even if he had the whole day. They would all have to wait. By far the most urgent task on his list was to finalize the NDA for Robert Carlson.

He had been awake most of the night, Rachael sleeping soundly beside him. Lying there, staring at the ceiling, he had gone over what Rachael had said about Maria Brennan's death. There was something strange about the case, something that didn't sit right the more he mulled it over. It just felt wrong. He had to admit that much to himself. But what it was exactly he couldn't be sure. Lewis knew nothing about science but he trusted Rachael's expertise. If she thought the circumstances of Maria's death were suspect, she was probably right.

But no matter how he figured it, Lewis couldn't believe that

Robert Carlson was involved. It just didn't fit. Carlson was a public figure, his name a constant presence in the media, promoting a new design of wind turbine or investing in a carbon-capture scheme. His character and motives seemed beyond reproach. If he'd had an extramarital affair and covered it up, that was one thing. But murder? Surely Carlson wasn't capable of that?

Riding the train east, Lewis was consumed by the gnawing feeling that he had to keep digging. It was what he was trained to do. Searching for facts. Finding the truth. Otherwise what was the point of being a lawyer? Was it only to make money for global corporations? Lewis wasn't sure he wanted to carry on under those terms. Solving the mystery of Maria Brennan's death would put his hard-won skills to some good use for a change. But to do it, he needed more information, more background on Maria's family. That appeared to be the key to solving the case. For information about the residents of Whitechapel, Lewis knew exactly where to go.

'Hello, stranger,' his sister said as she opened the door and saw him standing there. Angela's face broke out into a broad smile but Lewis could see a flash of disappointment in her eyes. A quick glint of emotion that she tried to hide but failed. Lewis cast his eyes down. He felt bad about the length of time that had passed since his last visit.

Angela reached out and hugged him close. She smoothed a proud hand over his shirt front and the lapel of his jacket.

'Look at you in your posh suit,' she said. 'I hardly recognized you. You look like the chairman of the board.'

'How are you, Angie? How are the kids?' Lewis asked.

'The girls are at school,' she said. 'Come in. The little ones are home. They'll be excited to see you.'

He stepped into the hallway. It was full of bikes and scooters and a folded-up buggy. The rack by the door was overflowing with coats and scarves. The two preschoolers, both boys, ran out of the living room and hugged Lewis round the knees. He gave them the bags of luridly coloured sweets he had brought.

'Oh, Lewis,' his sister said, 'they'll be awake all day now.'

He watched as they began to wolf down handfuls of sugary treats. 'I don't get to give them presents very often,' he said.

'Bring them some fruit then. Anything without so many chemicals.'

'What kind of terrible uncle would do that?' he laughed.

Angela made coffee and they talked together in the kitchen while the kids ran around like madmen. She was sandy-haired, like Lewis, and had an open, friendly face, the kind that kept her looking young. She was nearly a decade older than Lewis but the age difference didn't show. Angela was always smartly dressed and presentable and she prided herself on it. As his big sister, she could read him instantly.

'You look like you've got something on your mind,' she said.

'Is it that obvious?'

'You can't hide behind your lawyer act with me, Lewis. I know you too well. Tell me what's bothering you.'

Lewis felt himself relax. It was a relief to talk to someone who had known him his whole life. He could breathe out and be himself. 'I wanted to pick your brains, Angie. About a family from Whitechapel. It's for a case I'm working on. I know it's a long shot but I wondered if you'd heard of them.'

'Who are they?'

'The mother is East European. She's called Irina Koval.'

Angela held up her coffee cup and looked down at the dark surface while she wracked her memory.

'No,' she said finally. 'That name doesn't ring any bells.'

'What about Maria Brennan or Drew Brennan?'

Pursing her lips, Angela said, 'There used to be a Patrick Brennan who hung out with Dad. This was years ago, when you were still a kid. Patrick Brennan was a boxer – he trained at the gym Dad owned. He was a brawler. A drinker. He disappeared not long before Dad walked out on us.'

'I don't remember him,' Lewis said.

'You wouldn't. You were way too young.'

'Did he marry an East European woman?'

'He was a typical man. He had women all over the place. If he had a wife, I didn't know about it.'

'Were the Brennan family well off?'

Angela laughed at the notion. 'It was the East End. No one was well off. Patrick Brennan was a gambler on top of his other faults, just like Dad. If either of them had any money, they'd find a way to lose it in two seconds flat. Most people thought that was why Pat Brennan did a runner. He wanted to leave his debts behind. He just disappeared one day without taking so much as a pair of socks with him.'

Lewis let the information sink in. From what he was hearing, if Pat Brennan was indeed Maria's father, then it didn't sound like she came from an easy background. So why had her mother been so determined to walk away from Carlson's money? It would take a huge amount of willpower not to be tempted by such a large cheque.

'What's this all about?' Angela asked.

'It's a special case I've been given at work,' Lewis said. 'I have to finish it quickly or I'm in trouble.'

'What kind of trouble?'

'The kind I'll get sacked for.'

Angela could see the concern on his face. 'That's not fair, Lewis,' she said. 'I wouldn't work for anyone who could fire me just like that. It means they don't value you.'

'The people I work for don't value anyone. We're only there to make money for the clients. That's all. We're expendable. And the ones like me are most at risk.'

'The ones without a trust fund, you mean?'

'Exactly.'

Angela looked at him wistfully. 'Sometimes I wish I hadn't pushed so hard. After Mum died, and then Dad left, I wanted to keep you off the streets and out of harm's way. I made sure you had your head down in your schoolbooks. I thought it was best at the time but now I'm not so sure.'

'You were the one who wanted me to get out of this neighbourhood.'

'I wanted you to have a better life than the rest of us. I didn't want you to get trapped here, like I did.' Tears were coming to her eyes as she spoke.

'Don't start getting maudlin, Angie,' Lewis said.

'If I'd been a better parent back then, you might still be here with us. Instead, you're only a few miles away but you're in a different world, pushing yourself to be someone you're not.'

Lewis felt a lump in his throat. He put his cup down on the

table. 'I'd better go,' he said. 'I'm late already. The office will be searching for me soon.'

Angela called the boys so they could say goodbye. Lewis waited out in the hallway for them. On one wall hung a photo taken at the boxing gym their father used to run. He was standing in the ring, leaning on the ropes. Above him was a painted sign with the mantra he'd been so proud of.

WE ARE WHAT WE REPEATEDLY DO

Lewis tapped a finger on the picture frame. 'I can still hear the sound of Dad's voice when he used to say it to me. That note of pride he had, especially when he'd had a good day. I wish I could hear him say it one last time.'

Angela looked at the photo. 'He was broken after Mum died. It was never the same after that. All he did repeatedly was drink too much once she was gone.'

Lewis tried to laugh but it came out sounding false. 'He left you to take care of me on your own.'

'You can't blame him, Lewis,' Angela said. 'He loved her. He couldn't bear it after Mum died.'

Lewis cut the conversation off. It was too painful to dredge up the memories. The boys came out of the living room at a run, toys in hand, and bundled into their uncle. When they said goodbye, Angela hugged Lewis close.

'I'll be back soon,' he said, 'to see everyone properly.'

His sister's eyes glistened. 'Don't make promises you won't keep, Lewis. I know you find it hard coming back. Go and do what you've got to do. We'll be waiting for you when you're ready to come home.'

Lewis opened the front door and stepped out on to the terraced street.

Angela called out to him as she closed the door. 'If I were you, I would just go round and speak to this family myself. Keep it simple. It's always better to solve things face to face.'

15

TURNING AWAY FROM the autocue screen, Robert Carlson stalked to the edge of the stage, looking out at the silent crowd in the banked auditorium. Sweat was forming on his temples, his white shirt front damp. Clearing his throat, he willed himself to continue. The company was depending on him.

'For decades,' he said, 'the energy industry has been telling the world that the future is coming. That it's nearly within our grasp. Now it's finally arrived. And we can be the first to usher this vision we've long promised into the present. The key to this is hydrogen energy.'

The audience applauded lightly. He needed more enthusiasm, Carlson thought. He needed to turn up the razzamatazz.

Looking up into the high balcony, he signalled to the crew with a discreet nod and a spotlight came on, a single beam illuminating the centre of the stage. A glass tank of water had been placed there, standing unacknowledged throughout his speech. From his pocket, Carlson took a thin sheet of plastic and unrolled it. He held it up above his head, the material shining in the light. Like a stage conjuror, he draped the gossamer sheet over the top of the tank, letting it hang loosely. Bubbles started to drift up from a set of electric terminals immersed in the water. Slowly the sheet began to rise as it filled with gas. The audience stared in awe as it levitated over the stage and seemed to hang for a moment in the air like an apparition. The chemistry involved was breathtakingly simple.

'An electric current, passed through water. That's all that's necessary to create hydrogen. It can be used to power any machine on earth. A car. A plane. A factory. An entire city. Soon there will be no more need for oil wells or gas refineries. No more drilling or fracking. No more wars or corrupt regimes fighting over fossil fuels.'

The sheet hung suspended in the spotlight, the material ballooning with trapped hydrogen. There was silence in the auditorium. A knife-edge of suspense. Carlson reached up and plucked the plastic sheet out of the air. It dangled limply in his hand as the gas escaped.

'Hydrogen is the future,' he continued. 'It's here. Hydrogen production using my method will save the planet. And most importantly, it's going to make you all insanely rich.'

With that, the house lights came back up. Carlson waited for the thunderous applause to settle before taking questions from the audience.

An American from the back of the room spoke up first. 'This is very impressive,' he called out, 'but what's the catch?' He was groomed and gym-toned, slouching back in his seat like he was unconvinced by the whole presentation. His accent was highbrow New York, cynical and disapproving. The assembled investors turned to him. There were murmurs of agreement from their ranks.

Carlson held his hands up in a gesture of openness. 'Scale,' he said. 'To manufacture hydrogen in industrial quantities requires the building of a massive facility. This has to be situated close to London, where the consumers are concentrated, and also close to a source of water. A plentiful supply of water is essential.'

'Have you proposed a location yet?' the American asked.

Carlson's blue eyes glinted in the house lights. 'The perfect site has already been secured. Building permission has been granted by the government. All the formal documents have been signed. As of today, we're ready to break ground.'

'So soon?'

'The government needs this project to succeed,' Carlson said emphatically. 'London needs energy. It also needs jobs. The construction of the manufacturing plant will create both. This will be a significant boost to the economy. Government officials are providing full co-operation at the highest levels.'

The American appeared sceptical. 'This still smells funny to me. There has to be a downside to all this.'

Carlson took a moment before answering. He wanted his honesty to shine through. There was no benefit in dissembling, he thought. These people were among the world's most prestigious bankers and financiers. Transparency at this stage of the pitch was imperative.

'The biggest stumbling block is power,' he said. 'In order for this project to be profitable, the amount of electricity we need to produce is huge. Electricity is the key to making hydrogen.

At current prices, the cost of grid power would be greater than the price of hydrogen on the global market.'

The American looked smug. 'I knew it was too good to be true,' he said.

Carlson waved the objection away. 'It's a problem we've already solved. We're not going to be taking electricity from the network. We're going to be making our own.'

Another murmur of interest passed through the audience.

'How?' someone shouted.

'By building a new combined-cycle generator as part of the plant. Unfortunately, this will have to be powered by natural gas until we can find an alternative method that's cost-effective. Renewables can't yet provide the wattage we need at present. The huge quantity of hydrogen the facility can produce will be sufficient to balance its annual emissions. The construction of the generator will be the first stage to get underway.'

The investors seemed impressed. They cast appreciative glances at one another.

'Are there any more questions?' Carlson asked.

A positive silence emanated from the gathering.

'Then please take a prospectus as you leave. A brunch reception has been organized at the Savoy. It will be a chance for everyone to meet and relax. I'll join you there to discuss the proposal further at your leisure.'

The Ever Sine employees began to pass along the aisles, handing out brochures to the investors. Carlson gave a final bow as he left the stage.

In the wings, Olivia Ward was waiting, her assistant obediently at her shoulder. Stagehands milled around in the shadows, moving equipment and coiling cables. Ward gave a generous burst of applause as Carlson came off stage.

'You excelled yourself, Robert. Your magic show was a great touch. Very theatrical.'

'It wasn't too corny?'

'Not at all. The audience seemed to love it.'

'Good. We need these investors. I'm not sure how much longer we can survive with the ones we have.'

Carlson slumped down into a chair, loosening his tie, his blue eyes drained of energy. Ward poured a glass of water and handed it to him. Needing privacy, she glanced darkly at her assistant, who skulked off to a far corner.

'You look terrible, Robert,' Ward said gently. 'Are you getting any sleep?'

'You know the strain I'm under.'

'Does anyone else?'

'Susannah is preoccupied with Emilia's problems. She doesn't need to be burdened by mine as well.'

'That's probably for the best,' Ward said cryptically.

Carlson looked up at her. 'What do you mean?'

Olivia Ward's response was typically blunt. 'I heard that Maria's family refused to sign the NDA,' she said.

'Really?'

Ward nodded gravely. Carlson could see the seriousness etched on her face.

'Do you think we should offer them more money?' he asked.

'The amount was chosen forensically, Robert. Any less would look cheap. Any more would appear suspicious.'

'But if they don't accept the offer, it's all meaningless.'

'I think there might be another way.'

Carlson narrowed his eyes. He looked nervously at the stagehands bustling around to be sure their conversation couldn't be overheard. 'I don't want this to get out of hand,' he said.

Ward lowered her voice. 'Stop worrying. There's no way to connect any of this to you.'

'That doesn't reassure me, Olivia.'

She met his gaze and held it. 'We agreed that you'd follow my lead on this. There can be no sign of discord between us. That's imperative right now. It's vital we stay focused if we're going to keep our plans on track.'

Carlson hesitated. After a lingering moment, he said, 'Of course, you're right.'

'Good,' Ward said, smiling coldly. 'Because we both know what happened to Maria was her own fault. However tragic, she brought this all on herself.'

16

WHEN HE REACHED the estate, Lewis began to climb to the fourteenth floor of Crowmoor House, over the litter-strewn steps and shards of glass. From the windows, he could see the slab-like housing blocks of East London stretching out into the distance, the towers jagged on the skyline like broken teeth, the wind howling around as the weather closed in.

Walking along the exposed landing, past doors barricaded with steel grilles, he counted the flat numbers until he reached 149. He rang the bell and stood back. Footsteps hurried down the hallway. He could hear the click of metal as locks were unfastened. Irina Koval cracked the door open and peered out. It took a moment for her to recognize him.

'You?' she snapped. 'How do you know where we live?'

'Your address was on the NDA I brought to you yesterday.' Lewis held out the torn pages of the contract as proof.

'You have no right coming here.'

'I need you to hear me out,' he said. 'I want to make you an offer.'

'I told you already. I don't want that man's money,' Irina shouted and began to close the door.

Lewis stepped forward. 'That's not what I'm talking about. I want to offer you something else.'

'What else do you have?'

'Answers,' he said.

Irina paused. She eyed him suspiciously through the gap in the door frame. 'What answers?'

'To the questions you have about how Maria died. It seems you're not the only one who thinks there's something strange about it.'

Lewis watched a thousand thoughts fleet behind Irina's eyes. Slowly she opened the door.

'You'd better come inside,' she said. 'I don't want my neighbours thinking the police are here again.' She stood aside and ushered him in, pointing along the narrow hallway. 'Wait in the living room,' she said. 'It's cold outside. I'll make us some tea.'

The flat was cramped and sparsely furnished. Paint was flaking off the ceilings where damp had seeped in. Lewis had spent his childhood in identical flats. The same layout. The same features. He could have found his way around in the dark, navigating like a rat in a maze.

The television was playing in the corner of the living room. Lewis took a seat on the sofa, looking up at the framed photographs on the walls. School portraits and family pictures. A framed photo of Irina as a young pageant queen in a village covered in snow. On one wall, a bronze crucifix hung above a small shrine with a burning candle. Lewis recognized Maria Brennan's photo. It looked like it was taken at her confirmation ceremony. She was young and bright-eyed, wearing an ivory dress with a purple ribbon around her waist. A black lace veil had been hung over the photo frame, a rosary placed nearby.

When she came into the room, Irina was carrying a tray with cups, a sugar bowl and an enamel teapot. He could see how fragile she was, her arms only skin and bone, her hands gnarled and scarred by years of work. She took a seat in the armchair opposite and poured the tea. It was dark and pungent with the aroma of cloves and mint. Lewis thanked her, the cup hot and steaming in his hands. He blew on the rim of the mug as he drank.

'I've never had tea like this before,' he said.

'It's Ukrainian. My children hate it, but I like to remind myself of home. It's an old habit.'

'That's where you're from?'

She cast her eyes downwards. 'A long time ago.'

'Do you ever go back?'

Irina flashed him an impatient look. 'Did you come here to ask about my travel plans?' she said.

'Of course not. I should get to the point. I was discussing Maria's case last night and it seems there are details that aren't easy to explain. I want to look deeper into the case and report back what I find to you.'

'But you work for Robert Carlson?'

'And I think the facts will exonerate him once I get to the truth. I'm a lawyer. It's what I'm trained to do.'

Irina shook her head dismissively. 'I don't trust lawyers.'

'I don't blame you.'

'Then why should I trust you?'

'Because I'm going to keep looking anyway. I want to solve this case, even if no one's willing to help me. I've made a promise to someone that I'll keep digging. It's a point of principle now.'

'So you're a crusader?'

Lewis shook his head at the idea. 'No one's ever accused me of that before,' he said. 'I'm only a lawyer. A good one.'

He could see her softening as he spoke, the frown on her forehead relaxing. The deep, suspicious creases easing out.

'What do you want from me?' Irina asked.

'I need to hear your side of the story. To fill in the information I'm missing.'

'Such as?'

'Why don't you start at the beginning?'

Irina put her tea down on the table. Lewis watched her summon up distant memories. Her voice was sorrowful as she spoke.

'I was young when I first came to this country, just a girl really, from a small town near Kyiv. Soon after I arrived in London, I met a man. I should have known he was trouble when I first laid eyes on him. Everyone told me to keep away but I was too naïve to listen.'

'Patrick Brennan?'

Irina nodded. 'All he gave me was a few years of heartache and two children. I wanted them to have all the opportunities I never had. I tried my hardest with Drew but he was too much like his father. Maria fulfilled my dreams a thousand times over. She was beautiful and kind and intelligent. She really cared about people, about trying to save the planet. I thought it was a teenage obsession, something she would grow out of, but she was serious. It was her life. She made a career out of it and then one day it was all taken away.'

'You mean by Robert Carlson?'

'He tossed Maria aside like she was worthless. After that, she couldn't find another job even though she was so qualified. Maria was convinced he was whispering in people's ears, trying to ruin her reputation. She thought he was doing it to take revenge on her. She wouldn't say why.'

Lewis was trying to piece the story together from the fragments he was hearing. There were still too many holes for him to get a clear picture. 'Did she work closely with Robert Carlson?'

'Maria was like his right hand. They were together night and day.'

'And then he just fired her for no reason?'

'That's what she told me.'

'But why would Carlson do something like that if she was so valuable to him?'

'Because he's a spiteful man,' Irina said, her face tightening again. 'Because people like him don't care about anyone but themselves.'

'Had Maria done something at work? Made a mistake or had a disagreement of some kind?'

Irina shook her head. 'All Maria would say was that she was going to make Carlson sorry. She said when the truth came out, people would finally see who he really was. That's when Carlson began harassing her. Maria wouldn't talk to him. She didn't answer the phone when he called. He turned up here the night before she died, desperate to speak with her alone, but she refused.'

'Was he angry or upset?'

'They both were. Maria was crying. I saw Carlson pleading with her to stop.'

85

Lewis shifted in his seat. He needed to be delicate. 'Do you think there could have been something between them? Something personal?'

'What do you mean?'

'Were they . . . involved with each other?'

Irina pulled her sweater close, twisting the fabric in her fingers.

'No, of course not. Maria wasn't like that. She wasn't the kind to get mixed up with a married man.'

'What was she like?'

'Maria was dedicated to her work. It meant everything to her.'

'But that doesn't mean she had no personal life.'

Irina waved the suggestion away. 'I know my daughter. When all of her friends were having fun, she was studying. She had two part-time jobs at university and still finished top of her class. She wanted to work for Robert Carlson because he had the same ideals as her. Maria said that he used his money for good. To make the world a better place. She really looked up to him to start with. It was only at the end that she hated him.'

Lewis could see that Irina believed every word she was saying, but as she talked, it only confirmed his suspicions. What she was describing had all the hallmarks of a romantic relationship reaching a messy end.

'Mrs Koval . . .' he began.

'Please. Call me Irina.'

'Irina, I'm still concerned that this is only speculation.'

Her tone grew spiky and fractious. 'You don't believe me?'

Lewis didn't want to alienate her, but he had to be open about his doubts.

'Believing you isn't enough,' he said. 'I'm a lawyer. I need proof.'

She scowled at him in disappointment. 'Then you are not on my side.'

'It's not a matter of sides,' Lewis said. 'I don't know Robert Carlson personally. I've never met him. But I don't believe that he's the kind of man to do what you're accusing him of. It seems there's more to Maria's death than has come to light. You're not the only one who feels that way. But I can't take anyone's word for it. I need proof.'

Irina wrapped her arms tightly around her chest, struggling with herself to make a decision. Finally she stood from her chair.

'Come with me,' she said.

Irina led Lewis from the living room out into the hallway and pushed open the door to a small single bedroom. Opening the wardrobe, Irina reached inside and took out a green plastic sack. Lewis could see a pair of shoes and some clothes folded inside. Irina began taking the items out one by one. She handled them slowly, with a painstaking reverence.

'These are the clothes Maria was wearing when she died. The police gave them to me with the belongings they found in her car.'

From the bottom of the sack, Irina removed a Manila folder. Inside was a thick file of documents. She took a sheet of paper from the top and handed it to Lewis. It was brittle and delicate, as if it had dried out after being heavily waterlogged. On one side, a handwritten phrase was blurred but still legible.

He read it out loud. 'Beware. Do not open. Call police.'

Irina pointed to the sheet of paper. 'Now do you see?'

Lewis shook his head. 'I don't know what this is.'

'It was found on the windscreen of Maria's car, tucked under a wiper blade. The police say it was a warning to stop anyone from opening the car door and breathing the fumes trapped inside.'

'But I still don't see what this proves.'

Irina ran a finger over the spidery letters on the page.

'Maria didn't write this note,' she said. 'This isn't her handwriting.'

In the living room, Lewis waited alone while Irina made more tea. He read the note over several times. Water had caused the ink to run and fade on the paper. Now it was barely legible. Was it possible for Irina to know whether her daughter had written it? Lewis wasn't sure. But if she hadn't, it meant someone else had been out at Coldharbour Marshes when Maria died.

Flicking through the paperwork in the folder, Lewis was confronted with a sheaf of pages that made more sense to him. The document was a joint partnership agreement, a substantial one full of technical clauses and appendices. He looked the contract over quickly, scanning the text. It was drafted for the construction of a hydrogen fuel plant. The named parties were offshore shell corporations and holding companies registered in Panama and the Cayman Islands. The pages weren't executed, the signature lines and names of company directors still blank. Lewis wondered why Maria Brennan would have this kind of document in her car.

When Irina returned with fresh tea, Lewis replaced the pages of the contract in the folder. She handed him a cup and he thanked her. He looked down at the note that had been found on the windscreen of Maria's car.

'Do you think Robert Carlson wrote this?' he asked.

'Only if he understands the Cyrillic alphabet,' Irina said and leaned closer to the table. She traced a fingertip over the page. 'You see how this "N" is slightly odd? How the "E" is out of shape?'

Lewis looked closely. She was right. The letters were off-centre, strangely deformed. 'I see what you mean,' he said.

'The letters look badly written in English. But they're perfect in Ukrainian or Russian or Serbian. A whole host of Slavic languages. Whoever wrote this note was working so fast they mixed up two alphabets. It's easy to do.'

'Did Maria speak Ukrainian?'

'I taught her when she was a young girl. Maria was fluent.'

'Doesn't that make it more likely that she wrote the warning?'

Irina reached for a notebook among the belongings. She opened it and handed it to Lewis. 'This is Maria's handwriting,' she said. 'It's completely different.'

Lewis looked at page after page. Irina was right. Her daughter's writing was the most distinctive he had ever seen. It was ornate and cursive, each letter formed in long loops and tails, the pen hardly leaving the page. There were entries in English and Ukrainian and the writing was recognizable in each. The words in the notebook bore no resemblance to the hastily written warning sign that had been left on Maria's car.

'So if Maria didn't write it, then who did?' Lewis asked.

Irina shook her head. 'I have no idea.'

'Who else do you know who understands Ukrainian?'

'Me, obviously. And I know I didn't write it.'

'What about your son?'

'Drew never learned. He was too lazy.'

'So there's an unknown Slavic speaker out there who knows how Maria died.'

'That's who we need to find.'

This was a dangerous path to follow, Lewis thought. The idea of some shadowy East European being involved in the case was a chilling prospect.

'If what you're saying is true,' he asked, 'why don't you go to the police?'

Irina's voice was firm. 'Because the police only cause more problems.'

'But you think your daughter was murdered.'

'Look around you,' she said, with an expression of incomprehension. 'You think the police will listen to me? I'm an immigrant. A foreigner. Their job is to protect men like Robert Carlson. To make sure the rich always win.'

'I don't believe that,' Lewis said.

'Then you're not from my world. If you were, you'd understand.'

Lewis knew how he looked in her eyes. Distant and officious in his business suit and tie. The outer shell he wore to mask his true character.

'My world and yours aren't so different,' he said.

Irina looked sceptical. 'I doubt that.'

'I grew up in Stepney – the Ocean Estate on Mile End Road.'

She seemed surprised. 'You live there now?'

'No. I left a few years ago.'

'Your parents are still there?'

'They're both dead. It seems your ex-husband and my father knew each other. My dad ran the boxing gym where Pat Brennan trained.'

Irina paused. 'Ron Miller? I remember him. His wife was killed in a robbery.'

'That was my mum. She was working in an off-licence and there was a raid. She was stabbed. After that my dad ran off. He couldn't take it. My sister brought me up on her own.'

'That must have been hard. Losing your mother so young.'

'I always felt like it was my fault. Like I should have been able to save her. But there was nothing I could do. I was just a kid. I was asleep at home when it happened.'

Irina was examining him closely, as if she had discovered something about him that was previously hidden. 'You're not like them, are you?' she said. 'The other lawyers. The people you work with.'

'No. I'm not like them at all.'

'You're like Maria,' she said. 'That's what she wanted too.'

'What do you mean?'

'Escape.'

Lewis gave a wry laugh. 'I haven't escaped very far.'

There was a noise from beyond the room. The sound of curtains being drawn back and heavy footsteps on the floorboards. Irina suddenly looked rattled.

'You should go,' she whispered. 'My son is awake.'

She stood and began to usher Lewis from the room. He pointed to the folder of legal paperwork.

'Can I take this?' he asked.

'Of course,' Irina whispered, pushing him towards the front

91

door. Lewis tucked the Manila folder under his arm. Stepping out into the cold, he turned one last time before walking away.

'Can I ask you a question?' he said. 'If you really think Robert Carlson is involved in Maria's death, why would you want me to help you?'

Irina looked at him as she closed the door.

'What other choice do I have?' she said.

17

THE AMERICAN LEFT the conference hall with the other investors. Limousines were lined up to take them to the Savoy for
the brunch meeting. Uniformed drivers stood at the doors
with umbrellas, waiting patiently for their passengers in the
rain. Camera crews and eager reporters were waylaying the
investors as they ran for their cars, desperate for information
about Robert Carlson's latest mystery project. The American
sidestepped them, his head down. He slipped into the open
door of the limo at the head of the line.

A man was waiting inside, listening to the playback from
the computer resting on his lap. He slipped off his headphones
as the American took a seat opposite him.

'Did you get what you wanted?' the American asked.
He reached inside the lapel of his jacket and unclipped
the microphone hidden there. He held it out in his open
palm.

The man took the lapel mike. 'You did well.'

He spoke with an accent the American could hardly

understand. It was heavy and foreign, too many consonants in the wrong places.

'Carlson didn't like the pushback I gave him. I tried to sow as much doubt as I could.'

'You were very convincing.'

'Are you going to pay me now?'

'First we will go to the reception at the Savoy. I want you to continue there. Mingle. Make small talk. Keep pouring doubt on Carlson's hydrogen project.'

'Look, Mister . . .?' The American waited, trying to tease a name out of his employer.

Stony-faced, the man said, 'You can call me Andrei.'

'Look, Andrei, I completed my assignment back there. I don't know what you agreed with my agent but if you want more, we need to renegotiate my fee.'

Andrei looked at him with a thin smile that barely stretched his lips. 'Don't worry about money. Just keep doing as I ask. Spread the word that Carlson's project is a pipe dream. I will make sure you are handsomely rewarded.'

'Handsomely? What does that mean in real money?'

'I will pay double.'

The American relaxed visibly. He sat back with a broad grin on his tanned face. 'I don't know what you've got against this Carlson guy,' he said, 'but this is the best gig I've had in a long time.'

Andrei passed the microphone back to the American.

'I don't have anything against him,' he said. 'Quite the opposite. I'm his business partner.'

18

DREW BRENNAN HELD the fabric of his hoodie up to his face and breathed in the lingering smell of petrol. He should have washed everything when he came home last night. Or better still, thrown it all away. It was dangerous to leave evidence lying around for the police. It was stupid. This kind of sloppiness had landed him in trouble before.

His bedroom hadn't changed since he was a teenager. The same faded curtains and brown wallpaper and tattered posters taped to the walls. The same out-of-date stereo and Xbox he'd been playing for ever. He was stuck, flat broke. He'd been trapped in the same existence for years without anything to show for it. Glenn Egan was his friend from when they were kids and even he had stepped up and made something of himself now. They had been apprentices together, straight out of school. They'd been on similar paths, learning their trades, heading towards the same goals. Then disaster had struck. Drew had got caught.

The offer had been too tempting to resist. Hiding a stash of weed in return for an envelope full of money. He remembered holding the cash in his hands, counting the notes, fanning them out. Five hundred pounds for doing nothing. It had seemed like a fortune to a teenager, wide-eyed and reckless. It had taken the police dog three minutes to find the hiding place once they had broken into the flat at dawn.

Two years in Belmarsh had been an apprenticeship of a different kind. A crash course in the art of survival. He'd been forced to battle it out with the others on his wing for his place in the hierarchy. The brutality and nihilism of the place had seeped into him like poison. He remembered the long stretches of tedium. The frantic bursts of violence. Even on release, the smell of prison had stuck to him. He had made a reputation for himself and now he was forced to live up to it. Being back in Whitechapel didn't help. The place could bring down a saint, Drew thought. He remembered how Maria had gone downhill fast after she had lost her job and was forced to move back home. She had tried to hide it but Drew could tell how badly it affected her. Everything she had worked for was gone and she was back where she started. Trapped, just like him.

Drew gathered his soiled clothes and stuffed them into a plastic bin liner to carry down to the laundrette on the corner. He heard hushed voices out in the hallway as the front door creaked open and then gently closed again. It sounded like his mother was creeping around in her own house. He concentrated on the sound for a moment. Why was she being so cagey?

Stepping out into the hallway, he saw Irina locking the front door.

'Who was that?' Drew asked.

'Someone who wants to help me.'

'Who?'

Irina looked at him defiantly. 'The young lawyer we met yesterday. The one you threatened.'

Drew scowled. 'We'll be in big trouble if anyone sees him leaving here.'

'He's not the police.'

'He's a lawyer. That's just as bad.'

'I don't have a choice,' Irina said firmly. 'No one else will help us. I need to know what happened to Maria.'

His mother was torturing herself. No matter how hard he tried, he couldn't shake her out of this obsession.

'You're mad,' Drew said, pointing to his temple. 'Maria killed herself. There's no mystery to solve. Why can't you see that?'

'If there's no mystery, why would Robert Carlson offer us so much money to keep quiet?'

'To him, it's nothing. It's pocket change.'

'It's a bribe.'

'One that would change our lives.'

'What about Maria's life?'

God, he couldn't keep going over this. 'She's gone. You just have to accept it.'

Irina looked at him sharply for a moment. 'The lawyer just asked me who I knew that spoke Ukrainian.'

Drew shrugged. 'So?'

'I lied,' Irina said. 'I told him only Maria and I understood Ukrainian. But you do as well. Not fluently, but enough to mix up some letters if you write too quickly.'

He looked at her in confusion. 'I don't know what you're talking about.'

'You knew Maria worked for a rich man. You knew he'd offer money to us if she was dead. Didn't you?'

Drew began to understand what she was saying. 'I would never do that.'

Irina fixed him with a deathly stare, her eyes burning with rage. 'You hated Maria. You always have. I know you'd kill for money. Even your own sister.'

'How could you say that?'

'Because I know who you are.'

Suddenly Irina burst as if the emotion she had been bottling up inside her had boiled over. She came at him, beating her fists on his chest. She was spitting with fury. Drew dropped the bundle of laundry he was holding. He grasped his mother's wrists to stop her pounding him.

'Get out,' she said. 'Go!'

Slowly he released her from his grip. Irina seemed exhausted from the exertion. Without a word, Drew turned and opened the front door and stalked out into the harsh daylight.

19

THE COMMERCIAL DIVISION of Renfrew and Hall was a riot of ringing telephones and urgent voices. Lewis kept his head down as he made his way across the floor to his desk. He could feel the disapproving gaze of his line manager burning into his back. It was nearly lunchtime, his absence unexplained. The junior lawyer he shared a desk with seemed surprised to see him as he took a seat.

'Miller, where have you been?' she whispered. 'People have been asking for you all morning.'

'I'm on a special case.'

'Bullshit. You slept in.'

He leaned across the desk, his voice lowered. 'It's for Charlie King.'

She looked impressed. 'What's he asked you to do?'

'I can't say.'

'Well, whatever it is, you'd better get your story straight. I can't keep making excuses for you.'

The stack of files on Lewis's desk was piling up, the screen of his computer plastered with notes in fluorescent pink and yellow. He would have to work late again. There was no other way to get everything done. If he let his workload slide too far, the clients were going to start complaining.

He took the joint partnership agreement out of his bag. It was thick and heavy. Fifty pages at least. Lewis didn't have time to read it with all of the other work he had to finish. He looked at his colleague's desk. It was clean and empty, a picture of efficiency.

'Do me a favour,' Lewis whispered. 'Read this for me, will you? Let me know what you think.'

He tossed the file at her and she caught it. She flicked through the pages, her interest piqued.

'I'll read it for you if you buy me lunch next week,' she said with a wink.

Lewis nodded. 'Deal.'

He started working his way through the paperwork on his desk but his mind kept going back to the conversation with Irina Koval. If Maria Brennan had been in an employment dispute with Robert Carlson, there would be a paper trail. Her lawyer would have kept records. Every document told its own story. He couldn't resist seeing if he could access her legal history.

The receptionist at the Whitechapel Law Centre picked up the phone. In the background, a hubbub of office noise buzzed like static.

'It's Lewis Miller,' he said. 'From Renfrew and Hall. I came in yesterday to meet Martin Sobel.'

He could hear a tremor in the receptionist's voice. 'Yes, I remember. Thank you for calling. We're all devastated here. The news has come as such a shock.'

Lewis paused, confused. 'I'm not sure I understand.'

'The news about Martin.'

'Has something happened?'

The woman sniffed back tears. 'Martin is dead. It happened last night.'

Lewis was stunned. He wanted to ask her to repeat the words to make sure he'd heard her correctly. 'I'm sorry to hear that,' he said instead. 'I had no idea.'

'It's so awful. I can't stop worrying about his family. His kids. He was such a kind man. Such a dedicated lawyer.'

'That's actually why I was calling. I wanted to ask him about a young woman he was representing. Maria Brennan.'

The receptionist tried to recover her professional manner. 'Excuse me, of course. What were you looking for?'

'I was hoping to look at any transcripts or witness statements about the claim she was making. I need as much information as possible to look into her case.'

There was a long intake of breath. 'This is the second enquiry about that material in twenty-four hours,' she said.

'Someone else has requested it?'

'Yes.'

'Can I ask who?'

'Another lawyer – Olivia Ward. She's Robert Carlson's in-house counsel. She called here yesterday evening after your meeting with Martin. She demanded all the copies of the transcripts we'd taken.'

'Did you send them to her?'

'We reminded her that they were sent over weeks ago, in compliance with regulations. She must have overlooked them. The matter wasn't considered important back then.'

'Is it possible to request further copies?'

'Absolutely not. Martin isn't here to sign off on the matter now. Anyway, after the call from Ms Ward, he was worried he might have missed something. He took all of the drives containing the material with him when he left the office last night. They were with Martin when he died.'

Lewis was trying to piece together what he was hearing. 'Thank you for all your help,' he said. 'I'm sure I can pick this up at my end now. Again, I'm so sorry about Martin.'

He was about to hang up when another question occurred to him.

'One more thing,' Lewis said. 'Can I ask how he died?' He was praying that the answer was a heart attack or a stroke or some other natural cause.

The receptionist gave a sniffle. 'A cycling accident,' she said. 'Apparently he hit a pothole in the road and fell off his bike. A delivery lorry was behind him. It was going too fast and couldn't stop . . .'

Her voice trailed off into sobs. When he had offered his condolences and hung up, Lewis stared at the desktop for a moment, picturing Martin Sobel. His gaunt, sincere face and dishevelled appearance. The manner of his death wasn't overly suspicious, but it wasn't natural either. In the back of his mind, Lewis remembered the advice Sobel had given him.

Don't believe in coincidences.

He stayed in the office throughout lunch, keeping up a punishing work rate into the afternoon to clear the files from his desk. Rights contracts and tax loopholes. An insurance claim for a Norwegian shipping company. However hard he concentrated,

102

it was impossible to stop thinking of the Brennan case. The whole mess became murkier the more he tried to find a pathway through it. Now there was a mounting death toll. All afternoon, his mood alternated between intrigue and caution. There were already a host of different strands to the web he was trying to fight a way through. Now it looked like Carlson's legal team were getting involved. If he wanted to know the reason for their interest, he should go straight to the source, Lewis thought. The simple course of action was often the best.

He called the number for Carlson's company, Ever Sine. It was picked up by a switchboard operator.

'Hello. I need to speak to someone in your legal department. Her name is Olivia Ward.'

'Can I ask who's calling, please?'

'Lewis Miller, from Renfrew and Hall.'

She asked him to hold.

The line clicked back after twenty seconds.

'Ms Ward will speak with you at five p.m.,' she said.

'Today?'

'Yes. She can make a little time for you. Fifteen minutes at most.'

'Great. I'll give you my number . . .'

The operator interrupted. 'No, Mr Miller. She'll speak with you at five p.m., here at the office.'

'In person?'

'That's right.'

Lewis was caught off guard. 'Uh, OK. Great. Tell her I'll see her then.'

'By the way, Mr Miller,' the operator added, 'Ms Ward asked me to tell you that she's been expecting your call for some time.'

20

THE STEEL SKELETON of the new shopping centre was rising up out of the Isle of Dogs. Soon it would dominate the landscape, a shiny temple of modern consumerism. Drew Brennan rode along the access road. Above him, workmen swarmed over the scaffolding, fluorescent-clothed, calling out commands to each other over the din. Cranes working overhead lifted heavy steel beams high into the air, their loads twisting gently in the breeze. Everything was branded with the Egan Construction logo, from the cement trucks and pile drivers, to the signboards posted on the perimeter fence. The family understood the power of advertising.

Drew stopped his motorbike, a Ducati, at the site entrance and flipped up his visor. The security guard was leaning on a barrier, bored.

'I'm here to see Glenn Egan,' he said, and gave his name.

The guard ran a finger down his checklist. Satisfied, he hit the button and the bar began to rise.

'He's working on the plaza on the east side,' he said. 'You can't miss him.'

Drew nodded his thanks and pulled away. He rode slowly, giving way to the streams of forklift trucks and earth movers that crossed his path. Clouds of dust were blowing over the site, the sound of hammering ringing out. Sparks flew in bright arcs from welding torches. He saw Glenn standing in the half-built plaza, talking to another man, arguing over a set of plans. Sour-faced and ungroomed, both were wearing hard hats and high-vis jackets. Drew recognized Frank Egan at a distance. His reputation was fearsome. He had come over from the west of Ireland as a teenager and worked his way up by sweat and guile. The construction trade had been a cover for his less palatable activities. It was almost by accident that it had come to be so successful. Now the construction company dominated the family's interests but their business style hadn't changed. It was on Frank Egan's instructions they had torched the Bentley the previous night. He liked people to know he could still settle disputes the old-fashioned way.

Drew parked the Ducati on its stand and removed his helmet. Glenn waved him over. His body language was different around his uncle, Drew noticed. He was meeker, more subservient. The cocky swagger he usually adopted was gone. Drew wasn't used to seeing him like this. He looked smaller somehow.

'This is my uncle,' Glenn said. 'I told him it was time for you both to meet.'

Frank Egan took Drew's hand. He was a short, stocky man, solid and tough, his hair mostly gone. His face was wind-weathered and craggy, the Galway burr still prominent in his voice.

'Good job last night,' Frank said. 'That lying fool was on the phone to me first thing, crying like a baby, saying how sorry he was. He paid everything he owed. Just like that. He doesn't want his house going up in flames next time.'

'Glad to be of help,' Drew said.

'My nephew tells me your dad was Pat Brennan?'

'That's right.'

'I knew Pat. He was a good man. You're the spitting image of him.'

'That's what my mum says. I don't really remember him. He left home when I was still young.'

'Take it from me, he was one of the good ones. Any son of his is all right by me. We always need people we can trust. There's a new project coming up. A big one. I'm going to need some reliable people to help out.'

Drew saw his opportunity. 'That's what I wanted to talk to you about, Frank. I used to be a trainee welder. I nearly finished my apprenticeship a few years ago but I got sidetracked.'

'Why was that?'

'I got sent down,' Drew said. 'Two years.'

Frank nodded at him admiringly. 'Prison is a good place to learn some manners,' he said. 'That's what my nephew needs.'

Glenn looked stung. He turned his gaze to the floor.

'I'm looking to complete my apprenticeship,' Drew continued eagerly. 'I'm a fast learner. I need a chance, that's all.'

Frank shook his head. 'I've got all the welders I can use, son. It's your other talents I need right now.'

'I appreciate that. But I don't want to be setting fire to cars in my thirties.'

'I understand. And I'll see what I can do. But right now, those skills are in short supply.'

Glenn cut in. 'This new project is controversial,' he said. 'It's going to be targeted by protestors. Tree huggers and bleeding hearts. You know the type. We need people to dissuade them.'

Drew knew exactly what he meant. Breaking heads and scaring people. The same terror tactics he was paid for now. He tried not to let his disappointment show. 'Of course,' he said. 'Tell me when and where and I'll be there.'

'Good lad,' Frank said. He took a thick envelope from the inside pocket of his high-vis jacket and handed it to Drew. 'That's what I owe you for last night,' he said. 'There's a bonus in there to show my appreciation.'

Drew took it without pleasure. He gave a nod of thanks out of respect but his eyes betrayed his true feelings. He extended a hand and Frank Egan shook it. The meeting over, Frank strode away towards the half-finished grand entrance to his new shopping centre.

Glenn hooked an arm around his friend's shoulder. 'I told you I couldn't make any promises,' he said.

Drew was disappointed but he was still grateful for Glenn's attempt. 'Thanks for trying,' he said.

'Look, I've got another job for you,' Glenn said, his voice hushed. 'I need you to go and see a bookie in South London and collect some money.'

'Where?'

'The Old Kent Road. I'll text you the address.'

107

'How much money?'

'Ninety grand.'

Drew gave a low whistle. This wasn't the usual kind of job he was given.

Glenn sensed his hesitation. He shot him a stare with a glint of menace behind it. 'You wanted to meet my uncle,' he snapped. 'That means you owe me now.'

21

HYDROGEN. FUEL OF THE FUTURE! *Imagine an energy source that is cheap, clean and limitless. Hydrogen is highly efficient and creates no greenhouse gases. We can create it by passing electricity through water. It really is that simple. Hydrogen is the most abundant element in the universe, so why aren't we using it to heat our homes and power our cars?*

The voice echoed from the speakers as Lewis entered the cavernous industrial atrium of the Ever Sine building. On a giant video screen, Robert Carlson's face loomed in extreme close-up, studious and sincere. Even in his own lobby, Carlson was evangelizing for green power. He was a man obsessed, Lewis thought.

At the reception desk, Lewis announced his arrival and was asked to wait. Olivia Ward was sending someone down to collect him. He stood under the giant display screen as he waited, watching Carlson's face, studying him with interest. It was clear that Carlson was a great salesman, but there was something reticent about him. Something fleeting and shadowy behind his eyes, as if he was a man who kept a great deal of himself hidden. Lewis wondered if soon he'd find out why.

It was twenty past five when an assistant came down and announced that Olivia Ward was ready to see him. The assistant was plain and mousey but with a superior manner, as if Lewis's presence was an unwelcome imposition on her time. Gathering his things, Lewis followed her to the lift and they rode up to the executive floor in silence.

Olivia Ward was speaking on the phone as Lewis was shown into her office. She was facing the picture window with its views out over the city and didn't turn around as he came into the room. The assistant ushered him coldly over to a black-lacquered meeting table and he took a seat while he waited. He watched as Ward finished her call, her voice hushed. She stood poised and refined, her red hair cut straight across her forehead, her grey business suit expensively tailored.

When she hung up the phone, Olivia Ward turned and approached in confident strides. Lewis noticed that she wasn't smiling.

'You're Miller?' she said.

'Lewis Miller, from Renfrew and Hall. I'm working on the Brennan case.'

Ward took a seat opposite, perching on the edge of the chair as if she was only going to be there for the briefest time possible.

'There is no Brennan case,' she said. 'I hope you're not labouring under the misapprehension that there is.'

Her abrupt tone was unsettling. Lewis had been expecting a friendly discussion. Instead, Ward looked ready to do battle.

'I was asked to handle this case personally by Charlie King,' Lewis said. 'I intend to finish it.'

'We asked Charlie to prepare an NDA and get Maria's family to sign it. The generous fee was meant to make this simple, yet even then you managed to fumble it.'

'I'm still trying,' Lewis said. 'That's why I need to see the documents from Maria's employment dispute.'

Ward looked perplexed. 'Which documents?'

'The ones you requested from the Whitechapel Law Centre yesterday.'

'Those are off limits,' Ward said with a brisk shake of her head. 'We don't need you blundering around with sensitive materials.'

Lewis was surprised at her aggressive tone but his instincts urged him to keep pressing further. 'Maria was fired from this company for gross misconduct,' he said. 'What had she done? It must have been serious.'

Ward seemed to gather herself before she spoke. 'Perhaps you're not hearing me clearly. This matter doesn't require your attention. Maria Brennan was sacked legitimately. She thought lodging a legal claim would be an easy way to make some money. We fought back. As far as we're concerned this matter is closed.'

'Maria's family don't see it that way.'

'Maybe that's because you're stirring them up. We know you visited her mother this morning.'

Ward glared at him across the table as if he had committed an act of high treason. How could she know about his visit to see Irina? Lewis hadn't shared his movements with anyone.

'I met Maria's mother to hear her side of the story,' Lewis said. 'That's all. She's grieving. Any mother would be.'

'I sympathize. But the truth is simple – Maria took her own life. It's tragic but we have nothing to add to the matter.'

'There's been a development you should know about,' Lewis said.

Ward's interest was piqued. 'Go on.'

'Maria's mother is certain someone else was present when her daughter died.'

'Impossible.'

'She has proof,' Lewis said. 'A note was left on Maria's car. A warning. The note isn't in Maria's handwriting.'

Ward paused for a moment as she processed the information.

Lewis leaned forward. 'If Mr Carlson submitted a handwriting sample, he could rule himself out of any enquiries,' he said.

'Absolutely not,' Ward scoffed. 'Robert has nothing to prove.'

'It would be a big bombshell if Maria's family go to the media.'

Ward folded her arms across her chest. 'That is not going to happen. The police found nothing suspicious about Maria's suicide. It seems you're taking an unhealthy interest in this case, Mr Miller?'

He kept a straight face as he looked her in the eye. 'I thought there wasn't any case?'

She shook her head in disgust. 'We're done here.'

Ward rang for her assistant and she quickly appeared in the doorway, ready to escort Lewis back to the lobby.

Gathering his coat and briefcase, Lewis said, 'There was one other thing. Some paperwork was found in Maria's car. It looks like a joint partnership agreement. I haven't had a chance to examine it fully but it looked strange to me.'

Hearing this, a chink appeared in Ward's armour. It was the first time Lewis had seen her lose her steely composure.

'Do you have the file with you?'

'No. I left it at the office.'

'Why don't you send it over to me? I should probably take a look.'

Lewis frowned. 'I thought we weren't sharing paperwork with each other?'

Ward's look was withering. 'I want that file, Miller. Remember who you are.'

'If you want it, you'll have to send a formal request to my office,' Lewis said with a cool shrug. He couldn't disguise the note of satisfaction in his voice.

The assistant led him along the corridor in silence. Her frosty body language made Lewis think she must have heard the entire conversation from her desk outside the office door. She was loyal, Lewis thought. The disdain emanating from her was even more severe than from her boss.

They were walking towards the lift at the end of the corridor when the doors opened. An entourage of executives stepped out, engrossed in conversation. Lewis moved aside to let them pass. At the centre of the group was a face he recognized. The distinguished profile was unmistakable, striding forward, issuing commands, the team shoaling around him like acolytes. Lewis knew he'd not get another chance.

'Mr Carlson,' he called out, raising his voice. 'My name is Lewis Miller.'

He forced his way into the pack with his hand extended. The entourage stopped.

Robert Carlson looked at the outstretched hand with a bemused frown. 'What can I do for you?' he said flatly.

'I work for Renfrew and Hall,' Lewis said. 'I was hoping I could get a minute of your time.'

Carlson considered it. 'You can have thirty seconds.'

'I just had a meeting with Olivia Ward. I have some questions about a legal issue I'm trying to resolve.'

'Olivia wasn't able to help you?'

Lewis thought about the icy reception he'd been given. 'She gave it her best, but I still have a few unanswered queries.'

'What was the issue?'

Lewis glanced at Carlson's entourage. 'Maybe we could speak in private?'

Carlson brushed off the suggestion as if he kept nothing from his team. 'That won't be necessary.'

'It's regarding Maria Brennan,' Lewis said.

On hearing the name, one of the executives stepped forward, glaring at the impertinence. Carlson held him back.

'You're the lawyer that's speaking to Maria's family on my behalf?' Carlson asked.

'That's right. Charlie King asked me to handle it for you.'

Carlson's face softened. 'Thank you, Lewis. I appreciate your help. Maria's death has affected everyone here very badly.'

'The family have some questions. They'd like to meet you to discuss them.'

'What would they want to talk about?'

Lewis held his nerve. 'About your phone calls to Maria. About the visit you paid to her flat the day before she died.'

Carlson didn't flinch. 'Maria and I worked closely together.

114

We often spoke on the phone. There's no intrigue in any of this.'

'That sounds perfectly plausible, Mr Carlson,' Lewis said. 'If you could meet with the family and tell them exactly that, I'm sure they'll be reassured. It would be a great help.'

Carlson nodded sagely as he mulled over the request. 'I can try to find some time in my diary. I'll ask my office to call you and make an appointment.'

Lewis was about to reply when Carlson turned on his heel and resumed his procession down the corridor.

Riding down in the lift, Ward's assistant stuck close, staring at him in grim-faced silence. It was obvious Lewis had crossed a sacred boundary. He didn't care. He'd seen a chance and taken it. When the doors opened, he followed the assistant out of the lift, across the lobby and on to the street. As soon as they were outside on the pavement, she took him by the arm. Lewis was shocked at the strength of her grip.

'Be careful,' she said quietly. 'This place is rotten to the core.' The assistant was gritting her teeth as she spoke, keeping her face still like she was thanking him politely for his visit.

'Why?' he asked.

She kept her gaze focused on his. There was fear in her voice. 'Maria was my friend,' she said. 'She would never take her own life.'

'You think she was killed?'

'She had enemies. Powerful ones.'

Lewis was hanging on her words. 'Who?' he asked.

The assistant leaned closer. She spoke each syllable of the name clearly. 'Emilia Carlson.'

Without giving Lewis a chance to reply, she turned and marched away, back into the lobby. Lewis watched as she walked briskly to the lift and stepped inside. The assistant kept her eyes locked on his as the lift doors closed and she disappeared from view.

22

ROBERT CARLSON STORMED into the office, slamming the door behind him.

'Who is this jumped-up kid?' he raged. 'Why am I getting hijacked in my own office building?'

Olivia Ward closed the document on her computer screen and took off her reading glasses. 'I'm guessing you've just met Lewis Miller,' she said, her voice calm.

Carlson was practically frothing at the mouth. 'Met him? He had the nerve to challenge me about Maria in front of the staff. Who does he think he is?'

'Miller's harmless, Robert. He was chosen precisely because he knows nothing. He's wet behind the ears. Some underprivileged scholarship kid that Renfrew and Hall employed to improve their social diversity numbers.'

'He's smart enough to have arranged a meeting with Maria's family. He told me they want to speak to me privately. That can't be allowed.'

Ward dismissed the notion. 'Miller's a stray from the wrong

side of the tracks. He was given the task of delivering the NDA because he could speak to Maria's family on their terms. It was a gamble but it didn't pay off. Who cares if he wastes another day or two blundering around? He's not going to find anything, Robert.'

'Are you sure?'

'I've got this in hand. Stop worrying.'

'Stop worrying? My whole life is hanging in the balance. All I do is worry.'

'If Miller goes too far, he'll only hurt himself,' Ward said. 'You can rest assured of that.'

Carlson breathed out. He turned to the picture window and looked out at the bustling city below. All those people going about their lives, each wrapped up in their own world, their own problems. Each oblivious to the petty woes of the others. Maybe Olivia was right, he hoped. Maybe he was overreacting and this would all go away. The alternatives were too horrifying to consider.

23

DREW BRENNAN STOPPED his motorcycle in a lay-by on the Old Kent Road. South London lay before him, grey towers and smog. He rested for a few minutes, looking at the scruffy precinct of shops, watching people stroll in and out of newsagents and off-licences, carrying groceries in plastic bags. On the corner, a ragged piece of scrap land was being used as a car wash. Gangs of harried-looking men were toiling with pressure hoses and buckets, washing down the vans and taxis that queued up in the forecourt. Drew checked the address again, resting on the handlebars of the Ducati. It was definitely the right place. The car wash must be a smokescreen for the bookie operation, he thought.

He took his time, scoping it out, looking for any irregularities that caught his eye. Ninety grand was a lot of money to pick up on his own, enough to make him nervous. He couldn't afford for anything to go wrong with that much cash at stake. After ten minutes, Drew kicked the motorcycle off its stand, rode down to the junction and turned into the car wash. A fine mist from the hoses hung over the yard, catching rainbows as it caught the light of the street lamps. The workers paid no attention as he rode past and parked the bike next to the Portakabin at the back of the plot.

The hut looked derelict. The windows were barred, faded paint flaking off the walls. The only sign of life was a security camera mounted on a pole above the door. Drew walked up the steps and knocked lightly. He stood back so he could be seen clearly in the camera's field of vision. Weeds and nettles had grown up through the wooden stair treads, streaked green with mildew. After a few seconds, a voice called out from beyond the door.

'What do you want?'

'I'm here to see someone called Adem. Glenn Egan sent me.'

Drew could hear the sound of chains and bolts being unfastened. The handle turned and the door swung open. The doorman was a mass of muscles and tattoos in a tight T-shirt, restraining a fierce-looking bull terrier on a chain, the metal links wound around his balled fist. The dog snarled, baring its teeth, maddened at the sight of an invader on its territory. The man dragged it back.

'He's over there,' the doorman grunted, nodding to the far side of the cabin. Drew stepped cautiously inside, giving the dog a wide berth as he passed.

It was stifling in the cabin. A gas heater was blazing away in one corner, heavy blackout curtains over the windows sealing in the stale air. Plumes of cigarette smoke hung in the washes of lamplight. The place smelled of grease and sour milk. It was piled with boxes of cheap knock-off clothes and stacks of fake designer handbags. A rack of flashy leather

120

coats stood in one corner, a pile of counterfeit luggage in another.

Two men were seated at a plastic patio table, watching a boxing match on a fuzzy TV. One of them kept a phone pressed to his ear, giving a running commentary as the bout progressed. It sounded like he was speaking Turkish. The other man tallied scribbled figures on a notepad as the boxers pounded each other under the stadium lights. Neither looked like he'd slept in days.

'Which one of you is Adem?' Drew asked.

'Who wants to know?' the man with the notepad called over his shoulder.

'I do.'

The man glanced around dismissively. 'You'll have to do better than that,' he grunted.

'Glenn Egan sent me.'

The man gave Drew a sly grin. 'Why didn't you just say so?'

Adem was thin and narrow-faced, with bad teeth and a receding hairline. He wore a shiny, open-necked shirt with spots of grease dotted down the front.

'I'm here to collect some money,' Drew said.

'From me?'

'That's right.'

'Did Glenn tell you how much?'

The bookie was testing him, Drew thought. Playing dumb to see if he could find a way to wriggle out of paying what he owed.

'Ninety grand,' Drew said firmly. 'Not a penny less.'

The amount seemed to cause Adem pain. He winced as he gave Drew a grudging nod. 'Don't say it so loud. I hate losing that much money.'

121

Drew was impatient. 'Let's get this done. I'm in a hurry.'

'Wait until the fight is over. I've got a lot riding on it. You like boxing?'

'Of course.'

'You want to place a bet?' the bookie asked hopefully.

'I don't gamble.'

Adem nodded sagely. 'A wise choice.' He looked Drew up and down. 'You remind me of someone. A middleweight.'

Drew rocked on the balls of his feet. 'My dad used to box.'

'Who was your dad?'

'Pat Brennan.'

'The Shadwell Shocker,' Adem said, his face lighting up. 'Pat Brennan was a decent fighter. Solid and reliable. A great left hook. I made a lot of money on him back in the day.'

It felt strange to Drew to hear his father's name mentioned in such a place. In his imagination Patrick Brennan had been a heroic prizefighter, a champion. He didn't want to believe he was the kind of slugger who would associate with a low-rent bookie like Adem.

'Look, I don't have time to hang around,' Drew said curtly. 'Give me Glenn's money so I can get out of here.'

Adem rose from his chair slowly as if insulted by Drew's impatience. He went to a door in the corner of the cabin and closed it behind him. After a minute, he walked out holding a red nylon backpack. He opened it and shook the contents out on to the table. Stacks of twenty-pound notes, each bound by a thick elastic band, scattered across the table. Some of the bundles fell to the floor and Drew bent down and picked them up. He placed the stray bundles on the table with the others.

'Ninety grand. As agreed,' Adem said. 'Want to count it?'

Drew flicked through the edge of one of the stacks. He could smell the chemical scent of the brand-new bills. He began to scoop up the bricks of cash and stuff them inside the backpack. 'I don't have time. Glenn can check it when I deliver the money to him later.'

'Oh, there's one other thing,' Adem said casually, as if remembering something incidental that had slipped his mind. He walked over to a metal filing cabinet, opened the top drawer and took out a package wrapped in stained oilcloth. The sight of it made Drew uneasy.

'What's that?' he asked.

Adem gave a leering smile. 'Open it and take a look.'

He tossed it over and Drew caught the bundle in both hands. It was ominously weighty. Drew peeled back one corner of the cloth wrapping. The barrel of a sawn-off shotgun stared out at him. He dropped it on to the table and stood back as if distancing himself from danger.

'Glenn said nothing about collecting a gun.'

Adem stared at him through narrowed eyes. 'Why d'you think he didn't come here himself?'

Drew shook his head. 'This is too much for me. I've got a criminal record. If I get caught with that I'll get ten years.'

Adem tucked the barrel of the shotgun back inside the covering. He opened the backpack and shoved it on top of the bundles of cash. Zipping up the bag, he took a small padlock and locked the zip fasteners together, sealing the backpack shut.

'Here's the deal,' Adem said. 'You can take this bag or you can leave empty-handed. It's up to you. The way I see it, I owe this money to Egan. If the errand boy he sends refuses to take the cash, that's his problem. I've kept my part of the deal.'

Everything had stopped. Behind him, Drew could hear the panting of the bull terrier. The scratch of its paws on the faded lino. He glanced over his shoulder. The dog was desperate to be released, straining at the chain on its collar. A crackle of intimidation hung in the room. Drew made a stark calculation of his options.

He reached out, took the backpack by the straps and swung it up on to his shoulder. 'Looks like I don't have a choice,' he said.

Adem fixed him with a sinister look. 'Drive safely,' he said.

24

LEWIS LEFT THE Ever Sine offices and walked along the Thames. The name the assistant had whispered to him was still circling around in his mind. Emilia Carlson. Just the sound of it made Lewis nervous.

He found a park bench, took a seat and searched for her name online. It didn't take long to find what he was looking for. Her social media feed was accessible and Lewis scrolled through it quickly. Emilia Carlson's posts looked like an influencer's dream. An endless series of photos taken on tropical beaches and private jets. She was barely out of her teens but seemed to live the globe-trotting life of the ultra-wealthy, sipping champagne in glitzy nightclubs or sunbathing on the decks of luxury yachts. Emilia Carlson was reed-thin with perfect skin and the same bright blue eyes as her father. The resemblance to Robert Carlson was striking but there was something cold about her, something in her body language that was distant and remote. Lewis noticed how she never smiled in her pictures, no matter how exotic the location. She appeared to have the high-handed, disdainful manner of the uber-privileged. An indifference to the world that the rich seemed to flaunt as if it were a lifestyle accessory. But could this young woman really be involved in Maria Brennan's death? He remembered the stark look on the face of Olivia Ward's assistant as she whispered her name to him.

Was this warning a real lead or only gossip? Lewis couldn't be sure. So far, there was still no hard evidence that Maria Brennan's death wasn't anything other than suicide. He needed definitive proof. A first-hand witness he could speak with to confirm his suspicions. Sitting on the bench in the grim winter light, the cold seeping up from the river, an idea came to him. Lewis wondered why he hadn't thought of it before.

The hospital was only a short walk from the Ever Sine offices. It stood on the banks of the Thames, looking across the water to the Houses of Parliament. Lewis gave the patient's name at the information desk and the receptionist told him to go up to Chaucer Ward. She smiled and said there were only ten minutes of visiting time left so he needed to hurry. Lewis took the lift up to the third floor and followed the directions. Porters wheeled equipment along the corridors. Patients in surgical gowns shuffled along slowly, leaning on walking frames for support. When he found the room he was searching for, Lewis peered in through the porthole window. It was a small ward of four beds. Only one was occupied.

The man sat propped up on a thick stack of pillows. He eyed Lewis warily as he came in.

'Are you Arthur Cox?' Lewis asked, approaching the end of the bed.

'That's right.'

'I was hoping to speak with you, Mr Cox. About the dead woman you found out at Coldharbour Marshes.'

Arthur Cox let the words sink in. His skin was pallid and grey, his breathing laboured. 'Who are you?' he asked, his voice rasping.

'My name is Lewis Miller.'

'How did you find me?'

'Your name was in one of the news reports about the incident. It said that you were taken to a specialist hospital that dealt with gas inhalation. I did some research. There's only one in London.'

'So you're a detective?'

'Not really. I'm a lawyer.'

Arthur Cox looked disappointed. 'Another one?'

'I'm not the first to visit you?'

'Unfortunately not. I've had plenty of lawyers here but no police.'

Lewis was surprised to hear this. 'You haven't been officially interviewed?'

'I was told that some officers came to see me while I was unconscious. They left and never came back.'

'Which other lawyers have visited you?' Lewis asked.

Cox shook his head. 'I can't tell you.'

'Why not?'

'Because of the contract I signed.'

Lewis frowned. 'What contract?'

'One that stops me talking about what I saw that morning out at Coldharbour Marshes.'

'You mean a non-disclosure agreement?'

'That's it.' Cox pointed to the framed photos of dogs on the cabinet next to his bed. A pair of energetic-looking golden Labradors. 'I did it for them,' he said, 'in case I don't get back to my boys. They'll need looking after.' He stared longingly at the dogs he was desperate to return home to.

'Can I ask the name of the lawyer who visited you?'

Cox shook his head apologetically. 'I'm not even allowed to discuss that.'

'Was it a woman? Did she have red hair?'

Cox gave a shrug. 'It was a bloke. That's all I can say.'

'Look, Mr Cox. I want to ask about when you saw Maria Brennan's body. You were the first person to see her when you opened the car door that morning. Did it look like she'd taken her own life?'

The man in the bed looked up at Lewis with sad, rheumy eyes. 'I can't discuss it.'

'Maybe you could just nod for me if you think it was suicide,' Lewis said.

Cox lay back, his chest rising and falling steadily. His head remained still.

'Nod if you think she was murdered.'

Arthur Cox looked up at Lewis with a tired expression. He thought for a moment, his hands resting at his sides. Then, with a definite movement of his head, he dipped his chin to his chest and tilted it back up. He repeated the gesture again for good measure.

Lewis gave a grim smile of appreciation.

'Thank you, Mr Cox,' he said. 'You've been a great help.'

*

128

Outside, Lewis stood in the hospital forecourt, trying to work out what he was going to do next. This case was getting more complicated by the hour. Whoever had got to Arthur Cox was one step ahead of him and Lewis didn't like it. It had to be someone acting on behalf of Robert Carlson, he told himself. Silencing a witness with a gagging order was a cynical move. It was almost an admission of guilt. Lewis was mulling this over when his phone rang. It was the junior lawyer he shared a desk with at Renfrew and Hall.

'Lewis,' she whispered. 'Some men are here asking for you.'

'Who are they?'

'I don't know. But they're looking for the contract you gave me. They rifled through the files on your desk searching for it.'

It must be Olivia Ward's doing, Lewis guessed. She must want the file so badly she'd sent people to retrieve it without waiting for permission.

'Did you give it to them?' he asked.

'Of course not. I kept quiet about it. They're in the executive office right now, screaming about the sanctity of client privilege. It sounds to me like you're in a lot of hot water.'

'Did you get a chance to read through the contract yet?'

'Not all of it. But it looks pretty dodgy to me. I've never seen so many offshore shell companies listed on one document before. This deal looks like it was set up in a massive hurry. If you ask me, the whole thing stinks.'

'That's what I thought,' Lewis said. 'Look, I don't want to get you in trouble. Courier the contract over to a woman called Rachael Hudson. She lives in the flat above mine. I'll collect it from her when I get home.'

His colleague sounded genuinely concerned. 'Are you in trouble, Lewis?'

'I don't know. Just make sure no one knows what you're doing.'

'OK. Look after yourself.' She hung up.

Lewis switched off his phone. He knew that an angry call from his line manager was imminent. There was no way he was going to give up the contract before he had a chance to examine it himself. If Olivia Ward wanted it, there must be something important inside, something she didn't want any-one to see. At Waterloo Station, Lewis rode the escalator down to take a train heading north. The station was packed with commuters from the nearby offices. On the platform, they jos-tled and barged each other as they fought for position near the edge of the track. Their coats were slick with rain, umbrellas dripping on to the concrete underfoot. Lewis didn't notice. He was lost in thought, trying to figure out what it was that Ward wanted to hide so desperately.

He looked up at a cry from a startled commuter. An elderly man had dropped his hat on to the tracks. A smart tan trilby with a black silk band. It landed in the rubbish-strewn space between the rails. Lewis watched as the old man leaned for-ward, trying to retrieve it with the handle of his umbrella. The passengers alongside him cried out anxiously but the old man ignored them. The uniformed station attendants rushed to-wards him. Lewis was too far away to get involved. He stood in place, waiting for the train.

Soon the platform began to rumble. Lights began to glow along the dark walls of the tunnel, the rails shining as the train neared. A cool breeze blew along the platform. Lewis felt it on his face as he gazed down into the railbed, watching scraps of old litter stir. The noise grew louder, the platform vibrating underfoot. Around him, the scrum of people tightened, fighting for position.

A hand rested on Lewis's shoulder. Bodily contact was so common at that time of day that he barely registered it. He stood with his hands in his pockets, his head bowed as he waited. There was a sudden powerful shove from behind. He was caught off guard, completely unprepared. Below him, he could see the gleaming rails, the electrified circuits, the tangle of cables and switches. There was a moment of weightlessness. In one sickening instant, Lewis realized he was falling.

25

DREW LEFT THE hut and walked across the forecourt to his motorcycle. The weight of the backpack cut into his bones as if it contained his entire future. He could feel eyes watching him from the Portakabin windows as he mounted the Ducati and started the engine. This was way too dangerous, he thought. Carrying a shotgun across London like this was madness. Glenn didn't want to take the risk himself so he'd set Drew up. It was a dirty, low thing for a friend to do.

Riding out of the yard, Drew turned on to the main road, merging with the other traffic, heading back towards the river. He kept his speed in check, his riding smooth and conservative. Beneath his helmet, beads of sweat were forming on his brow.

There was no way he'd be able to keep his temper in check when he caught up with Glenn. What that lying snake had asked was more than a favour. He was gambling recklessly with Drew's life. He didn't care who Glenn's uncle was, he was going to let rip once he was safely back home.

As the traffic moved around him, Drew shook the thought from his head and forced himself to concentrate. He couldn't afford any mistakes. Anything that might attract unwanted attention.

He had travelled less than a mile when he noticed a silver car in his mirrors. It was unmarked but it seemed to be tracking him, keeping its distance but maintaining an even pace. He kept a check on its movements as he rode. The silver car stayed fifty metres behind, never turning or overtaking, always there, shadowing him.

He slowed as he approached a roundabout and checked for oncoming traffic. When he glanced back at his mirrors, the silver car was gone. Maybe he was just being paranoid, Drew thought. Surely there was no way a police car could be tailing him already?

Suddenly a siren sounded. He looked over his shoulder. The silver car was coming up fast, blue lights flashing in its windscreen. Drew had a split second to make a decision. A thousand factors weighed up at once.

Possession of a firearm meant ten years. He could picture himself in the dock at the Crown Court, wearing a cheap suit, the next decade behind bars stretching out before him. He could hear cell doors clanging shut. The shouts of desperation on the block. He pictured his mother's face, heavy with disappointment, telling him again that he was no good, the same way she had done his whole life. He thought of Maria. The golden child. How she would never have been stupid enough to get caught like this. His mother was right. He did hate Maria. But he hated himself more.

133

Drew forced himself to focus. He had to act. The silver car was almost on him, the flashes of blue light filling his vision. Fate seemed to hang over him for an instant. A resolute conviction filled his mind. The decision to run was made in an instant.

26

LANDING HARD FROM the fall, Lewis rolled on to his side instinctively to protect himself, his head striking the corner of a sleeper, his face scuffing the grit and gravel scattered between the rails. He could feel the shuddering of the tracks as the Tube train thundered towards him. Shrieks of blind panic rose up from the platform above. Lewis sprang to his feet and looked up. There was a metal barrier above him and he jumped and seized it with both hands. He could taste pure adrenaline as he tried to haul himself up. His feet were trying to find purchase on the smooth track walls but he could feel his fingers slipping. He could hear the train speeding towards him and glanced round, terrified. Through the windscreen, he saw the driver's face, staring, open-mouthed. Sparks flew from the emergency brakes but the weight of the train, travelling at speed, powered relentlessly forward.

It was almost on him when, from above, a cluster of hands reached down, grasping at his clothes. Lewis felt himself dragged upwards, and then the cold wet safety of the platform was once more beneath him as the train screamed past, the brakes still sparking, the windows rattling violently.

A forest of faces looked down at him. A uniformed attendant took Lewis by the hand, his face pale with shock.

'You are one lucky man,' he said, helping him up. 'When the old guy dropped his hat on the line, the alarm system triggered. The train was already braking, otherwise you'd be squashed flat.'

Lewis began to rise to his feet, his head pounding.

'He's drunk!' a woman shouted.

'No, he fainted,' someone else called out.

'I was pushed,' Lewis said, breathless. 'Someone shoved me.'

People looked at each other accusingly, starting to argue among themselves. Lewis stood on tiptoe to see over their heads. About twenty metres away, a man was fighting through the throng, making for the exit. He was wearing a baseball cap, the brim pulled low, obscuring his features. Lewis set off after him, forcing a way through the mass of passengers crowded around him. The exit led from the platform to the foot of a rising escalator. About halfway up, a figure was running. On the opposite side, panicked station staff were pounding down towards the platforms. Lewis kept running, a righteous anger pulsing through him. Someone had just tried to kill him and the realization made him sprint harder, the escalator treads bouncing beneath his feet. Suddenly he stumbled forward, landing on his hands. When he looked up, the running man was gone.

At the head of the escalator, the ticket hall was thick with irate commuters. The barriers were closed, the Underground workers trying desperately to quell the anger of the crowd.

Lewis jumped the gate and tried to force a path through the pack of bodies. He swayed with their motion, his feet lifting from the floor. Finally, shoving headlong, he made it to the exit and out on to the street. He looked each way along the length of Waterloo Road. People, cars, taxis. All the usual sights but nothing to attract the eye. No one running or hurrying. Lewis cursed. There was no sign of his attacker. He was gone.

27

THE FRONT WHEEL of the Ducati lifted off the road, the torque surging uncontrollably as Drew twisted the accelerator. He aimed for a gap between two slow-moving cars, his handlebars almost touching the sides as he shot through. Behind him, he heard the sound of squealing tyres as the silver car gave chase.

Near the river, he saw traffic lights turn red and accelerated, shooting over the junction without looking. There was a heavy thump of colliding bodywork behind him. Glass smashing. Angry horns sounding in unison. The road beneath his tyres was slick and treacherous. In the winter dark, the headlights of approaching cars flared dangerously in his vision.

From a side road, Drew saw a regular patrol car speed towards him, its siren wailing. It was blue and yellow, lit up like a carnival ride, its roof lights spinning, casting strange shadows on the tarmac. Drew crouched low over the handlebars to reduce his drag. He was in real trouble now. It was only a matter of time before they sent the whole cavalry after him. He could outrun one car, but not a whole fleet.

He turned up a one-way street, leaning hard, his exhaust pipe scraping along the tarmac. A van turned into his path and he mounted the pavement sharply, the wheels of the motorbike rattling and juddering over the uneven paving slabs. Drew raced on, heart pumping. Blue beams swept over him, spectral shapes flickering and shimmering in the windows of buildings he passed. Faces leered in his peripheral vision, slack-jawed as they watched him shoot back on to the main road like a roaring apparition. Checking above him, Drew scanned the darkness. He was looking for the helicopter beam that would mean disaster. Each way he looked, the night sky was empty. The light from the patrol car was receding but he couldn't shake it off.

Weaving in and out of traffic, car horns blaring as he threw the bike around, Drew tried to figure out what he was going to do. Heading towards Tower Bridge, he could smell the thin salty brine of the Thames. He unslung the straps of the backpack from his shoulders and grasped the carry handle in one fist. He could explain the money inside to the police, but the shotgun was another matter. The bag was locked, the padlock holding the zippers together. There wasn't enough time to stop and rip the backpack open to separate the contents. He thought of Glenn, safe and sound at home. It would be insane to go down because of him.

He clawed back the accelerator and screamed up the rise towards the centre of Tower Bridge. Beneath the granite pillars, the police car out of sight, Drew slowed the bike and mounted the pavement. Pedestrians scattered in his path. Swinging the backpack high, he tossed it over the railings and watched it sail down, splashing heavily as it hit the black river below.

28

STANDING UNDER THE protection of a café awning, Lewis laughed to himself. Passers-by shot wary looks at him as if he was some kind of madman. He was still breathing. That was all that counted. He was bruised and scuffed from the fall on to the tracks. His hands were bleeding, an egg-shaped lump forming on the back of his head. He was shaken but he was still alive.

As the fear and adrenaline began to subside, Lewis could taste an acidic anger rise up from his gut. He had to think straight. He was making people scared now, he told himself. Scared enough to want him dead. It had to be the questions he was asking. No one had expected him to dig so deep. That meant he must be close to the truth now. Close enough that people were prepared to kill to stop him. Lewis was scared but he was determined to fight back. It was in his nature. There was no way he was going to take this lying down.

The best revenge would be solving the case, he thought. To do that, he needed the documents Olivia Ward had refused to give him. The copies of Maria Brennan's witness testimony. Lewis was certain they would give him the information he needed.

So far, he had done everything by the book. From now on, screw professional etiquette, Lewis thought. This was personal. If Ward refused to hand over the paperwork, there were other ways he could get what he needed. It would entail some subterfuge, enough to get struck off if he was found out. But weighing up his options, Lewis decided it was a step he was prepared to take. After all, it wasn't as if anyone else was playing fair.

29

RIDING THROUGH THE Barbican, Drew spotted the entrance to an underground car park. He turned the bike sharply and dropped down the steep ramp into the concrete basement. Sirens screamed past, speeding along the road behind him. He slowed and turned into an empty space between two parked cars, the soles of his shoes scraping along the smooth cement. He kicked the Ducati on to its stand and shut the engine down. Leaving the keys in the ignition, Drew turned and walked calmly towards the stairwell. The bike was stolen, the number plates false. It was impossible to trace it back to him. Drew's breathing was heavy, his visor misted, but he kept his helmet on. Security cameras blinked from every corner. He needed to keep his face hidden.

Outside, the street was quiet. A bus stop stood fifty metres ahead, a red double-decker pulling in, a line of passengers waiting to board. Under the cover of the bus shelter, Drew took his helmet off and pulled up the hood of his jacket. He tapped his bank card and climbed the steps to the upper deck.

He didn't care where the bus was headed. Suddenly the windows were bathed in blue streaks as another police car screamed past, its siren blaring. Drew's heart pounded like a fist against his ribcage. He kept his eyes lowered, staring down at the scuff marks on the tips of his shoes. The lights faded as the patrol car sped away in the opposite direction. For the next thirty minutes, Drew kept his head down, not even glancing out of the window as the city passed by, praying for deliverance.

30

THE HOUSE WAS quiet, the curtains drawn. Lewis was apprehensive but held his nerve. He walked up the gravel path to the front door and rang the bell. It was a street of neat bay-fronted homes, tree-lined and secluded, their hedges trimmed. Colourful children's paintings were stuck in the top-floor windows. On the covered porch, a bamboo wind chime rang gently in the breeze.

The face that appeared in the doorway was pale and drawn. Her hair was wild, her eyes damp.

Lewis stood in the glare of the porch light so he could be seen. 'I'm sorry to disturb you, Mrs Sobel,' he said. 'I was hoping to speak with you about a case I shared with your husband.'

She seemed surprised. 'You worked with Martin?'

'We were working on the same case when he died.'

'On the same side?'

Lewis shook his head. 'Actually, we were opponents.'

Sobel's widow looked outraged. 'Then what are you doing here? How did you find me?'

'I called his office and told them I wanted to send you a letter of condolence. They gave me your address.'

'You lied to them?'

Lewis shifted uneasily. 'If you let me in, Mrs Sobel, I can explain.'

'Which company do you work for?' she asked.

'Renfrew and Hall.'

'The City firm?'

'I'm afraid so.'

'Then you're definitely on the wrong side,' she said, and began to close the door.

Lewis stepped forward. He spoke with urgency. 'Please, Mrs Sobel. Martin told me that a client in our case had been murdered. I didn't believe him at first but now I think he was right. I need your help to get justice for her.'

She looked at him guardedly. 'Murdered?'

'I'm sure of it.'

'And you think I can help?'

'Without it, I'm finished.'

Lewis stood back, patient and unthreatening. Sobel's widow chewed her lip as she watched him. Gradually she began to ease the door open and stood aside.

The hallway was decorated for a child's birthday party. Lines of pink bunting and silver balloons that had floated up against the ceiling. At the head of the stairs, looking down, three young girls were watching, peering around the bannisters. Lewis recognized them from the family photos he had seen on Sobel's windowsill.

Showing him into the living room, Sobel's widow took a seat on the sofa. The house was cold, the floorboards creaking underfoot. The life had been sucked out of the place, Lewis thought. He had only met Martin Sobel once but he had seemed like a decent man. His family had lost a husband and a father. They looked like their whole world had fallen in.

'This is an unusual request, Mrs Sobel,' Lewis said, 'but I don't have any choice. Without access to some important files, the case I'm working on will go unsolved. The material was stored on memory sticks that Martin took from his office on the night he died. They should still be in his bag if it wasn't damaged in the accident.'

Sobel's widow shook her head. 'Martin's bag was thrown clear. It's upstairs.'

'Then I really need to take a look at the memory sticks inside.'

'Aren't those kinds of files confidential?' she asked.

'They are, but not to other lawyers working on the same case. We're all bound by professional ethics.'

She cast her eyes down, trying to digest what he was saying. Lewis sensed her gut reaction was to refuse. It was a huge stretch for her to give out her husband's legal material.

'I'm not sure I can do this,' she said.

Lewis was tempted to accept her answer. He didn't want to push a woman in such a vulnerable state. But if he gave up, his search into Maria Brennan's death was over.

'I can't begin to imagine the pain you must be feeling,' he said. 'The case I was working on with Martin also involves a bereaved family. Without those drives, they'll never reach a resolution. Their suffering will go on. I'm sorry to put you in a difficult position, Mrs Sobel, but I wouldn't ask if I had any other option.'

Her brow furrowed. 'What would Martin have done if he were here?' she asked.

Lewis leaned forward in his chair. 'Your husband knew that the system favours the wealthy. They always find a way to win. Right now, a rich man is about to use his money to beat the system. Martin wouldn't want him to go unpunished just so some rules don't get broken.'

'Is this the only way you can access the files?' she asked.

'There are people who are so scared of the truth coming to light that they're prepared to do anything – to threaten, even to kill.'

She looked at him with a sense of desperation. 'Do you think this has anything to do with Martin's death?'

Lewis chose his words carefully. 'I can't speculate,' he said. 'But the case is becoming more dangerous the harder I look. I can only find the truth if I keep searching. To do that, I need those files.'

The shadow of a smile passed over her face. 'Now you sound like my husband,' she said.

Lewis nodded silently. He knew she meant it as a compliment.

Sobel's widow took a long breath as she stood from the sofa.

'Wait here,' she said. 'I'll go and fetch Martin's bag.'

31

THE END OF the line was Limehouse Basin. The bus driver blinked the interior lights to show he was going no further. Drew glanced out of the window to check there were no police cars waiting as he left the bus. His hood was up, his face hidden as he walked along the bank of the canal. Mist was drifting in from the river, hanging over the frozen pathway in a thick sheet. Drew wished it would swallow him up. He knew he couldn't go home. He needed somewhere to lie low and wait for the chaos to subside. Somewhere he could hide without fear. Walking through Limehouse, he thought of the perfect place.

The Church of the Holy Cross was hidden among Victorian housing blocks near the old gasworks. It was where he used to come as a boy, dragged there by his mother. He walked up to the heavy oak entrance door and looked inside. Mass was still underway. He could smell the candle smoke and incense floating out into the dark. There was only a handful of people spread out in the vast gloomy interior. The church was hung with ancient icons.

Portraits of obscure saints and anguished depictions of the blessed Virgin, bordered in burnished gold. A line of worshippers gathered at the rail to take communion. Drew could hear every movement, every whisper in the echoing space. He found a pew in a quiet corner and typed a message on his phone.

I'm at the Church of the Holy Cross,
Broughton Street. Come and meet me. It's urgent.

Drew crossed himself as he sent it.

By midnight, the church was almost empty. The final worshippers were kneeling and lighting candles in the shadowed transept. Drew was watching them when he heard feet shuffling behind him. The sound of a pew creaking as someone lowered themselves down. He turned around.

'Start talking,' Glenn said.

Drew glared at him in anger. 'You've got a lot of nerve sending me to do your dirty work. I thought we were friends.'

'We are, but you work for me. Sometimes I need people to do what they're told. No questions asked.'

'You put my life on the line, Glenn. I'd have got ten years if I'd been caught with that bag.'

'Ten years for carrying some money?'

'Not the money. The sawn-off.'

Glenn looked confused. 'Sawn-off? Adem wasn't supposed to give you that. I was going to send someone else to collect it tomorrow.'

'Well, he did. He insisted on it.'

Glenn peered over the back of the pew, scanning the floor at Drew's feet. 'So where's the bag?'

149

'I haven't got it.'

Glenn's face darkened. 'Why the hell not?'

'As soon as I left the car wash, the police were on to me. It was like they were waiting. They must have been keeping a watch on Adem. You're mad doing business with a scumbag like that.'

'What are you telling me? You got stopped by the police?'

'No. I shook them off.'

'Then where's the damn bag?' Glenn growled.

'I tossed it.'

'You better be joking?'

'I'm serious. I thought I was done for. There were two police cars at least. I managed to lose them as I came across Tower Bridge, but I didn't know how long for. I couldn't risk getting caught with a shotgun so I threw the bag over the rail.'

'You chucked away all that money?'

'I was about to get nicked.'

'But yet here you are, free as a bird, sitting in a church. How do I know you haven't stashed the bag somewhere so you can pick it up later?'

Drew was outraged. 'I'd never do that to you, Glenn. You know that.'

Glenn shook his head. 'I can't believe what I'm hearing.'

'You won that money gambling, Glenn. It was a windfall. Losing it only takes you back to square one.'

'Is that what you think?'

'That's what Adem told me.'

Glenn's voice was trembling, his eyes wide with fear.

'Those weren't my winnings,' he said. 'Those were my uncle's.'

32

ROBERT CARLSON WOKE in the dark. He was thirsty, his fore-head covered in sweat. Susannah was sleeping beside him, lying peacefully on her side. Carefully he folded back the covers, slid his feet inside his slippers and pulled on his silk dressing gown.

In the kitchen, he poured himself a glass of water and stood at the sink as he gulped it down. The house seemed to thrum with an ominous dread. He glanced around the opulent room, the gleaming stove and endless kitchen gadgets. What was the point of it all? Was this what he was working himself into the ground for? He wondered whether Maria had been right – that too many possessions just drag people down in the end. Did he even want this life any more or was it all pointless vanity?

Carlson thought of Maria, remembering how she would speak in business meetings, the forthright way she had of articulating herself. She had a brilliant mind and a fierce dedi-cation to their shared mission. He'd favoured her over his other employees, trusted her and given her the most high-profile projects to manage, despite the animosity this had created at the company. But Maria's abilities were always head and shoulders above those of her rivals. She had deserved the attention. Her input helped the business to thrive. Was that the best way to run a company? Carlson wasn't sure. But he'd been true to his instincts and that was the best he could do.

If only she had suspended those damn principles of hers, she could have had it all. She was on the fast track to the top. But keeping quiet wasn't Maria's way, he thought. She never could have compromised like that.

Beneath his feet, Carlson noticed a rhythmic pulse vibrating through the floorboards. Surely Emilia wasn't having yet another party down in the basement? She was treating the house like a nightclub. Listening to the pounding bass line, Carlson felt his blood boil.

Storming down the stairs, he could hear the bass growing louder as he neared the doors to the swimming pool. He threw them open without announcing himself and gaped in shock at the sight before him. There were over fifty teenagers in the pool, all strangers, cavorting in his house. Carlson was enraged. Bottles of wine and champagne lay half drunk at the pool's edge, scattered among broken furniture and discarded clothing. The heady stench of cannabis hung thick in the air. A young woman he'd never seen before was reclining on the diving board in her underwear.

'Where's Emilia?' he demanded over the deafening music.
'Who?'
'Emilia Carlson.'
She looked completely nonplussed.
'The girl who lives here!' he shouted.

'Oh, I think I saw her in the sauna.'

Carlson marched from the poolside to the gym and along the corridor that led to the spa. What on earth was Emilia doing? She was supposed to be going to therapy, talking about her problems, getting better. God knows it was costing him enough money. Instead, she was distracting herself with this chaos. Inside the sauna, the air was filled with clouds of searing vapour escaping from the glass-walled steam room. He could make out a figure inside. A message had been written on the glass, traced into the moisture by a fingertip.

Emilia Carlson is a junkie.

Someone had crossed out the word 'junkie'. Beside it they had written,

Killer.

Carlson blanched. Who would write such a thing? As he reached out a hand to wipe the message away, he noticed the unusual form of some of the letters, as if they belonged to a foreign language. Looking through the smeared glass, he could see his daughter in her swimwear, her eyes half closed, high as the stars. A half-smoked cigarette was balanced on the edge of the marble countertop, slowly burning down. Beside it was a square of tinfoil, blackened and burned. Carlson crumbled inside.

Oh, Emilia, he thought, *what you have you done?*

33

LEWIS ARRIVED AT Highbury Corner and set off towards his flat. A hundred metres from his front door, he slipped through the gates of the park and walked along the empty pathway. Behind the cover of some tall oak trees, deep in the darkness, he scanned the road outside his building. A car, a black BMW, was parked in a side street, its windows down. Inside, two men were talking, their seats reclined. On the pavement beside the driver's door was a pile of cigarette ends and a paper coffee cup. They had parked the car where they could get a clear view of the entrance to his building. It looked like they'd been there for some time, waiting for him to come home.

Lewis's nerve endings jangled. How did these people know where he lived? Who'd sent them? This situation was starting to slide out of control. The only way to fight back was to solve this case once and for all. Lewis knew he couldn't go up to his flat. It was too dangerous. He'd have to find somewhere else to go. Quietly, he slipped deeper into the dark and headed back towards the station. He knew where he'd be safe.

When he knocked on his sister's door in Stepney, Angela immediately sensed he was in trouble.

'What's wrong, Lewis?' she said. 'And don't say nothing, because you wouldn't show up here twice in one day otherwise.'

'I'm fine,' he said. 'I need a place to stay for the night, that's all.'

She hugged him, running a maternal hand through his hair. Her fingers found the egg-shaped lump on the back of his head. 'What's this?'

'Nothing.'

'I told you not to say "nothing".'

He knew it wasn't a good move to tell his sister how he'd been pushed in front of a Tube train. 'I fell over,' he said. 'That's all. Can I come in, please? It's freezing out here.'

The kids were in bed, the house quiet. Angela made tea while Lewis went into the living room. It felt good to be in a normal house, somewhere safe and welcoming for a change. Lowering himself on to the sofa, Lewis winced at the bruising all over his body. The fall on to the tracks had been heavier than he'd realized. Adrenaline alone had got him through the last few hours.

Angela came into the room with two steaming mugs of tea. 'Are you going to stay the night?' she asked.

'If that's OK with you. I'll sleep on the sofa.'

'It's fine by me. Expect the kids to wake you up early, though.'

He laughed. 'I'll look forward to it.'

'So why's your place off limits?' Angela asked.

Lewis hated to do it, but he knew that telling a white lie was best for everybody. 'Someone's trying to serve me with a court summons,' he said, waving a hand breezily. 'It's just lawyer stuff. Nothing serious.'

'Is this the case you were telling me about earlier?'

'Yeah. I went to speak with the family, face to face, like you said. The woman I spoke with remembered how Mum was killed. She said she knew Dad too, from the gym.'

Angela looked uncomfortable, as if old wounds were being reopened. 'So you went there and discussed our family ghosts?'

Lewis shook his head. 'This woman has enough ghosts of her own, believe me. I'm trying to help her, that's all.'

'Don't do anything dangerous, Lewis. It's not worth it. I don't want you to get hurt.'

'I'm not going to get hurt. I'm fine.'

'You're like Mum,' Angela said. 'Too proud to back down.'

'Look, it's late, Angie. Go to bed. I'll still be here in the morning.'

Lewis waited while his sister fussed over him, making up the sofa with a fresh duvet and some spare pillows. She kissed him goodnight, switched off the TV and crept upstairs.

When he was alone, Lewis took out his laptop and the memory sticks that Martin Sobel's widow had given him. He loaded the first one into his computer and began to open the files.

It wasn't long before he found what he was looking for. Sobel had meticulously catalogued all of the paperwork regarding

Maria Brennan's case. Particulars of claim, disclosure statements. Everything Lewis needed. Reading the list, Lewis stopped, his eyes brightening. At the foot of the index was a transcript of a private meeting that had taken place in Sobel's office.

Lewis opened it and began to read.

For the benefit of the tape, I think we should state our names. Perhaps I should begin. My name is Martin Sobel, senior solicitor at the Whitechapel Law Centre. And you are?

Maria Brennan.

MARTIN SOBEL: Could you state the nature of your grievance?

MARIA BRENNAN: You just want me to say it?

MS: Yes, as plainly as possible.

MB: I'm accusing Robert Carlson of being a lying bastard.

MS: (*laughs*) Well, perhaps not that plainly.

MB: OK. My complaint is that, after working for Robert Carlson's company for a number of years, I've been unfairly dismissed for absolutely no reason. I don't think that's right.

MS: The company claim that your contract was terminated for gross misconduct?

MB: That's a lie and I can prove it.

MS: There'll be plenty of time for that. First, can you tell me about the alleged misconduct, please?

MB: The accusation is so ludicrous that it's embarrassing to say it out loud.

157

MS: This meeting is confidential. What you tell me here is completely privileged.

MB: (*sighs*) I'm accused of using drugs at a social function where I was representing the company.

MS: You deny this?

MB: Of course. I've never used drugs in my life.

MS: Mr Carlson offered you a substantial cash settlement to encourage you to drop this case. I understand that you've rejected this offer?

MB: Yes. And I object to the way he's trying to force me to take it.

MS: Force you?

MB: By coming to my house. By calling me repeatedly.

MS: Why would he feel the need to do this?

MB: Because he always gets his own way. He's frustrated that I'm prepared to stand up to him. And he's scared.

MS: Scared of you?

MB: Scared of what I know.

MS: Maria, please can you explain in more detail how you came to work for Mr Carlson?

MB: It was my dream job. Ever Sine is a world leader in green tech. Everyone I studied with wanted to work there. Some of the early designs Robert patented revolutionized the green energy industry. He's a legend among environmentalists.

MS: This doesn't sound like a man you're enthusiastic about suing?

MB: I'm not. I mean, I wish there was another way to make him see sense. Recently he's changed. Become unstable. There are sides to him that I never knew existed. It frightens me that I could have spent so much time with a man like Robert and never really known him.

MS: Did relations with Mr Carlson sour gradually?

MB: No. It happened one night. About two months ago.

MS: Tell me what happened on that night, please.

MB: Robert's wife, Susannah, had organized a charity fundraiser at the Carlingford Hotel in Mayfair. It was for high-society types. Wealthy tech investors and media people and the like. Robert was going to make a keynote address. It was a big night for him. I'd helped Robert write the speech so he asked me to be there, to support him. I thought the evening was going to plan but then it took a strange turn. Everything got out of hand after that and I ended up in this situation where I'm unemployed, with my career in tatters.

(*A long pause*)

MS: Is there anything the matter, Maria?

MB: There are some parts of the story I'm not sure I can tell you.

MS: Why?

MB: Because I think the information could be dangerous.

MS: Why do you think that?

MB: Because of the people involved. I never thought Robert would do business with men like that. They frighten me.

MS: Don't worry about speaking openly or omitting anything sensitive. I can assure you this meeting is totally confidential. You have nothing to be scared of here. Please tell me everything.

34

Two months earlier

MARIA KNEW THE night was going to be a test of endurance as soon as she arrived at the house on Lowndes Square. She waited patiently in the limousine while the Carlson family finished getting ready, a uniformed driver seated silently beyond the glass partition. Maria always felt like a fraud in these situations. Sitting on plush Italian leather, surrounded by chrome fixtures and polished teak veneer. No matter how many times she travelled by limo, it still seemed painfully unnatural.

It was Susannah Carlson's big night. She had been organizing the gala for months. The event was in aid of a new children's wing at a London hospital. The rich loved giving money to sick kids, Maria thought. That way no one could hold their wealth against them. Robert wanted her to help revise the speech he was due to give that night. He was the star turn and he wanted to make sure his performance would be perfect in front of such a prestigious crowd. There would be time enough to go over the speech on the drive to the Carlingford, Robert had told her. Maria had sensed how nervous he sounded on the phone. It wasn't like him, she had thought. He was always so composed when it came to his work. Confident and self-assured like a man at the top of his game. But it wasn't the speech that was unsettling him, she guessed. That part was easy. It was the prospect of an evening with his dysfunctional family that was troubling him.

She looked up at the five-storey mansion, its windows ablaze in the dark. She could see people hurrying from room to room in search of coats and shoes, the chaotic last-minute preparations for a black-tie event. The Lowndes Square mansion was such an opulent home for a green energy tycoon. Maria knew that Robert would have preferred living in a modest eco-house, one he had designed himself, but Susannah had insisted on buying this palace in the heart of Belgravia. Anything smaller would have been shameful in her eyes. Status symbols and the trappings of wealth meant so much to people in her circle. Maria sometimes wondered how Robert could stand living with such a family. His wife and daughter were caricatures of the idle rich. They were always so needy, demanding more and more of Robert's attention, no matter how much he gave them. They were a huge drain on his energy. Distracting him. Dragging him down.

Maria often thought that the time she spent alone with him, flying on business trips or attending international conferences, gave Robert a chance to relax and be himself. Spending time one-on-one with the CEO was beneficial for her as well. It was priceless to be able to watch a man like Robert Carlson work so closely. Sometimes Maria worried that he enjoyed her company too much – that boundaries were becoming blurred, intentions mistaken. It was a concern that constantly needled away in the back of her mind, but one she tried to ignore. Maria loved her job too much to tackle the issue head-on.

When the front door finally opened and the family came down the wide stone steps, Maria could see they'd been arguing. Susannah was walking with her teeth gritted, her eyes alive with rage. When she opened the door to the limousine, she stopped in her tracks.

'Maria?' she said, shocked. 'What are you doing here?'

Maria tried not to let her cheeks redden. It was obvious Carlson hadn't told his family she was joining them.

'Uh . . . uh, Robert asked me to help with some changes to his speech,' she stammered.

Susannah scowled at her husband. 'Oh, I see. How convenient.'

She regained her composure and stepped into the limo, hitching up the hem of her gown. Her daughter and husband followed in her wake. This was going to be an uncomfortable ride, Maria thought.

'I like your dress,' she said to Susannah. 'And yours, Emilia.'

Susannah was wearing a silver brocade evening gown, her hair set in a tight chignon. Emilia had chosen a black cocktail dress and towering heels. Maria wasn't giving empty compliments. They really did look amazing. A life with private chefs and Pilates instructors had not been in vain.

'Thank you, Maria,' Susannah said, her voice polite but cold. She smiled thinly at the compliment but didn't offer any praise in return.

Carlson was seated opposite. He was wearing a black

dinner jacket and a neat bow tie. A crisp white dress shirt with silver button studs. He always acted differently when his family were present, Maria noticed. More formal and distant. As if he didn't want his wife to see how close he was to his young female employee.

'Thank you for joining us, Maria,' Carlson said. 'I just want to check the statistics at the end of the speech. I'm not sure they're up to date.'

He took the typed pages of the presentation from the pocket of his dinner jacket and unfolded them.

'Please, Daddy,' Emilia said petulantly, 'you've been rehearsing all day. I can't take any more talk about rainforests and windmills.'

Carlson gave a huff of disappointment. 'My speech is important. Think of the people who'll be listening tonight.'

'But you're obsessed,' Emilia whined. 'It's all you ever talk about.'

'Perhaps you should be a little more occupied with your own work,' Carlson scolded. 'You should be more like Maria. She's a fine example for you to follow.'

Emilia looked stung at the criticism. Maria shrank back in her seat, shying away from her employer's praise.

Carlson slipped on his reading glasses. He looked at Maria. 'Shall we start at the top?' he asked.

'Of course,' Maria said.

Carlson was about to begin when Emilia interrupted spitefully.

'No one at the gala will care about your stupid speech,' she spat. 'They'll all be too busy enjoying the party to listen to you.'

Maria wondered what made the rich so unhappy? Their good

fortune seemed to weigh so heavily on them, especially their children. Emilia Carlson was a product of her environment – a spoiled rich kid who had grown up flying in private jets and staying in six-star hotels. She had recently interned at the Ever Sine offices for a few months, working as a junior in the legal department. Maria had sometimes seen her toiling away at her desk or trudging through the lobby on the morning coffee run with the other assistants. It had been obvious that Emilia hadn't enjoyed the experience. She had probably expected to be appointed straight to senior management, Maria supposed.

The grand entrance of Carlingford was a barrage of camera flashes as guests made their way along the red carpet. Saudi playboys. Grey-haired investment bankers. Silicon Valley types and their glamorous partners. To Maria, they all looked like disciples of some elaborate cult, practising a dark ritual. Worshippers at a temple of empty opulence.

Climbing from the limo, Carlson whispered one final instruction. 'I know what a great networker you are, Maria,' he said. 'I want you to keep Emilia with you tonight. It would do her good to see you in action. She pretends to be confident but she's very shy really.'

Maria was appalled at the prospect, but there was no chance to argue as they swept up the red carpet, fighting through the blinding flashes of the paparazzi. In the cocktail bar, the guests were mingling, standing in circles and making polite conversation. They were dazzling people, extroverts, poised and refined, who carried themselves as if everything in the world belonged to them by right. Olivia Ward was there with some of the other Ever Sine staff. Carlson went over to greet them like a dutiful employer.

Maria looked around at the glitz and wealth. It was supposed to be impressive but she found it all disgustingly superficial. Taking Emilia by the elbow, she began a passage around the room. Some of the assembled guests she had met before, others were strangers. The secret to networking, Maria knew, was to speak with knowledge and sincerity. Emilia, it was obvious, lacked both. She stood at Maria's side like a prisoner, making no disguise of her boredom. When they were alone together, Maria took the chance to talk frankly.

She took two glasses of champagne from a passing tray and handed one to Emilia. 'You don't really want to do this, do you?' she said.

'What do you mean?'

'A career in the green energy sector. It's not what you want, is it?'

Emilia shrugged disinterestedly. 'Not really.'

'Why don't you tell your father?'

'Because I don't know what else I can do with my life.'

'It's a big world. You have lots of options. Go and find your own way.'

'I want Daddy to be proud of me.'

'He will be if you live your own life.'

Emilia's eyes widened as she had an idea. 'Maybe you could help me? Give me a crash course on how the business actually works. All that jargon you and Daddy use . . .'

Maria could see how naïve and sheltered Carlson's daughter really was. 'Climate science isn't something you can learn in a couple of hours,' she said. 'It's takes years of studying and dedication. You have to be really interested in it.'

Emilia's shoulders slumped dejectedly. She had the same clear blue eyes as her father. She fixed them on Maria. 'I see the way my father talks to you,' she said. 'I wish he'd show me the same kind of attention. That's what I care about really.'

'You don't have to put on an act to get his respect,' Maria said. 'Robert will think more of you if you follow your own path in life.'

Emilia raised an eyebrow. 'Robert?'

Maria corrected herself quickly. 'I meant to say Mr Carlson.'

It was a slip that Maria regretted. Emilia looked pleased to exert her superiority. She took a long sip of champagne, a smug smile creasing her lips. Maria bit her tongue. She knew better than to pick a fight with a spoiled princess. It was a battle she could never win. A moment seemed to hang between them. An awkward silence.

'Tell me,' Emilia asked finally, 'are your family successful?'

Maria laughed at the idea. 'God, no.'

'What are they like?'

'My mum's tough. She's an immigrant so she had no choice. It was the only way she could survive in our part of London. I have a brother too. But he's another story.'

'How?'

Maria thought of Drew, of the chaos that followed him around like a shadow. 'A story without a happy ending,' she said.

Emilia excused herself to go to the bathroom and Maria continued her sweep of the room alone. Soon it was time to go to the ballroom where dinner was served. The guests descended a crowded winding staircase. Maria found herself alone, moving with the flow of people. She felt a hand on her shoulder and glanced round. A man she had never seen before was standing at her back. He was tall and confident, about thirty-five, with an expensively tailored tuxedo and platinum wristwatch that twinkled in the light from the ballroom chandelier. He was handsome and well groomed, but there was an undercurrent of menace about him.

'Hello,' he said, extending a manicured hand. 'My name is Andrei.'

Maria shook his hand politely. Andrei held on longer than necessary, holding her gaze like a pick-up artist. Behind him, a group of his friends were giggling, urging him on. Maria's attention was caught less by his actions than his accent. It was Russian but with a hint of Ukrainian, as if he came from a southern city near the border.

'*Vy rozmovlyayete ukrayins'koyu?*' Maria asked. 'Do you speak Ukrainian?'

A bright smile spread over his face as if he'd won a prize.

'*Absolyutno,*' he answered. 'Of course.'

Maria switched to speaking in her second language. Something about the ease of the conversation seemed to make Andrei open up.

'How do you know Ukrainian?' he asked.

'My Mum is from a town near Kyiv.'

'Have you visited?'

'No. I'd love to go.'

Andrei considered the idea with distaste. 'I'd recommend a trip to Moscow or Saint Petersburg instead,' he said. 'Russia is much more interesting. I only learned Ukrainian because I have business in the country.'

'What do you do?' she asked.

'I make money for people,' Andrei said flippantly. 'Lots of it.'

His arrogance was astounding but typically Russian. He was pumped up on his own self-assurance and vanity. Maria was losing interest in the conversation but decided to keep humouring him.

'And how do you make so much money?' she asked.

'By magic.'

'You pull rabbits out of hats?'

'In a way,' Andrei said. 'I work for my father. We find troubled energy projects. Wounded animals in need of protection. We revive them and take the profits.'

'You've found one of these troubled projects in London?' Maria asked.

Andrei nodded. 'I think it could be our biggest yet.'

'Where is this golden opportunity?'

'I forget the name. Coldharbour Messes. Or Meshes. Something like that.'

'Marshes?' Maria corrected him. 'Coldharbour Marshes?'

'That's right,' Andrei said.

It had been a long time since Maria had visited that part of East London, out on the fringes of the city by the river. She remembered it as one of the only unspoiled natural habitats for miles around. A pristine hideaway for rare species of birds and plants. It wasn't a place for any kind of energy project. She was sure Andrei must be mistaken.

'Those marshes are protected,' Maria said. 'You can't build anything on that land.'

A flicker of cold nonchalance passed over Andrei's face. 'Work starts in a few weeks.'

169

'But that's illegal.'

He shrugged. 'That's what expensive lawyers are for.'

'Which developer are you working with?'

He looked uncomfortable at her questioning, as if the flirtation wasn't working out as planned. 'Why do you want to know?' he asked.

Maria gave a casual shrug. 'Idle curiosity,' she said.

'You probably don't know him.'

'Try me.'

Andrei hesitated. He was trying to keep his mouth shut but didn't want to be disbelieved by a mere woman. He couldn't bear to appear as an empty blowhard who was just showing off.

'We're working with a man called Robert Carlson,' he said.

As soon as the name left his lips, Maria could see how much he regretted it.

35

MARIA SLIPPED AWAY and found a quiet spot in a corner of a corridor. Taking advantage of the semi-darkness, she took out her phone and logged on to the company database. Using 'Coldharbour Marshes' as a search term, she scanned for documents containing that name. A long list of files was returned. Clicking on them, Maria found they were all locked. Alarm bells sounded in her mind. Robert trusted her with the highest level of access to the database. Why would these files be restricted? It must be some mistake, she thought. Although it was late on a Friday evening, Maria knew the IT engineers would be working the night shift back at the Ever Sine building.

She called the switchboard and pressed '3' for the IT department.

'It's Maria Brennan,' she said. 'I'm with Mr Carlson at a charity gala. I need access to all the files on the Coldharbour Marshes project but I'm locked out. Can you help me?'

The engineer was eating a snack. She could hear him chewing loudly down the line.

'Those files are off limits,' he said, mid-mouthful.

'On whose instructions?'

'Mr Carlson's.'

'Why would he restrict access to them?' she asked.

'I have no idea. He ordered them all to be kept private.'

'But I need to view them as a matter of urgency.'

'Sorry. You're not named on the distribution list.'

'Who is?'

'Only Mr Carlson and Ms Ward.'

Maria fumed at what she was hearing. She had never liked Olivia Ward, had always openly distrusted her motives when they worked on projects together. Ward was too calculating, too devious, in Maria's opinion. They treated each other cautiously around the office, maintaining a polite, safe distance from each other whenever possible. It came as a blow that Olivia Ward was held in closer confidence than her.

Back in the ballroom, Carlson had begun his speech. He was standing at a podium at one end of the room, lit by a single spotlight. The assembled guests listened in rapt silence. Susannah was watching him admiringly. Emilia was nowhere to be seen. An empty chair stood at the table where she was supposed to be seated. Maria found a spot at the back of the room and looked on from the shadows.

'Most of us here tonight have dedicated our working lives to helping others,' Carlson said. 'In the course of our work, we've become wealthy. For this, I believe none of us should apologize. We've worked tirelessly to improve people's lives. This is no empty sentiment. At Ever Sine, it's in our DNA. It's the keystone on which the company is built.'

The audience applauded heartily at the compliment. It was a balm to the hedge funders and asset strippers to hear that they were on the side of good for a change. Carlson had them in the palm of his hand after that.

'Many years ago, I started out with nothing,' he continued. 'I built the company up from humble beginnings and forged success through sheer force of will. Ever Sine is now a global brand. An integral part of the planet's future.'

As Carlson was speaking, Maria noticed Olivia Ward's assistant, Anya, loitering at the far side of the room. She caught her eye and beckoned her over. Anya scurried towards her, keeping herself hidden in the shadows.

Olivia Ward's assistant always looked depressed and withdrawn. Maria assumed it was a result of the constant stress that her boss put her under. Maria and Anya had grown quite friendly recently, even seeing each other for drinks outside of work. Lately though, Anya had been refusing to socialize with anyone from the office. Maria was always saddened to see such a carefree person lose their shine so completely.

'How are you, Anya?' Maria asked tentatively. 'Enjoying yourself?'

Anya shrugged. 'Olivia's in a bad mood again. That makes enjoying anything impossible.'

'Are you going to take your seat for dinner? It looks like the first course is about to be served.'

Turning her eyes to the floor, Anya said, 'Olivia didn't reserve a place for me. I'm not even on the table with the other assistants.'

Maria felt terrible for her. She held up the invitation with her table number.

173

'You can have my place if you like? I'm not really hungry anyway.'

Anya accepted it with a shy smile. 'Thanks, Maria. I'm starving. But I'll have to hide my face. If Olivia sees me eating, she'll bawl me out again.'

Maria took her chance. 'Actually, it was Olivia I was looking for,' she said. 'Is she around?'

'She's in the bathroom fixing her make-up. She told me she'd heard Mr Carlson make enough speeches to last a lifetime.'

Maria thanked her and left the ballroom by the side door. She walked along the dimly lit corridor until she came to the women's bathroom. She pushed open the door and stepped inside. Olivia Ward was standing in front of the large gilt mirror, applying black mascara to her lashes. She was alone.

'I want to know about the Coldharbour Marshes project,' Maria said abruptly.

Olivia Ward eyed her in the mirror. Her face was heavy with pale foundation. The fringe of her fiery red hair ran perfectly straight across her forehead.

'Why on earth would I know anything about that?' Ward answered bluntly.

'Because you've been granted access to the planning documents. I'm guessing that means you've already read them despite their top-secret status.'

Ward gave her a sly smile. 'Andrei told me about your honeytrap,' she said. 'How you teased out the information about the project from him like a little flirt. You have quite a history of doing that sort of thing, don't you?'

Maria ignored the insult. 'How do you know Andrei?'

'None of your business.'

'Why do I know nothing about this deal we've struck with him?'

Ward smirked at her discomfort. 'That really bothers you, doesn't it?'

'Finding out that our company is in business with some shady Russians bothers me, yes.'

'I wouldn't upset Andrei any further. He's already fuming about your underhand tactics tonight. He's not the kind of man I would antagonize if I were you.'

'*He's* upset?' Maria said. '*I've* just found out we're going to destroy a nature reserve.'

Olivia Ward inspected her mascara. Satisfied with the effect, she turned and faced Maria head-on. It looked like she was enjoying Maria's distress. 'You really do think this whole company revolves around you, don't you?'

'I'm going to speak to Robert about this,' Maria said.

Ward rolled her eyes. 'To manipulate him into doing what you want, as usual?'

Her words were designed to sting. Maria felt them hit home.

'I would never do that,' she said.

'Oh, come on. Everyone talks about the two of you. How you've got him wrapped around your little finger. You make him look pathetic.'

'That's a lie.'

'The whole office knows about it. It's an open secret that Robert only promoted you because he's obsessed.'

'I live and breathe for my work,' Maria said. 'It's my whole life.'

175

'Stop kidding yourself,' Ward said scathingly. 'You're not some eco-saviour. You're just Robert's little crush. That's all.'

With that parting shot, Olivia Ward breezed past Maria and marched out of the bathroom, heels clicking on the tiled floor.

Maria stood at the washbasin for a moment, letting the conversation sink in. The sound of someone moving around came from one of the toilet stalls.

'Who's there?' she called out hesitantly.

The door opened. It was Emilia Carlson. Maria suddenly felt unbelievably foolish. It was a set-up, she thought. Ward had known who was in there all along. The conversation had been aimed for Emilia's ears. That was why Ward had been so brazen.

'Please,' Maria said. 'I can explain.'

Emilia's face was drawn, her eyes bloodshot. 'Don't bother,' she said petulantly.

At first Maria thought she'd been crying and she took a step forward to comfort her. Then she saw the white powder dotted around Emilia's nostrils. A small bag of cocaine and a bank card were lying on the marble shelf at the back of the toilet stall.

'You shouldn't be doing that,' Maria said.

Emilia ignored her. 'At least now I know why my father prefers your company to mine. No wonder I can't compete with you.'

'None of what you heard is true. Olivia was making it all up. You've got to believe me.'

'Do I?' Emilia said curtly. She took the bag of white powder and tipped out some on to the corner of her bank card and

snorted it loudly. She made her actions exaggerated and delib-
erate, like a child displaying a naked defiance.

'You should give that stuff to me,' Maria said, holding out
her hand. 'It's dangerous. I've seen the damage drugs can do.'

Emilia laughed derisively. She opened her evening bag and
tossed the cocaine inside.

'Don't try and order me around,' she spat as she headed for
the door. 'You're nothing but my father's plaything.'

36

BACK IN THE ballroom, the gala dinner was underway. Waiters were moving around the room with trays of food under silver covers. Maria looked for Carlson, sitting in pride of place on the head table. Susannah gripped his arm tightly as she saw Maria approach.

'Robert, I really need to speak with you,' Maria said.

He looked uncomfortable at being addressed so directly in front of his wife. 'Can't it wait?'

She held his gaze. 'This is important.'

Apologizing to Susannah, Carlson excused himself and followed Maria out of the ballroom. To find some privacy, she led him through the heavy swing doors and into the hotel kitchen. It was hot and steamy inside. The staff were hurriedly plating up meals, too occupied with their work to notice the couple's presence.

'What on earth is this about?' Carlson snapped.

'Coldharbour Marshes,' Maria said. She spoke without

warning or preamble so she could gauge his reaction. Carlson couldn't disguise his shock.

'I was going to tell you,' he said guiltily.

Maria was incredulous. 'Then it's true? We're destroying a nature reserve?'

'I need you to trust me on this. It's not what it seems.'

'Then what are we building out there?'

Carlson's eyes lit up. 'A hydrogen plant. One big enough to supply London.'

'And you had to partner with some dodgy Russians to finance it?' Maria's voice was full of righteous indignation.

'There are things you don't know about the state of the company,' he implored. 'Not everything is as healthy as I pretend. There are balance sheet issues. Cash flow problems. Crises that I have to keep to myself or else the whole business could be destroyed. Some decisions I make might look compromised but they're for the good of us all. Believe me.'

Waiters were running through the swing doors, pirouetting around each other with trays held aloft. Harried chefs were shouting at the kitchen porters. The heat from the stoves was intense. Maria was growing angry and flustered at what she was hearing. It was like she was having her dreams desecrated by the very man she had hoped would fulfil them.

'Why didn't you discuss any of this with me?' she asked plaintively. 'Why am I the last to know?'

Carlson looked like the answer should have been obvious. 'Because I knew how you'd react,' he said.

He took a step towards her, resting his hands on her shoulders. The gesture was meant to soothe her but all Maria could think of was Olivia Ward's accusations. She shied away, shrugging him off.

'Don't touch me,' Maria barked.

As she backed off, she moved too close to the edge of a hot stove. Her arm pressed against the searing metal and she cried out in pain. The kitchen staff turned to see the cause of the commotion.

'Oh my god,' Carlson said. 'Are you hurt?'

He swept a concerned arm around Maria's waist to move her away from danger. Taking her wrist in his hand, he held it gently, examining the skin and the red welt branded there. As he pulled her close, he felt Maria's body tense. She was staring past him, her eyes wide.

Carlson turned and followed her gaze. Through a porthole window in the kitchen door, Susannah was staring in. She looked at them grimly, reading the obvious signals in their embrace. She lingered for a moment, her face clenched tightly as if all of her darkest suspicions had been confirmed. Then, without a word, Susannah turned and stormed away.

'Please, Susannah. Wait . . .' Carlson called after her despairingly.

His wife kept walking.

Maria's shoulders slumped. The night had become the ordeal she had always predicted.

37

THE HEAD CHEF ran a stream of cold water into a sink and insisted Maria hold her burned arm under its flow. He was Italian, gesticulating wildly as he scolded Carlson for using the kitchen as a private meeting room. Carlson tried to placate him, apologizing profusely. He looked mortified at the turn of events. The porters and waiters flashed disapproving glances as they carried on working around them. The chef demanded that hotel rules be followed; the accident had to be recorded in the kitchen log. Carlson obediently filled in the paperwork. It was laborious and time-consuming. When it was done, he and Maria stepped out into the corridor.

'I think it's best if I went home,' Maria said, looking like she wanted to get out of there fast.

Carlson stood and blocked her way. 'You can't leave like this,' he said. 'It will only look worse to Susannah if you go now. We have to find her and explain what she saw. Tell her it was all a misunderstanding.'

Maria shook her head sadly. 'I don't think she'd listen to me. Especially with all the gossip that's going around.'

'What do you mean?'

'I saw Olivia Ward earlier. She told me people are whispering about us spending so much time together.'

Carlson paused, reading her eyes. 'And that embarrasses you?'

'I don't want any special favours, from you or anyone else. I want to be respected for my work.'

'You think I want something else from you?'

'It doesn't matter what I think. It's what others are saying that's the problem.'

'You don't trust me?'

'Don't turn the tables on me, Robert,' Maria said. 'You're the one who doesn't trust *me*.'

'That's ridiculous.'

'What about this Coldharbour Marshes project? You've kept me completely in the dark about it.'

'That's different.'

'Is it?'

'You have to believe me.'

'I'm not sure I believe you about anything any more.'

Carlson looked crushed. 'I'm horrified you could say that to me.'

Maria fixed her eyes on his. 'If you want me to trust you, give me access to the Coldharbour Marshes files. The ones you've taken offline.'

A wave of suspicion passed over his face. 'How do you know about those?'

'I called into the office,' Maria said. 'The IT engineers told me you'd issued instructions to keep the documents top secret.'

'You have to stop snooping, Maria. Leave this project alone. That's an order.'

Maria was indignant at the idea. 'You don't give me orders,' she said. 'No one does.'

With that, she turned and marched along the corridor towards the lobby. Carlson hurried after her. At the cloak-room, Maria gave her ticket stub to the attendant and waited as she disappeared to retrieve her coat. When she returned, a uniformed security guard was beside her.

'Does this belong to you?' he asked, pointing at her coat.

The question was phrased like an accusation.

'Yes,' Maria replied innocently. 'Is there a problem?'

The security guard gave her an officious scowl. 'I think you'd better come with me,' he said.

38

THE SECURITY GUARD led her up to the first floor. Carlson accompanied them up the grand sweeping staircase. In an office at the end of a long corridor, the hotel's chief of security was seated behind a large desk. He was grim-faced and stern, his manner unwelcoming.

'Take a seat,' he said, motioning to the chair opposite.

Maria did as she was asked. Carlson remained standing behind her.

'What's going on?' she said.

The security guard placed Maria's coat on the table.

'Is this yours?' the chief of security asked.

'Yes. Why?'

'I want to search your pockets,' he said. 'You're within your rights to refuse. If you do, I will have to call the police. Do I have your permission?'

Maria looked up at Carlson for help. She had no idea why this was happening. He seemed wary of intervening.

Finally she said, 'Go ahead. I don't have anything to hide.'

The security chief reached inside the left-hand pocket and rummaged around. He pulled out a packet of chewing gum and a broken hairgrip. He tossed them on to the table.

As he reached into the right-hand pocket, Maria could tell immediately from his reaction that he had found what he was expecting. A self-satisfied smirk spread over his jowly face as he triumphantly removed his hand from her pocket and laid a small plastic bag on the table. It was full of white powder. It must be cocaine, Maria thought.

'I think you might have some explaining to do,' the security chief said.

'That isn't mine,' Maria blurted out, her voice panicked.

She could immediately hear how false the denial sounded. The chief looked like everyone in her position always made the same protest. He pursed his lips in distaste.

'We've had a complaint of drug dealing in the hotel,' he said. 'You were named as the culprit.'

'These drugs have been planted,' Maria said. 'I've never taken cocaine in my life.'

'Hotel policy states that we have to inform the authorities. It's up to them if they take the matter further. I don't think the charge of drug dealing will stand, but nonetheless, possession of a Class A drug is a serious offence.'

'But I swear it's not mine,' Maria insisted. 'I don't use drugs.'

'You think someone else put this in your coat?'

'They must have done.'

'Who?'

Maria glanced awkwardly at Carlson. 'I'm sorry, but I think Emilia did it.'

She watched as his face dropped in shock and then, just as quickly, hardened into an expression of fierce protectiveness.

'That's nonsense,' Carlson snapped.

'It's the only explanation that makes sense.'

'Why would Emilia do that to you?'

Maria was sincere but adamant. 'She overheard an argument I had earlier with Olivia Ward. About how people think we're having an affair. She was upset. I think she's done this to take revenge.'

Carlson looked disgusted. 'That's a bare-faced lie. A fantasy. I can't believe you'd say something so hideous about my daughter.'

'It's the truth,' Maria said. 'I saw Emilia taking drugs in the bathroom. I'm sorry. I should have told you . . .'

Carlson held up a hand to stop her. He turned to the officious-looking chief of security. 'My name is Robert Carlson,' he said. 'I employ this woman. She's here tonight as my guest. I'd like to deal with this as an internal company matter if that's agreeable to you.'

The chief nodded gravely.

Carlson looked down at Maria, his eyes full of scorn. 'You should be ashamed of yourself, Maria.'

'I'm telling you the truth,' she pleaded.

Her answer only seemed to enrage him further.

'Get out,' Carlson said. 'You're fired!'

39

TEARS FROZE IN her eyes as Maria walked out of the doors of the Carlingford into the bitter wind that was blowing through Mayfair. Her thoughts were pinballing around wildly. She had uncovered secret plans to destroy a nature reserve, been accused of trying to seduce her boss, then been set up by a spoiled princess. Finally she'd been sacked from her job. The night couldn't have been more disastrous.

As she played over the events in her mind, there was something unsettling about the sudden and ruthless way in which Carlson had fired her, as if he was using the situation to cover up some hidden intention. Was this a convenient way to discredit her because she'd found out about his plans for Coldharbour Marshes? Or was it because of the office gossip about his feelings for her? Whatever the answer, Maria couldn't help the surge of outrage welling up inside her. Was this all she was worth? Tossed aside at the first sign of trouble? She thought of all the time she had spent with Carlson, travelling to seminars and on research trips. Talking about their private lives and their hopes for the future. Their shared desire to play a part in solving the climate crisis. Now all those moments seemed no more than a heap of lies.

The rich always protected themselves, Maria thought. It was their nature. She wasn't one of them and would never be more than a pawn in their plans. Robert Carlson was no different from the rest. Maria promised herself that she wasn't going to walk away quietly. Simply leave him to carry on with his plans to destroy a beautiful nature reserve with his megalomania and his money. That was not her style.

On the hotel patio, she spotted one of the giggling Russian men who had been with Andrei earlier. He was alone, half drunk, smoking a cigarette. He recognized her, his eyes glassy, his bow tie crooked. Maria approached him with a bright, flirtatious smile.

'Got a cigarette?' she asked.

He was surprised to have female company and fumbled with the packet, almost spilling the contents. He took a matchbook branded with the hotel's logo and struck it. Maria leaned towards him as he lit her cigarette, touching his hand gently.

'Can you do me a favour?' she said. 'Andrei forgot to give me his phone number. He wants to take me out next time he's in town.'

The Russian looked eager to help. 'No problem. I'll write it down for you,' he said. He took a pen and flipped open the matchbook. He wrote quickly on the inside cover and handed it to Maria.

'Will you write Andrei's surname for me, please?' she said. 'I'd hate to forget that too.'

He scribbled the name down next to the phone number.

'I can give you my number too, if you'd like?' he said hopefully.

Maria was repulsed at the suggestion. 'No, that won't be necessary,' she spat.

She flagged down a passing taxi and gave the driver her address. As he pulled away, she read the name written inside the matchbook several times, trying to dredge her memory. It wasn't a name she recognized from the usual list of financiers the company did business with. This name was completely new to her. She placed the matchbook in her handbag. Of all the revelations that night, it was the one about Coldharbour Marshes that Maria couldn't stop thinking of. It was outrageous that Robert was going to destroy such a beautiful place so blithely. Someone had to stop him.

Watching the city pass by outside the window, Maria took out her phone and redialled the number for the Ever Sinc IT department.

'Hello?'

Her luck was in. It was a different engineer. He sounded groggy and half asleep. Maria adopted Ward's cut-glass diction to disguise her voice.

'This is Olivia Ward,' she said curtly.

The engineer perked up instantly as if frightened by the announcement. 'What can I do for you, Ms Ward?'

'I need hard copies of some documents on the database. It's urgent.'

'Of course. Which ones?'

'All of the Coldharbour Marshes files. I need the paper copies taken up to my office as soon as possible.'

'No problem,' the engineer said, sounding eager to please. 'I'll print them out and bring them up straight away.'

Maria hung up, smiling to herself. The staff were too scared to argue with Olivia Ward. She had a reputation for ruining the career of anyone who challenged her. Now that high-handed disdain was going to come back and bite her. Leaning forward, Maria spoke quickly to the driver.

'Change of plan,' she said. 'Take me to the Ever Sine building on the South Bank. I need to pick something up.'

40

Martin Sobel: So what happened next?

Maria Brennan: Half an hour later, I arrived at the Ever Sine building and went up to Olivia's office. It was late and the place was almost deserted. The copies were all there, hot off the press, stacked on her desk just as I'd asked. I took them home and read through every word, especially the joint part-nership agreement that had been drawn up to finance the hydrogen plant. It gave the full scale of the project that Robert was planning. What I saw really scared me. Those beautiful marshes were going to be completely destroyed if he wasn't stopped. I'd never seen him do anything like this before. It was like he'd lost his mind.

MS: What was so unusual about the proposal?

MB: Building any kind of facility at Coldharbour Marshes would be an outrage. But the scale of the project Robert was planning was breathtaking. He was overreaching himself. The plans were far too ambitious. There was no way he could pull it off.

MS: Even though he had secured the money from the Russians?

MB: Andrei and his father had agreed to invest a fortune, but that was still only a fraction of what was needed. Robert would run out of money well before the project was completed unless he found additional investment. But the financing structure was so opaque, no one else would dare put their money in. They could stand to lose everything if the plans failed. Robert's hydrogen facility was a fantasy, in my opinion. He could start it, but there was no way he could finish it. Coldharbour Marshes were going to be destroyed for nothing. No wonder Robert had to rely on Russian money. No reliable investor would dare buy into the scheme. Now I had Andrei's full name, I did some research into him and his father. What I found frightened me. They're both very dangerous men.

MS: You're scared of them?

MB: Of course. Men like that are capable of anything. They have to stay hidden because no reputable business will touch them. Whoever drafted the contract for the hydrogen plant had worked magic. The Russian money was funnelled through a host of shell companies and blind trusts. Andrei's father is barred by Magnitsky sanctions so he has to remain anonymous. His identity has to be concealed to evade the attention of the UK authorities. That's why he sent his son to represent him.

MS: You mean the government has banned Andrei's father from doing business in the UK?

MB: Along with all the other corrupt Russian and Belarusian nationals. Crooked politicians. Gangsters. Money launderers. Other assorted scumbags. Andrei's father deserves his place on the list.

MS: Can you tell me who he is?

MB: It's safer for you if I don't. I kept the matchbook from the Carlingford with their family name written inside. I've hidden it somewhere safe. When the time is right, I'll reveal who they are.

MS: And on top of this, you think Carlson was blacklisting you?

MB: After he fired me, I began to call other green tech companies, looking for work. Everywhere I turned, I got the same response. They knew about the scandal I'd supposedly caused at the charity gala. I was now unemployable. I kept researching the Coldharbour Marshes project at the same time. Asking around, making enquiries. Then one day, Robert called me out of the blue. He was frantic. He offered me money to drop my wrongful dismissal claim. I refused. He kept increasing the offer. He said the money didn't matter. I told him that not everyone has a price. Some of us have principles and mine weren't for sale. That's when he began calling me relentlessly on the phone. Following me and stopping me in the street. I thought he was losing the plot. I started to get scared about what he might do next.

MS: Did you try to reason with him?

MB: He wouldn't listen. Overnight, I'd become his adversary. My fall from grace was complete. I needed to save money so I gave up my flat and moved back in with my mother. I'm sleeping in my childhood bedroom. Living with my younger brother and all his madness. But I couldn't cave in and take Robert's money. Not now I knew the kind of people he was working with.

MS: Are you worried for your own safety?

MB: (*pauses*) These men will stop at nothing if they think their wealth is threatened. They're all the same really. Everything comes down to money with them. But I know how to fight back, especially now I have the thing that scares them the most.

MS: Which is?

MB: The power to make them poor.

41

LOOKING UP FROM his computer screen, Lewis could see the sun streaming in through the slatted blinds over the window. It was Saturday morning, nearly seven a.m. He had spent the night lost in the pages of the transcript, reading and re-reading it, taking copious notes. He was numb from sitting in one position for so long. His neck ached. He stretched and tried to shake out the tension in his back and shoulders.

Now that he'd read her words, heard her voice, Lewis was beginning to understand who Maria Brennan was. From what he had learned, he liked her. She was earnest and determined, an activist for a noble cause. Despite this, she wasn't above subterfuge when it suited her. That was a useful quality to have, in Lewis's opinion.

In many ways, the transcript had only complicated things. Lewis had more questions than answers now. Who were Andrei and his father? If Andrei was Russian, did he write the note that was found on Maria's car? If Emilia Carlson had been callous enough to frame Maria for taking drugs, was she also capable of murder? The web was tightening, entangling Lewis the more he tried to find a way through it. But one thing was certain now: Robert Carlson knew more about Maria's fate than he was prepared to admit. It was clear that Carlson had been careful to cover his tracks. Lewis had to find out why.

At the end of the transcript, Maria had mentioned the files she had taken from Olivia Ward's office – the joint partnership agreement for the Coldharbour Marshes project. That must be the contract that had been found in her car, Lewis thought. The paperwork he had taken from Irina Koval and couriered to Rachael for safekeeping the previous day. He urgently needed to read that document.

Taking out his phone, Lewis called Rachael. She answered quickly.

'Lewis,' she said breathlessly, 'you didn't come home last night. I was worried about you.'

'I stayed over at my sister's in Stepney,' he said. 'It was a last-minute decision.'

'Are you all right?'

'I'm fine. I'm working through the Brennan case. I think I might be on to something.'

'A courier came with a package yesterday,' Rachael said. 'It was sent by someone in your office. I assumed it was meant for you.'

'Have you still got it?'

He could hear the sound of the duvet being folded back as Rachael got out of bed. Quick footsteps on the bare floorboards.

'I've got it in my hand now,' she said.

'Good. What are you doing this morning?'

'I don't have any plans. Why?'

'Can you bring the folder over to my sister's house? I'll send you the address.'

Rachael thought for a second. 'OK. I'll drive over.'

'Afterwards, there's something I thought we could do together,' Lewis said. 'Just the two of us.'

'What did you have in mind?'

'It's a beautiful day,' Lewis said. 'I thought we could go for a walk out at Coldharbour Marshes.'

By the time Rachael arrived, Lewis had spent an hour making breakfast and playing with his nephews. Angela was in her pyjamas, her hair crumpled from the pillow. She saw Rachael's car, an old brown Volvo, pull up outside the house.

'Invite your girlfriend in so I can meet her,' Angela pleaded, pulling open the blinds so she could peek out.

'Another time,' Lewis said. 'I'm in a hurry.'

Angela pressed her face to the window, squinting. 'She's pretty. And she looks intelligent too. I wonder what on earth she sees in someone like you?'

Lewis ignored his sister's teasing. He gave her a hug goodbye and gathered his coat and bag from the living room.

Angela followed him out to the doorstep. 'Be careful, Lewis,' she said, her voice turning serious. 'Call me later so I know you're safe.'

He turned and smiled at her. 'Stop worrying, Angie,' he said. 'I've got this totally under control.'

42

IRINA KOVAL MADE coffee in the tiny kitchen. When it was ready, she knocked on her son's bedroom door. He answered, looking pale and haggard.

'What's wrong?' she asked. 'Are you sick?'

Drew looked at her scornfully. 'Yesterday you accused me of being involved in Maria's death. Now you're worried about my health?'

A look of regret passed over Irina's eyes. 'I'm sorry. I was angry.'

'It feels like you're always angry lately.'

'I made you coffee,' Irina said.

'I don't have time. I've got to go out.'

'So early? Where are you going?'

'I'm meeting Glenn. He's picking me up in ten minutes.'

'I don't like you hanging around with him. He's trouble.'

Drew shook his head. 'You've been saying that for years.'

Irina sighed. 'That's because it's true,' she said.

*

When he came out of the stairwell at the foot of the tower block, Glenn was waiting. He looked nervous, chewing his fingernails as he sat at the wheel of a black Audi A5. He started the engine when he saw Drew approach.

'Come on,' Glenn said curtly. 'My uncle's waiting.'

'Did you get a chance to explain what happened yesterday?'

'I tried but he wouldn't listen.'

'What do think he's going to do?'

Glenn glared at him from the driver's seat. 'What would *you* do if you'd just lost ninety grand?'

They drove out through the grim housing estates and forlorn streets, heading east into the Isle of Dogs. Soon the steel skeleton of the half-built shopping centre came into view. The huge earth movers and cranes stood idle. The muddy access roads lay empty. Dark clouds were gathering overhead, birds wheeling in sinister flocks in the slate-grey sky.

Glenn drove down the ramp leading into the underground car park of the shopping centre. It was half built, the walls unfinished. Loose wiring hung down in tangles from the ceilings. The wheels of the Audi trundled over the rough, unpaved road surface as they headed down deeper into the darkness. In the gloom of the basement level, a dirty white van was parked next to a freshly dug pit. A cement-mixing lorry stood beside it, its heavy drum slowly spinning. A few men stood around smoking. Drew recognized them from previous jobs. They were street thugs, ruthless and dangerous.

Frank Egan stepped forward when he saw the Audi, his hands shoved deep in the pockets of his coat. He spat a great ball of phlegm on to the dirt at his feet as Drew got out of the car and walked towards him. Frank looked like he was in a bitter mood.

'My nephew tells me you've found a brand-new way to lose my money,' he said.

'I can explain.'

Frank Egan dismissed the attempt to placate him. 'Glenn's already filled me in on your story. There was a chase. You tried to outrun the police. You had no choice.'

'It's the truth.'

'And you think I should just take your word for it? Where's the proof?'

Drew blew on his hands to warm them. It was freezing in the depths of the car park where daylight never penetrated.

'I don't have any,' he admitted.

'That's why I decided to get a second opinion,' Frank said.

He strode to the side of the white Transit van and slid open the panel door. A figure lay huddled inside, trussed up with cable ties around his wrists and ankles, a black hood over his head.

Frank dragged the whimpering figure up to a sitting position and pulled off the hood. It was Adem. Frank slapped him hard across the face to stop his snivelling.

'Why don't you tell these lads what you just told me,' he said.

Adem's teeth were chattering. He looked at Drew. Words fell out of him in a frantic tumble.

'The . . . the gun was Drew's idea,' he stammered. 'I tried to talk him out of it. He wouldn't listen. He wanted to rip you off, Frank.'

'This is bullshit,' Drew said, stunned. 'That gun was nothing to do with me. Why would I do something like that?'

'I can think of ninety thousand reasons,' Frank said.

'He's a thief!' Adem cried. 'He must have stashed your money somewhere, Frank. The gun was just a smokescreen. He needed it to give him a reason to explain why he'd tossed the bag away.'

Drew was shocked. Adem was inventing a crazy story to save himself. He was trying to pin the blame on Drew to get himself off the hook.

'I thought it was weird when I picked up the money,' Drew said. 'I didn't want to take the gun. I tried to refuse but Adem insisted.'

'Don't listen to him,' Adem squealed. 'He's conning you.'

Frank turned to Drew with a scowl. 'Was the money all there?' he asked. 'Did you count it?'

Drew made an instant calculation. He couldn't admit that he had neglected to count a single note. Not checking such a large amount of cash was an unforgivable error. Telling the truth now would land him in even deeper trouble.

''Course I checked it, Frank,' he said reassuringly. 'It was all there.'

'So you knew how much of my money you were tossing off the side of Tower Bridge?'

'What else could I do? That shotgun spelled ten years for me if I got caught.'

Frank turned to Adem. 'Your story doesn't add up. This kid's already done time. Why would he ride across London with a gun, stash it in a bag with my money, and then go all the way back across town?'

Adem tried to answer. His words came out in an incoherent stutter. His fear was causing him to seize up. 'I . . . I don't know. I . . . I'm telling the truth. You have to believe me.'

Frank Egan looked from one to the other, his gaze sharp

and unyielding. Drew could see that his temper was about to break. Finally Frank hissed, 'Right. I've had enough of this nonsense. I know how to get to the bottom of this.'

He strode to the Transit van and opened the side door. From a pile of tools he took a wooden pickaxe handle. To test its weight, Frank slapped the heavy stave against his calloused palm. It sounded like a joint of raw meat hitting a butcher's block. He nodded over at the freshly dug pit.

'Want to change your story?' he asked Drew bluntly.

'I can't,' Drew said. 'I don't have another version to tell you.'

'Then kneel down.'

Drew looked down into the dark hole. 'Come on, Frank,' he pleaded.

'Now.'

Drew glanced over at Glenn. His friend refused to meet his eye. Reluctantly Drew lowered himself on to the wet earth.

'One of you is lying to me,' Frank said. 'I can't have that.'

With steady footsteps, Frank walked behind him, out of sight. Drew looked down into the pit. The bare earth seemed to beckon him. The sound of the pickaxe handle smacking into Frank Egan's hand echoed around the basement. The heavy slap of wood against flesh. Drew waited, his senses on alert, his stomach churning. He heard a sharp intake of breath as Frank lifted the pickaxe handle over his head. Then there was a deathly swoosh as it was brought down with full force. Drew's whole body tensed, ready for the blow. Suddenly his ears filled with the sound of bone splintering and blood spilling.

Drew froze, his eyes clamped shut. Seconds passed. He was amazed to find he was still breathing. Slowly he opened his eyes and blinked in the gloomy half-light. Behind him, he heard a body being dragged, heels scraping against the dirt. With a heave, Adem's corpse was flung into the pit. His head was split wide open, his lifeless limbs horribly contorted as he landed.

Drew looked up. Frank was standing over him.

'Tell me where my money is,' he said. 'Or you're next.'

43

AS RACHAEL DROVE, Lewis told her what had happened since they had last been together – Martin Sobel's mysterious death; the frosty meeting with Olivia Ward; the near miss he'd had with the rush-hour train. Rachael alternated between disbelief and concern as she listened.

'You're saying that someone tried to kill you at Waterloo Station?' she asked incredulously.

Lewis gave a fatalistic shrug. 'It wasn't an accident. I know that much.'

'Surely you need to go to the police, Lewis? This is becoming way too serious now.'

'But then I'd never get the chance to find out who killed Maria Brennan.'

Rachael was surprised to hear that he'd changed his mind. 'So now you believe she *was* murdered?'

'I think you were right all along,' Lewis said. 'There's no way Maria's death was suicide. But I still don't know who killed her. That's what I have to find out.'

He opened the folder of legal paperwork that had been couriered to Rachael's flat and flicked through the pages.

'What is all that jargon?' Rachael asked. 'I took a peek at it earlier but I don't understand a word. It means nothing to me.'

'It's a joint partnership agreement,' Lewis said. 'A contract for the construction of a new hydrogen fuel plant. A massive one.'

'Do you know who's trying to build it?'

'A client of mine.'

'Who?'

Lewis thought the time for discretion had long passed. 'Robert Carlson,' he said.

Rachael immediately recognized the name. 'The famous environmentalist? Surely he can't be caught up in a murder case?'

Lewis registered the shock spreading across her face. He remembered having an identical feeling when he first heard the name. It was so out of character with Carlson's public persona that the idea was practically unbelievable. But that didn't rule him out of suspicion. In a way, it only made him seem more dangerous. It meant he was able to hide his true motives from scrutiny.

'Maria Brennan worked at his company,' Lewis said. 'She was a climate scientist, someone who had access to his secrets. Carlson fired her from her job over a scandal where Maria maintained her innocence. She insisted that he'd done it to discredit her. They were locked in a legal dispute when she died.'

Rachael took a moment to process the information. 'I can't believe a man like Robert Carlson would be capable of killing someone. He's spent his life trying to make the world a better place.'

'I agree. But all the evidence points to him being up to his neck in this. He's definitely hiding something. I know that much.'

'Where does Carlson want to build his hydrogen fuel plant?'

'Guess.'

Rachael looked at him through narrowed eyes. 'Coldharbour Marshes?' she said, her voice full of disbelief.

'That's why we're going out there. I want to see if he's serious.'

Rachael was stunned. 'But he'll destroy an unspoiled wilderness. Why would a man like Robert Carlson want to do that? That would be against everything he stands for. He's practically a saint.'

Lewis gave a resigned shake of his head. 'I'm afraid his halo might be about to slip,' he said.

Driving further east, the density of the city thinned. Trees and hedges appeared, the sky grew larger, the horizon widening to the far distance. Soon they were an hour from the heart of London but it felt like a different world. There were no buildings, no people, only the sound of wind through the trees and birds calling back and forth in the high branches.

When they arrived at the entrance to the nature reserve, Rachael pulled off the road and stopped in front of the wooden gateway. The place was deserted. A tall metal fence had been erected over the entrance, barring the pathway that led on to the wetlands. The whole nature reserve was closed to the public, the gateway locked with heavy chains and padlocks. Lewis read the sign attached to the metal fencing.

Do Not Enter. This Site is Under Development by Egan Construction.

44

DREW TRIED NOT to look at the lifeless body twisted in the pit beneath him but he couldn't tear his gaze away. He was only seconds away from following Adem down into the hole.

'Where's my money?' Frank Egan demanded.

'I already told you,' Drew said. 'I had to get rid of the bag. I couldn't get caught with a gun. The thought of going back to prison was too much for me. But I swear I didn't steal your money.'

'You just expect me to believe you?'

'I don't have any other way of convincing you, Frank.'

With heavy steps, Frank Egan walked behind him. Drew could hear him standing there, breathing hard. It was inevitable, Drew thought. There was no way out now. He tensed as the shadow of the pickaxe handle swung high above him, poised to strike. Drew closed his eyes.

'Wait!' Glenn shouted. 'He's telling the truth.'

The words seemed to puncture the silence, the unbearable

pressure of the moment released in an instant. Drew breathed out, his shoulders slumping.

'How do you know it's the truth?' Frank hissed.

Glenn's voice was shaking with fear. 'Because it was my idea. I bought the gun from Adem. I didn't know he'd send it with the money, I swear. That was his decision, not mine. But it was my fault that the gun was there in the first place, not Drew's.'

Frank cursed under his breath. 'I should have known you were behind this,' he said.

'I'm sorry, Frank,' Glenn pleaded.

'What the hell did you want a shotgun for?'

'For Coldharbour Marshes. In case it gets heavy out there. Some of those protestors are dangerous. If they break in and start sabotaging our equipment, we'll be screwed. They've done it before. The gun was to scare them off.'

'But I can get as much firepower as you need,' Frank said. 'Why buy a gun from a low-life like Adem?'

Glenn was begging, his hands clenched before him. 'I'm sorry, Frank. I messed up. It was my fault.'

Frank pointed the end of the pickaxe handle at his nephew's chest. 'This is all part of your drug-dealing sideline, isn't it? I told you to end that.'

'I've stopped selling drugs, I promise. I did what you asked.'

Frank took a moment to digest what he was hearing. He shook his head ruefully. 'If you weren't my blood, I'd smash your brains in right now,' he said. 'This is your last chance.'

He strode over to the Transit van and returned with a heavy bottle plastered with toxic warning stickers. He thrust it into Drew's hands. Drew looked at the label. It was acid.

'Pour that over him,' Frank ordered, pointing the pickaxe handle down at Adem's body. 'I don't want him being identified.'

His hands shaking, Drew unscrewed the cap. He began to drench Adem's corpse with the liquid. A trickle of acid spilled on to his arm and he winced in pain as it scorched his skin. Frank laughed at his distress.

'Be careful, boy. That stuff can take your flesh clean off.'

Drew emptied the bottle over the body in the pit. When he was finished, Frank swung the chute of the concrete mixer over the edge of the hole and released the lever. Gallon after gallon of wet cement began to cover Adem's remains.

Drew cradled his injured arm against his chest. The skin was peeling away where the acid had burned him.

'Now there's only one thing I want from you,' Frank told him. 'My money.'

'I haven't got ninety thousand pounds,' Drew said.

Frank kicked the empty bottle of acid down into the pit. It sank quickly beneath the flow of cement.

'Then get it. Or that stuff will be scorching more than your arm.'

45

LEWIS STOOD BEFORE the chain-link fence, looking at the wild expanse of Coldharbour Marshes. The fence stood about ten feet high and ran for miles around the perimeter of the nature reserve. Beyond it, acres of scrub grass and reed beds stretched out to the horizon. He looked at Rachael.

'Come on,' he said. 'We're not going to let this fence stop us, are we?'

'What do you suggest?'

'Back the car up and I'll show you.'

Rachael started the engine and manoeuvred the Volvo until it was pressed against the metal barrier. Lewis climbed on to the roof and reached up to the top rail of the fence. He pulled himself over and dropped down to the muddy track on the other side.

'Are you coming?' he said with a grin.

Rachael followed him. She was wearing jeans and a flannel shirt beneath a thick duffel coat, with a woollen scarf wrapped around her chin to keep out the cold. Lewis caught her as she lowered herself down and together they set off along the pathway leading into the wilds of the marshland. About fifty metres along the track, they saw a pile of wilted flowers and faded photographs with a few sympathy cards discarded in the hedgerow, sheltered from the rain. Lewis picked up a card and opened it.

'For Maria Brennan. My beautiful cousin,' he read. 'Rest in peace.'

Some of the condolence cards contained what appeared to be Ukrainian, the messages written in bold Cyrillic script. Lewis remembered the warning note that Irina had showed him. Maria and her family were part of a large Ukrainian community in London. Could one of them have written the note?

Rachael gripped his hand. She looked around her sadly. 'What a lonely place to die,' she said.

Lewis hugged her close. A cold wind was whipping in from the river, blasting against his skin like ice. It was an exposed, wild expanse of land, seemingly far from the comforts of civilization. It wasn't the kind of place anyone would want to visit alone at night.

'I still don't understand why Maria came out here in the first place,' Lewis said. 'It makes no sense.'

'Maybe she wanted to see for herself exactly what Carlson was planning to destroy?'

'But it was night-time in the middle of winter. Maria was dressed for the office, not for a hike in the countryside. I saw the shoes she was wearing. They were formal, with heels. Imagine walking around here with those on your feet? Maria was smarter than that. She would have come prepared if she'd known she was going to hike round a place like this. She'd even brought her laptop and a folder of legal paperwork.'

'Maybe she'd agreed to meet Robert Carlson out here?' Rachael suggested.

Lewis mulled it over. 'I'm not sure,' he said, with a shake of his head. 'Carlson had gone to her mother's flat the night before she died. She refused to speak to him then. Why would she change her mind and agree to meet him all the way out here?'

'Maybe it was a stranger who just happened to find her out here alone?'

'No way,' Lewis said definitely. 'It had to be someone Maria knew, because she let them into her car. There was no struggle. She allowed them in voluntarily. Then she was murdered and the killer tried to make it look like a suicide. It was well planned.'

Rachael looked pained at the thought. 'Do you really think Robert Carlson is capable of that?'

'I don't know,' Lewis said. 'But right now, he's still the number-one suspect.'

Bending down, Rachael picked up a crumpled photo of Maria from among the remnants of the floral shrine abandoned in the hedgerow. 'It seems wrong to leave these here,' she said. 'We should take them back with us.'

Lewis agreed. He began to gather up the cards and pictures and shoved them in his pockets. 'I'll take them back and give them to Irina,' he said. 'It's the least I can do.'

At the end of the long track was a small copse of stubby leafless trees. Lewis and Rachael walked up to it together and followed the path through the copse to the clearing beyond. Out of the cover of the trees, they heard a dull rhythmic thudding in the distance, only faintly audible over the rushing wind.

'What's that, do you think?' Rachael asked.

Lewis shook his head. 'Let's find out.'

Following the sound, they crossed a small bridge over a waterway and turned south at a fork in the path. As they approached the river, the thudding became louder and clearer. Looking over a small rise, Lewis saw that a construction site had been recently erected. There were rows of shipping containers and stacks of building materials. Bulldozers and dumper trucks were parked in lines. The pristine grassland had been torn up by their heavy tyres. He scanned the site but it looked deserted.

The juddering sound was coming from an engine mounted on the back of a flatbed truck parked by an embankment. Cautiously Lewis walked towards it. Rachael followed close behind. The sound of the diesel motor grew louder as they neared. They could see a series of pipes running from one side of the engine, down the steep embankment and into the water of the lake. A family of egrets were wading below, searching for fish. Groups of white-tailed ducks paddled past, ripples fanning out in the lake behind them. From the other side of the pump, water was sluicing out into the Thames. It was exactly as Maria had feared, Lewis thought. The marshes were being drained. The destruction she had hoped to expose had already begun.

Lewis was standing beside the truck when a sudden shout startled him. A face appeared in the wing mirror of the cab, wide-eyed and rattled. The door swung open and a workman climbed down. He was grey-haired with a pot belly that hung over his belt. His shirt bore the Egan Construction logo they had seen on the perimeter fence.

'What are you doing?' the workman demanded.

Lewis thought fast. 'We're lost,' he said. 'We're trying to get back to the main road.'

'You're not meant to be here. This nature reserve is closed.'

'We were following a public footpath,' Lewis lied. 'We must have taken a wrong turn.'

The workman looked at Lewis's suit and black brogues, scuffed and muddied from walking on the sodden ground. It was obvious he was lying. 'Turn around and head that way,' he said, pointing back the direction they had come. 'And go quick. My boss is paranoid about trespassers. He's got some nasty-looking people guarding this site.'

'What are you doing out here?' Lewis asked.

'Why do you want to know?'

'I'm just curious.'

The workman looked around hesitantly. He seemed reluctant at first but couldn't resist the chance to talk. It was lonely work, stuck out in such a remote place, all alone. He spoke quietly, as if sharing an intimate secret. 'I'm preparing the ground,' he said. 'Draining the land to get it ready for building.'

'Building what?'

'A new power station. A huge one. I've seen some major projects before, but this is the biggest yet. There'll be an army of workers out here soon. Digging foundations. Pouring concrete.'

'We heard there was going to be a hydrogen production plant out here,' Lewis said.

The workman shook his head. 'There won't be any hydrogen made out here. This facility is designed to burn gas, not produce it.'

'What makes you say that?' Rachael asked.

The workman laughed dismissively. 'Because I've seen the plans, haven't I? Hundreds of smokestacks belching out fumes. Miles of pipework. The loading docks and storage tanks alone are vast. All for bringing in shipments of methane to power the electric turbines. Whoever gets the contract to supply this place will be printing their own money.'

Rachael looked saddened at what she was hearing. 'Isn't it a shame to ruin such a beautiful place?' she asked.

The workman shrugged. 'It's progress, I suppose.'

Lewis was about to speak when an angry shout sounded over the cranking of the water pump.

'Hey! You!'

They all turned towards the cry. Two young men were running at full tilt along the river path, charging like they were going into battle. They were carrying lengths of steel piping in their hands like clubs. The workman looked terrified.

'Run!' he said. 'And be quick. Don't let them catch you.'

Lewis grabbed Rachael by the hand and they set off back along the pathway at a sprint, racing over the wooden footbridge and through the small copse of oak trees. They could hear the sound of heavy footsteps pounding behind them as they ran.

'Faster!' Lewis shouted.

They passed the place where Maria had died and ran towards the fence. When they reached the barrier, they stopped. Lewis knotted his fingers together and boosted Rachael up. She

215

gripped the top rail and hauled herself over. Lewis began to climb up, using the wire links of the fence as a ladder. He was almost at the top when he felt a hand seize his ankle and pull him back down. He grasped a fence post to break his fall as he landed on the stony ground. The photos and cards spilled from his pockets as he rolled on to his back and looked up at the two men standing over him, veins bulging angrily in their necks. One of them dragged Lewis to his feet and pushed him up against the wire fence.

'Who are you?' he demanded. 'What are you doing here?'

'I'm lost,' Lewis insisted.

'Don't give me that bullshit. You're spying.'

The second man picked up one of the photos of Maria from the pathway. 'What are you doing with these?' he asked.

'Taking them back to her family.'

The man showed the photo to his companion. They whispered to each other in hushed, suspicious tones.

'Isn't that Drew Brennan's sister?' one asked. His brow was creased in confusion.

Lewis recognized Drew's name as it was spoken aloud. It shocked him to hear it. 'How do you know Drew Brennan?' he said, his voice full of surprise.

The first man turned to him. 'Shut up,' he snarled angrily. 'I'm asking the questions. Now tell me why you're out here?'

Lewis gave an insolent shrug. 'I told you already,' he said. 'I'm lost.'

The man swung the length of pipe into Lewis's stomach and he doubled over. A fist hit him hard in the back of the head and he tensed instinctively, covering himself as he waited for more punishment. Instead, there was a fizzing sound followed

216

by a wail of pained screams. Winded, Lewis glanced up. His two assailants were crying out, clutching their faces. An acrid, stringent smell hung in the air, strong enough to make Lewis gag. Rachael had pushed her hand through a gap in the fence. She was holding a small metal canister.

'It's pepper spray!' she shouted. 'Quick! Climb over.'

Lewis grabbed the fallen photos from the path and began to scramble up the fence. Rachael helped him as he dropped to the other side. His attackers were still blinded, stumbling around as they tried to claw the spray from their eyes. Rachael threw open the driver's door of her car and jumped in, waiting for Lewis before starting the engine and pulling away in a shower of gravel. When they were back on the main road, Rachael looked at him with an exhilarated smile.

'Thanks for the romantic walk in the country,' she said.

46

THEY DROVE IN silence. Glenn was speeding through the city, trying to get out of the Isle of Dogs, back to the safety of Whitechapel. He was jittery with nerves, beads of sweat running down his face. The skin on Drew's arm was blistered and burned from the acid. He cradled it against his chest as they drove.

Drew couldn't stop thinking of Adem. Of how he'd been buried under a ton of fresh cement, never to be found. Remembering the sound of his skull splitting open made Drew want to throw up. He realized how close he'd come to joining him. He wondered why Adem would have made up such a convoluted story about Drew insisting on taking the gun with the backpack full of money. It made no sense, no matter how hard Drew thought about it. There had to be some purpose behind such an outlandish tale, but Drew couldn't figure out what it was. He had no idea what Adem was trying to hide.

As they reached the safety of Commercial Road, Glenn seemed to relax. He felt safer among the familiar sights and sounds of home ground. He slowed down, the danger far behind him.

'I can't believe my uncle did that,' he said with a shudder. 'It was messed up.'

Drew crossed himself. 'I thought I was next. I was just waiting for that pickaxe handle to fall.'

'I wouldn't have let Frank do that to you.'

'Really?' Drew asked. The disbelief was heavy in his voice.

''Course not,' Glenn said.

'You took your time speaking up.'

Glenn turned to him, his brow furrowed. 'What do you mean?'

'You knew Adem's story was bullshit,' Drew said. 'You kept quiet until I was about to get my brains bashed in.'

Glenn looked outraged. 'I had to choose the right moment to make sure we didn't both end up in that pit. It's not the first time Frank's done it.'

'Who else has he buried like that?' Drew asked quizzically.

Glenn turned away, casting his eyes back to the traffic moving on the road ahead of him. 'Trust me,' he said, 'you don't want to know.'

Drew thought of the crazy tale Adem had told in the underground car park before he died. It still didn't make any sense. 'Why did Adem come out with such a pack of lies back there?' he asked. 'About the gun and my plan to steal Frank's money. Why would he make up a story like that?'

Glenn gave a dismissive shrug. 'Adem was a slimeball. A low-life bookie. He was just saying whatever came into his head.'

'No,' Drew insisted, 'there had to be a plan behind it. He couldn't have invented all that nonsense for no reason.'

'Who knows what he was thinking? He was a crook.'

'If he was such a crook, why did you send me down there to collect all that money on my own? Your dumb plan nearly got me killed.'

'You work for me,' Glenn snapped. 'If you don't like it, find yourself another job.'

Drew bit his lip. He knew it was the truth. He was free to walk away any time he chose. No one was forcing him to carry on working for the Egans. But Drew knew there was no other way he could earn a living. He was trapped. And now he owed Frank Egan ninety thousand pounds.

'How am I supposed to come up with the money to pay your uncle back?' Drew said.

Glenn shrugged. 'What about that compensation you told me about?'

'From Maria's boss? No way. That's impossible.'

'Why? It's more than you owe.'

Drew shook his head. 'My mum would never agree to it. She'd rather see me in a hole next to Adem before she accepted that money.'

'That can't be the truth?'

'Believe me, it is.'

'Well, you'll have to get the money from somewhere. Frank's not going to wait for long.'

Drew looked darkly at his friend. He wanted to say how all this craziness was Glenn's doing. How it had been Glenn's idea to send him down to the car wash to collect the money in the first place. Now the situation had gone south, it had fallen on Drew's shoulders to correct a problem he had no part in creating. He knew if he asked Glenn to pitch in and give him some cash, there would only be one answer. Glenn had side-stepped any blame from his uncle and he wasn't about to put himself in the firing line out of charity. Drew decided to keep quiet. There were other factors in play that might help solve his problems.

Glenn swung the car into the entrance of the housing estate. He stopped at the foot of Drew's tower block to drop him off. Drew wasn't in the mood for friendly goodbyes. He opened the door without a word, stepped out of the car and began to walk towards the looming stone crag of Crowmoor House. As the car pulled away with a squeal, he heard it stop suddenly and back up. Drew turned around to see Glenn reverse towards him. His window was wound down.

'I want to ask you something,' Glenn shouted.

Drew could see his friend's face was tight with anger. 'What?'

'Why didn't you say anything to my uncle back there? About the gun being my idea. You could have told him before I spoke up. You knew the truth but you kept your mouth shut. Why?'

Drew didn't hesitate. 'Because I'm not a grass,' he said.

The flat was empty. He went into the bathroom and ran his arm under a flow of cold water to soothe the angry blister where the acid had splashed him, gritting his teeth in pain as the water washed over the wound. He thought again of Adem and the wild story he had told. Drew couldn't shake the feeling that there was something more to it. Something Adem had held back. An ulterior motive that had forced him to lie.

After he had dried himself and wrapped the wound in a

bandage from the medicine cabinet, Drew went into his bedroom. He bent down and reached under the bed, searching with his fingertips beneath the mattress. There was an envelope taped to the wooden bed frame and he pulled it out. Inside was a wad of twenty-pound notes. He sat on the bed and stared at the cash, thumbing quickly through the stack. Five thousand pounds in fresh bills. This trivial sum had almost cost Drew his life.

He remembered how Adem had spilled the bundles of banknotes on to the table that night at the car wash. Some of them had tumbled to the floor. In the confusion, Drew had stashed a stack of notes inside his jacket as he gathered up the bundles. It would be easy to explain, he had thought at the time. Adem was a crook. He couldn't be trusted. After he had taken it, Drew had refused to check the money so that Adem wouldn't realize any was missing. Five grand had seemed like a fair commission for the errand he'd been asked to run.

But the money he'd stolen was not the key to the puzzle. No way. Adem hadn't died to protect anyone else from Frank's wrath. He was too selfish and scared to think like that when his life was threatened. There had to be some other reason he'd stuck to his story right to the end. Suddenly the answer came. Drew ripped off the elastic band that held the banknotes in place. He lifted one up to the light coming in through the window and examined it closely. He gave a snort of wry laughter.

The banknote was fake. He tilted it from side to side. The holographic image of the pound sign didn't change as he moved the note. It was a dead giveaway. He rubbed the paper between his fingers. The feel of the material was all wrong. It was printed on cheap pulp, the foil strip missing. The money wouldn't pass even the most basic of checks. It was all worthless.

That explained Adem's wild tale. He had to lie to Frank because he'd ripped him off so brazenly. The gun must have been a distraction, Drew thought, to prevent him from checking the cash before accepting the bag. He thought back to the moment he'd left the car wash. How the silver car was on to him almost immediately. That must have been a fake too. A decoy. Adem had known he would try to outrun it. Any real police patrolling the area would see this and give chase. Once he was caught, Adem was safe and his plan would have worked. He was home and dry. If the news of the fake money was ever made public, Adem could blame it on corrupt police officers. Frank would have no way of checking. It was a genius plan and it had almost worked.

Thinking of it now, Drew was glad the bookie was dead and buried. He'd deserved everything he got, the low-life thief. Adem had set him up to take a fall but now he was dead because of his own lies. There was a harsh sense of justice in it. But Drew still had to come up with the money to pay Frank Egan what he owed. He knew there was only one way to solve that problem.

47

LEWIS TOUCHED A fingertip to the bruise swelling under his eye. *We are what we repeatedly do*, he said to himself. In the last twenty-four hours, he had been chased and beaten and thrown on to train tracks in an Underground station. He had to turn the tables if he was going to come out of this on top. The case was not going to get solved unless he began to fight back.

The cards and pictures from Maria's shrine were stuffed in his pockets. Lewis remembered what the thugs at the marshes had said when they saw the photos. They knew who Maria was straight away and they also knew her brother. They had spoken Drew's name out loud. At a stretch, it could be a coincidence, Lewis supposed. But in Martin Sobel's wise words, it was better not to believe in simple explanations like that.

The deeper he considered it, the more there was something unsettling in the connection. Maria Brennan had been an environmentalist, opposed to any development at Coldharbour Marshes. How could the sort of men who guarded the site be friendly with her brother? Wouldn't that have put Drew and Maria at loggerheads? Drew Brennan was a violent man, that much was obvious. Could Carlson have paid him to get rid of his own sister? That would explain how she let her killer inside the car with her. Lewis felt a chill even thinking of it as a possibility. It would be a hideous turn of events if it were true.

As they neared the outskirts of London, Lewis spotted a service station at the side of the road. Rachael pulled over into the car park and they went inside and took a table in the café.

'I still don't understand what that workman told us,' Lewis said. 'About the site not being designed to produce hydrogen. How it's really going to be a huge gas-burning power station.'

Rachel stirred sugar into her coffee. 'It's mind blowing that Carlson thinks he's going to get away with it. The whole project is just some elaborate scam.'

'I really thought a man like Robert Carlson was better than that. That he was a force for good. He poses as a kind of saviour but really he only cares about making money.'

Rachel looked disgusted at the notion. 'It's so cynical,' she said. 'Men like Carlson know how to cheat the system. It's all a game to them.'

Lewis thought of the interview transcripts he had read overnight at his sister's house. Maria Brennan had had the same thoughts about her employer in her statement. Maybe she was right. Maybe Carlson wasn't as green as he liked to pretend. Maybe it was all an act to enrich himself. He remembered how Maria had learned that Ever Sine was struggling financially.

'Carlson admitted to Maria that he has money problems. Bad ones. This project is vital to keeping his business afloat. He needs the Russians for their cash and they need him for his eco credentials. Each of them is using the other.'

Rachael gazed at him over the rim of her coffee cup. She was thinking quickly, fitting the pieces of the puzzle together in her mind.

'The whole project is a Trojan horse,' she said. 'The hydrogen plant is a smokescreen. It's just an excuse to get planning permission, then they'll build a power station burning fossil fuels instead. Carlson is going to destroy the marshes to save his business. And if his Russian partners have a monopoly to supply the natural gas to the power station, they'll be cashing in on the scam for ever.'

Lewis grimaced at the thought. 'If Maria discovered this, she would have been in a lot of danger.'

'From Carlson?'

'From everyone who stood to lose money. Any one of them would have wanted to silence her.'

Rachael tapped her spoon against the rim of her cup. 'Silence her how?'

'Any way that kept suspicion away from her killers,' Lewis said.

'Like staging her death as a suicide?'

'Exactly.'

As Rachael drank her coffee, Lewis went to the bathroom and tried his best to clean himself up. His suit was streaked with mud and grass stains, his face scratched and bruised. When he was done, they returned to the Volvo. Rachael pulled out of the service station and continued the journey back to London. While they drove, Lewis flicked through the joint partnership agreement that had been found in Maria's car. It was a maze of unnamed directorships and hollow shell organizations based in obscure jurisdictions. Cyprus. Panama. The Cayman Islands. A series of offshore banks and obscure trusts. It looked like the contract had been drafted to make it impossible to follow the path of the money that was moving through its clauses. Carlson was trying to shield the Russian cash from scrutiny, Lewis thought. He wanted to hide how rotten the project really was.

The contract was so Byzantine that, even as a trained lawyer, Lewis could barely unpick it. How had Maria made sense of it? Why had she deemed the document so important that she took it out to Coldharbour Marshes on the night she died?

Lewis wanted answers to his questions and there was only one way to get them. He took out his phone, dialled the number for the Ever Sine head office and waited, tapping his foot impatiently as the ringtone sounded in his ear.

The woman who answered the phone was bright and cheerful. 'Robert Carlson's office,' she said.

'My name is Lewis Miller. I spoke with Mr Carlson yesterday about arranging a private meeting.'

Lewis was expecting to get rebuffed but the PA seemed relieved that he had called.

'Actually, Mr Carlson left a note for you,' she said. 'He asked if you would meet him for lunch today. I was planning on calling you but I'm snowed under here.'

Lewis was surprised. 'Lunch today? Where?'

'Mr Carlson has reserved a table for two at his club. I'll email the address to you if you can make it?'

'Of course,' Lewis said. 'Tell him I'll be there.'

He hung up and made a second call.

48

IRINA HURRIED HOME. She stepped through the front door of the flat with two bags of heavy shopping and dropped them in the hallway. The lights were on in the living room, the television blaring. She found Drew dozing on the sofa. A bottle of painkillers stood on the coffee table. Irina seized him by the arms and shook him wildly.

'Wake up!' she shouted. 'I want to talk to you.'

He was groggy and slow. 'What's wrong?' he asked.

'Lewis Miller called me. He says he went out to Coldharbour Marshes today. Some people out there know you. What's going on? What is it you're not telling me?'

Drew rubbed a hand against his tired eyes. 'I don't know anyone out at Coldharbour Marshes. I've never been there.'

Irina narrowed her eyes at him. 'Then how do they know *you*?'

'I have no idea. I know all kinds of people.'

'Lewis told me they were nasty thugs. Dangerous. They could be the people who hurt Maria.'

Drew clutched his arm and winced in pain. The burn was throbbing beneath the tight bandage.

'Right now, the only person who's hurt is me,' he said.

'What happened to you?' Irina asked.

'A misunderstanding.'

'Do you need to go to hospital?'

'No. I'm fine. I need money. That's all.'

'How much money?'

Drew took a deep breath before he answered. 'Ninety thousand pounds,' he said.

Irina gasped. 'Where can we get hold of that kind of money?'

'You know where,' Drew said.

She paused for a moment as she realized his meaning. 'You're talking about Robert Carlson?' she said.

'Who else?'

Irina shook her head firmly. 'No way. I can't go to him. If I do, I'll never find out what happened to Maria.'

Drew lifted back the edge of the dressing to show her the wound. It was scarlet in colour and raw.

'Then this is only the start,' he said. 'Next time, they'll kill me.'

Irina went into the kitchen. She took a seat at the table and held her head in her hands. Her whole world was falling in, piece by piece. Maria was dead and now her son was in danger of getting killed over money. Was this all her fault? Had she been such a terrible mother that she couldn't keep her children safe? Ninety thousand pounds was more than Irina had ever seen. But she knew the kind of people Drew mixed with. They would kill for a lot less than that. Could she

230

abandon one child so that she could avenge another? It was an impossible dilemma.

When Drew came in to the kitchen, Irina looked up at him, her eyes full of tears.

'Maria never would have put me in a position like this,' she said.

'That's because Maria was an angel. I've been hearing the same story my whole life.'

'She would never let me down the way you have.'

Drew looked at her grimly. 'You've never done anything for me, not like you did with Maria. I always came second. I know I haven't been the best son to you. But I need your help now. I haven't got anywhere else to turn.'

'What about Maria? Do you expect me to just give up?'

Drew placed a hand on his mother's shoulder. 'If you get that money, I'll find out what happened to her.'

'How?'

'How do you think?'

'I don't want you to do anything illegal.'

Drew looked at his mother like she was a starry-eyed newborn.

'It's too late for that,' he said.

49

RACHAEL STOPPED THE car at the kerb and peered up at the dark Gothic façade of the Pantheon Club. Snarling stone gargoyles stared down from the high ledges. A large Union flag fluttered above the doorway. The building was solid and imposing, a venue that made no secret of its Establishment credentials.

'Do you want me to come in with you?' Rachael asked.

'You can't,' Lewis said. 'My meeting with Carlson is privileged. I'll be speaking to him as his lawyer. It's the only way he'll open up.'

'Shall I wait for you here?'

'No. Go home. I'll call you later.'

'OK. Good luck.'

Lewis kissed her goodbye. 'Thanks for saving me today,' he said.

He waved Rachael off and watched the Volvo drive away into the heart of St James's. With quick steps he mounted the wide stone staircase and walked into the hallowed lobby of the private members' club. At the desk he gave Robert Carlson's name and a porter was sent for. Lewis was led through the reading rooms and oak-panelled lounges to the dining room at the rear of the grand building. It was like stepping back in time to a vanished world of empire and deference. Lewis caught the glances of the whiskery colonels and their watery-eyed peers as they spied him over the tops of their newspapers. In his crumpled suit and mud-splattered shoes, they sized him up instantly as a lowly tradesman, there to perform some mundane task or other. Silently he dismissed them in turn as he passed.

The dining room was full. Carlson was sitting alone by the window at a table draped in white linen, staring out over the deserted lawns of Green Park.

'Thank you for coming,' Carlson said, standing and offering his hand.

'I'm pleased we can finally meet properly, Mr Carlson.'

'Call me Robert, please.'

Lewis shook his hand firmly. Carlson took a business card from his breast pocket and handed it to Lewis.

'I thought you should have my direct line,' he said. 'Seeing as you're now heading my legal team at Renfrew and Hall.'

Lewis smiled politely. He could see it was meant as a gesture of goodwill. He slipped the business card inside his jacket and took a seat. White-gloved waiters fussed around them, pouring wine and straightening the cutlery. Carlson tried to make small talk about the menu but Lewis decided to get straight to the point. This was no time to beat around the bush.

'Can we talk freely?' he asked, looking around at the neighbouring tables.

'Of course,' Carlson said. 'All meetings here are completely confidential. The members value their privacy above all else.'

'I'm sure that helps if you're involved in a conspiracy to destroy a nature reserve.' Lewis was deliberately blunt and Carlson shrank from his hostile tone.

'That's quite an accusation. I hope you have some evidence to back it up.'

'I've spent the morning out at Coldharbour Marshes. I've been chased and beaten but I think I've discovered what you're really planning out there. "Conspiracy" is a polite word for what I've found.'

'Which is?'

'That you're building an old-fashioned, methane-burning, planet-destroying power plant. It couldn't be more against your public image if you started pumping oil out of the marshland.'

Carlson's eyes betrayed his guilt. 'I admit that the project isn't what I'd hoped it would be,' he said.

'That's what Maria Brennan found out, wasn't it? That you're not some kind of saviour. That really you're just like the rest of the men in this club. A naked profiteer. Your eco-friendly image is just a disguise. I'm wondering if you'd kill to protect it.'

'Remember who you are,' Carlson said, pushing back. 'I could have you fired with a click of my fingers.'

'Tell me why you went to Maria's mother's flat the night before she died.'

Carlson waved away any suggestion of an illicit motive for his visit. 'I wanted to persuade her not to reveal sensitive information,' he said. 'That's all.'

'About your Russian business partners?'

A flicker passed over Carlson's face. A faint twitch of the muscles at the corners of his mouth. 'So you know about Andrei and his father?'

'I've read Maria's witness statement,' Lewis said.

'I thought that material was restricted.'

'It wasn't too difficult to obtain.'

Carlson leaned forward. He dropped the volume of his voice to a hushed whisper. It sounded like a warning. 'Take my advice,' he said. 'Forget about my Russian partners.'

'Is that a threat?'

'A friendly suggestion.'

'So you won't tell me who they are?'

'For your own protection.'

'Why would you go into business with people who have to remain hidden from public view?'

'Perhaps for all the reasons you think. For wealth. For power. For my own selfish desires.'

Lewis shook his head at his own folly. 'To think that a few days ago I looked up to you. I thought there was no way you could have hurt a woman like Maria Brennan.'

Carlson jabbed a finger on to the tabletop at the accusation. 'I couldn't,' he said adamantly. 'No one is more devastated that Maria is dead. The police concluded that she took her own life. I'm as upset about that as anyone, but there's no evidence of foul play.'

Lewis thought of the note left on the windscreen of Maria's car. The mystery of the strange handwriting that Irina had brought to his attention.

'A warning was left on Maria's car,' he said. 'It was supposed to prevent anyone from hurting themselves inadvertently. Her

235

mother insists that Maria didn't write the note. She says that's it's not in Maria's handwriting. That means at least one other person was present when she died. Some of the lettering suggests it was written by someone from Eastern Europe.'

'Well, that rules me out,' Carlson said gruffly.

'But not your new business partners.'

Carlson checked around him carefully before answering. 'Andrei was with me when Maria died. I can vouch for him. I know he wasn't out at Coldharbour Marshes that night.'

'So you're providing him with an alibi?'

'I am.'

'Will you tell me Andrei's surname?'

'No. For your own safety.'

'What about the construction company you've employed? Judging by the men they've stationed out at the marshes, they'll happily use violence when it suits them.'

Carlson dismissed the question. 'Andrei deals with the sub-contractors. I've never even met them.'

'Maybe you should. They look like they're readying for war out there.'

Carlson was on the verge of losing his temper. 'Take my advice, Lewis,' he said. 'Leave this case alone. You're out of your depth.'

Lewis gave a sardonic smile at the warning. 'You're desperate to stop anyone finding out what you're really up to, aren't you? Everything you're doing is shrouded in secrecy, but Maria saw through it and she was threatening to expose you. Either you killed her or you arranged for it to be done. Well, I'm going to find out what you're trying to hide and I'm going to tell the world. That's a promise. Believe me.'

Carlson didn't flinch. 'If you persist with this crusade, I'll have you thrown on to the scrapheap. Take it from me that you'll never work again.'

Lewis stood abruptly from the table, a look of righteous determination on his face. He pushed his chair back into place and paused for a second, looking down at his companion with disgust.

'You might scare most people, Mr Carlson,' he said, turning to walk away, 'but you don't scare me.'

50

CARLSON WATCHED LEWIS leave. He admired him for his youthful spirit. The world hadn't yet drained him of his convictions. There was plenty of time for that, he thought. Amidst the clatter of glasses and silverware, a tall man from a neighbouring table stood and walked over to join him. He was well groomed, wearing a sharp designer suit and silk tie. He carried himself with a regal air. He took the seat that Lewis had vacated.

'I thought that went pretty well,' he said. His voice was husky, his accent Slavic.

Carlson frowned at his new companion. 'You really think so, Andrei?'

It was clear the other man had been able to overhear the entire conversation from his original vantage spot.

'Miller knows nothing of any importance,' Andrei said. 'If he had any evidence, he would have presented it to you.'

They stared at each other coldly over the starched linen tablecloth. There was no sense of camaraderie between them.

'I accepted your father's funding because I had no alternative,' Carlson said firmly. 'You assured me that we would build a hydrogen facility together. Foolishly I believed you. If I'd known your real plans, I never would have accepted a penny from you, Andrei.'

Andrei appeared unmoved at Carlson's words. As if distracted, he brushed a fleck of stray lint from the table and then looked across with an expression of pity. 'If I was in your position, I would be grateful to have any business partners at all.'

'Grateful? After all I've endured at the hands of your family?'

'My father and I have the same goals as you, Robert.'

'Which are?'

'To make money.'

'The trouble you've caused recently isn't good for that.'

Andrei smiled condescendingly. 'I think you've done most of the damage yourself.'

From the corner of his eye, seated alone at the adjacent table, Carlson caught sight of the man Andrei had been lunching with. Carlson recognized his silver hair and patrician bearing. It was the Minister for Energy, the politician who had participated in the video conference from his office. Knowing he'd been spotted, the Minister squirmed awkwardly in his seat. He seemed keen not to meet Carlson's gaze.

'I see you've got your hooks into the government now,' Carlson said.

Andrei shrugged. 'It's prudent to keep powerful friends.'

'That explains why no restrictions were placed on the land use out at Coldharbour Marshes.'

'Why should we be hemmed in by petty rules?' Andrei said with a nonchalant shrug. 'The Minister shares our desire to produce cheap energy for London. A methane-fuelled power station will achieve that. He knows it will pay dividends in the long run. Of course, I've made a generous donation to the party in return for his co-operation.'

Carlson struggled not to raise his voice. 'If you trusted me, we wouldn't need to bribe politicians. With my plans we can produce sustainable energy that's cheap, clean and profitable. Let me complete the project in full and I'll show you. Hydrogen energy is the future. It's your father's insistence on sticking with old-fashioned technology that's dragging the entire project down. You're a young man, Andrei. Be a force for good. Join me.'

Andrei waved away such evangelizing. 'My father and I are in agreement. You knew our rules when you accepted our money. Your progressive ideas are merely an indulgence. A pipe dream. We need you as our public face. That's all. In return, we'll save your company from ruin. This way, we all win.'

Carlson sighed wearily. 'I should have listened to Maria,' he said. 'She warned me about you.'

'Maria was a fantasist. People like her don't survive long in this world. Life has a way of snuffing them out.'

'What about this note? The one Miller talked about. Do you know who's responsible for it?'

'There are many Russian and Ukrainian people in London,' Andrei said dismissively. 'I can't keep track of them all.'

Carlson wiped his mouth with a corner of his napkin and then tossed it on to his half-finished plate. 'This chaos is more than I can bear,' he said. 'I have a family to think of. Once the

Coldharbour Marshes project is finished, I think it's best for us to go our separate ways.'

Andrei nodded. 'Agreed.'

'Will your father feel the same way?'

Smiling from one corner of his mouth, Andrei said, 'My father is a man of his word.'

Carlson made no reply. He really would have to be a fool to believe that, he thought.

51

LEWIS CHECKED THE coast was clear as he left the Pantheon Club and walked up towards Piccadilly. He kept a wary eye out as people crossed his path. The men who wanted to silence him could be anywhere, waiting, ready to strike. He needed to stay vigilant.

The meeting had left him unsettled. Before it, he had only known Carlson by reputation. His public image was carefully curated: the benefactor saving the planet with his technological prowess. Now Lewis's worst suspicions had been confirmed – Carlson was just another vulture capitalist, as corrupt and compromised as the other oligarchs that haunted London.

Turning the corner at Duke Street, Lewis headed for Green Park Station, fighting through the afternoon crowds. He was at the entrance, about to descend the steps into the dark, when his phone buzzed in his pocket. He took it out and looked at the screen. It was a text from a number he didn't recognize.

The message was blank but there was an attachment. Lewis clicked on it and a photograph sprang into life on his screen.

It was a picture of a car, the occupants visible through the windscreen. Maria Brennan was sitting behind the steering wheel, her head turned to a woman in the passenger seat. Remembering the posts on social media that he'd scrolled through previously, Lewis recognized the passenger as Emilia Carlson. She was gesticulating wildly. The photo was taken from far away, but the body language between the two women suggested they were in the middle of a heated argument.

Lewis needed to find out who had sent the photograph. He called the number it had come from and listened to the line ring. He stood and waited, his phone pressed to his ear as people hurried past him, down the steps towards the ticket hall. After a few rings, the line went dead. Lewis tried again but was cut off once more. Changing tack, he sent a text message instead.

Who are you?

As he stood, waiting for a reply, Lewis looked again at the photo. He checked the date stamp. It had been taken on the day Maria died. Lewis remembered Maria's testimony – how Emilia had planted cocaine in her coat pocket at the charity gala. He knew that Carlson's daughter bore a grudge against Maria. That was beyond dispute. But did she hate her enough to commit murder?

Thirty seconds later, his phone buzzed as a message arrived. He looked at the screen.

Another searcher for the truth.

52

SUSANNAH CARLSON CHECKED her watch. It was after two p.m. Emilia should be awake by now, she reckoned. She remembered how Robert had carried her up from the swimming pool last night and put her to bed. He had stayed with her until morning, watching over her, checking her breathing every few minutes. Susannah knew that if her daughter's past behaviour was any guide, it was best to assume she had shovelled a cocktail of narcotics into her body. Emilia was a girl without any boundaries when it came to drugs.

Susannah knocked lightly on her daughter's bedroom door. When there was no answer, she knocked again, louder this time. 'I need to speak to you,' she called out, her face pressed to the surface of the door. 'I'm not going away.'

After a few seconds of silence, a hollow voice said, 'You'd better come in, then.'

The room was dark, the curtains closed. Emilia sat propped up in bed, her phone clutched before her, the ghostly glow of the screen illuminating her drawn features. She looked a complete wreck, her hair lank and greasy, her skin dry.

'It's time to get up now,' Susannah said.

'I want to be left alone.'

Susannah scanned the make-up, empty coffee cups and discarded tissues scattered across Emilia's nightstand. She tried to be discreet but it was obvious what she was looking for.

'I don't have any drugs,' Emilia snapped impatiently. 'You don't have to worry.'

'Lately all I do is worry.'

'You're being melodramatic.'

'Last night was the final party. I don't think your father can take any more.'

Emilia was defiant. 'After all he's done, he deserves to suffer for a while.'

'You're talking about the gala at the Carlingford? The problems he had with Maria Brennan?'

'We both know what Daddy was doing that night. I don't know why you allow him to treat you like that.'

Susannah took a seat on the edge of the bed. She tried to maintain her patient demeanour. 'It's not that simple, Emilia,' she said. 'Your father was acting in the best interests of the family. Sometimes he has to make decisions that we don't understand.'

'I understand what he was doing just fine. He was cavorting with his mistress. It would be embarrassing if it wasn't so disgusting.'

'Your father and I make sacrifices that you know nothing about.'

Emilia glanced up darkly from her phone. 'I'm prepared to do what's necessary to keep this family together, even if you're not,' she said.

'What does that mean?'

'It means that I refused to let a jumped-up whore take advantage of us. She reckoned she was so clever, making Daddy lust after her like that. Well, I brought her down a peg or two.'

'What did you do?' Susannah asked warily.

Emilia tried to sound tough. 'Put it this way,' she said, 'Maria regretted acting so high and mighty around me once she was knocked off her pedestal.'

Susannah recoiled from the steely glint in her daughter's eye. She remembered how Robert had told her of the message scrawled on the misted glass of the steam room when he found her passed out the previous night.

Emilia is a killer

Susannah knew how self-destructive her daughter could be. How impulsive. She was already facing a long and arduous stretch to get clean. That was bad enough. But was there something even more harrowing Susannah needed to be aware of? The thought made her cower inside. As a mother, she was growing terrified. But it was better to know the truth, she told herself. She didn't have the strength for any more nasty surprises.

Susannah took Emilia by the hand. She looked into her bright blue eyes.

'Darling,' she said gently, 'is there anything you want to tell me?'

53

THE HOT WATER sluicing on his body was a welcome relief. All the stress and tension seemed to dissolve as Lewis stood under the shower stream. He had a permanent locker at the gym with fresh clothes and underwear. It had saved him before, during long negotiations at the office when he had no time to make the journey home to change. It was too risky to go back to his flat in case it was still being watched. He would have to stay away until the case was solved.

Stepping out of the shower, Lewis towelled himself dry and opened his locker. He selected a clean shirt, shrouded in dry-cleaning wrap, and began to dress. The crisp fabric felt good against his skin.

He thought about the anonymous photograph he'd been sent. Why had Emilia Carlson met Maria on the day she died? Emilia had never come forward to admit that the meeting had happened. Had the argument led to Maria's death? If this was the key to the case, then he'd been looking in the wrong place all along. He'd assumed the catalyst for Maria's murder was her relationship with Robert Carlson and her discovery of his true plans out at Coldharbour Marshes. Perhaps he was completely off target, Lewis thought to himself. Maybe Maria's death was really down to Emilia Carlson's jealousy.

But something about it didn't feel right. The photo had been taken in a residential street. There were houses and cars in the background. Maria was found dead in the depths of the countryside. That meant the picture wasn't taken where Maria was killed. Could Emilia have done the deed and then driven a dead body all the way out to Coldharbour Marshes? Lewis doubted it. The car was filled with toxic fumes. It was sealed shut. The dog walker who found Maria had almost died when he opened the door. That meant the car couldn't have been driven after her death. It was impossible.

Lewis became more frustrated as he tried to think through the possibilities. What did the photograph really reveal? Only more confusion, he decided. The biggest question of all was the identity of the sender. *Another searcher for the truth*. What did that really mean? Whoever it was, they wanted to put Emilia Carlson in the frame for murder. Sending Lewis the photograph was designed to paint a target directly on her.

Gathering his coat and bag, Lewis left the basement gym and walked up to the ground-floor exit. His phone buzzed in his pocket as it regained signal and he took it out to check his messages. There were eight missed calls, all from the offices of Renfrew and Hall. Lewis called back reluctantly, sure he was about to be reprimanded for not showing his face at work.

'Where have you been?' his line manager raged. 'I've been leaving messages for over an hour.'

'I can explain—'

'Charlie King is looking everywhere for you.'

Lewis had almost forgotten about the man who had sent him on this mission in the first place. 'I thought he was in New York?'

'He came back this morning. He's in the office now. He wants you to come in right away to help wrap up the Brennan case.'

'Wrap it up?'

'Maria Brennan's mother is coming in to sign the NDA today.'

Lewis was confused. 'I don't understand.'

'She's agreed to everything. Charlie wants you to be here when Mrs Koval puts pen to paper. He insists that you share in the glory.'

'When is she coming?'

'Any minute now.'

Lewis couldn't understand what he was hearing. He had to get to the office quickly before events slipped out of his control.

'Don't let anyone sign anything,' he said. 'I'm on my way.'

He hung up and looked around, scanning the traffic for a taxi. There were no black cabs on the street. It was a fifteen-minute walk back to the office, seven if he ran. He knew he didn't have much time before it was too late. Taking a deep breath, Lewis set off along Farringdon Road at a dead sprint.

54

RAIN PATTERED DOWN on the umbrellas filling Paternoster Square. Irina looked up at the offices of Renfrew and Hall. The building was a towering stone edifice with a façade the colour of bone. It was like a mausoleum, she thought. A fitting place in which to lay her hopes to rest.

An officious-looking lawyer in a grey suit was waiting for her in the lobby. He escorted her up in the lift to the top floor and showed her into a corner office. Charlie King was seated behind a large teak desk, his hands folded over his generous stomach. He stood as Irina entered and graciously offered her a seat. He was wearing an ivory silk shirt with his initials monogrammed on the chest, his chalk-striped trousers held up by a pair of wide braces. Irina glanced around the office at the opulent furniture, the framed portraits of the company grandees and shelves of leather-bound legal volumes. She kept herself upright and resolute in her chair, refusing to be overawed by her surroundings. On King's desk the copies of the non-disclosure agreement were laid out, each turned to the signature pages.

'I'm so pleased we can finally resolve this matter,' King said. 'What happened to your daughter was a tragedy. Taking her life at such a young age. Please accept my condolences.'

Irina was unmoved. 'Maria's death was no suicide. The only mystery is who killed her.'

King was taken aback by her directness. 'You can't think my client was responsible?'

'Can't I? Only Robert Carlson is sure what really happened that night. So far, he's refused to reveal what he knows.'

'I can assure you that Robert is a good man. He had nothing to do with this.'

Irina stared at him across the desk. 'You expect me to take your word for it?' she asked.

The meeting wasn't the triumphal procession that Charlie King had expected. He adjusted the reading glasses perched on the end of his nose. There seemed little point in continuing with this line of conversation.

'Perhaps we should just complete the signing of the paperwork?' he asked delicately.

Irina looked reluctant but she nodded in agreement. King took a pen and handed it to her. He indicated the dotted lines on the NDA where she was required to sign.

'I wanted Lewis Miller to be here to see this,' King said. 'I understand he's been making extensive enquiries around London on your behalf.'

Irina shook her head. 'It's better that he isn't,' she said. 'I'm not sure he'd agree with my change of heart.'

*

Lewis ran into the lobby of Renfrew and Hall, throwing open the huge glass doors in his path. The receptionist looked startled as he burst into the hallowed space.

'Where is she?' Lewis shouted.

'Who?'

'Irina Koval.'

'She's on the top floor, in Mr King's office.'

There wasn't time to wait for the lift so Lewis sprinted up the emergency stairs. Reaching the executive floor, his lungs bursting, Lewis ran out into the corridor. The lights were on in Charlie King's office at the end of the hall. Lewis raced down and stopped in the doorway. He was breathless, his clothes soaked with rain.

Charlie King's face broke out in a beaming smile. 'Miller. So pleased you could make it,' he said. 'We were just talking about you.'

Irina saw him and looked away in shame.

'Don't sign anything,' Lewis panted.

His words came out in heaves. Irina pointed down at the signed pages of the contract on King's desk.

'It's too late now,' she said. 'It's over.'

Charlie King stood from his office chair. He passed the cashier's cheque to Irina. 'One hundred thousand pounds, as agreed, Mrs Koval.'

Irina thanked him quietly. She gathered her things and began to walk to the door. She looked on the verge of tears. Lewis tried to think of something to say but it was futile. The deed was done. Irina brushed past him without a word and headed silently along the corridor to the lift. Lewis watched her go. There was something broken about her now, a tired fragility that showed in her movements.

'Congratulations,' King said to Lewis. 'Robert Carlson will be a very happy man tonight when he hears that this ordeal is over.'

Lewis searched himself for any feeling of victory but he was hollow inside. The injustice he had spent days trying to redress would now go unpunished. He could feel the disappointment gnaw at the very heart of him.

'I . . . I have to go,' he stammered. 'Excuse me.'

King looked perplexed. He was about to speak when Lewis turned and ran back along the hallway.

He reached Irina as she was leaving the main exit of the building, stepping out on to the rain-drenched square. People were scurrying past under umbrellas, the deluge of water sluicing around them.

'Leave me alone,' Irina said, her voice faltering. 'There's nothing more to say.'

Lewis stood in her path. 'I think you owe me an explanation.'

'I don't owe you anything.'

'I've been all over London trying to solve this case!' Lewis yelled in frustration. 'Now you spring this on me? Were you just using me all along to get a better settlement?'

Irina looked disgusted at the accusation. 'There are other problems I have to sort out. Things I can't explain. It's over now. Leave me in peace.'

She turned and began to walk away. Lewis wasn't going to let her leave so easily.

'Do one last thing for me,' he said. 'Maria wrote a name inside a book of matches from the Carlingford Hotel. She hid the matchbook somewhere safe. I have to know the name she wrote down.'

Irina waved the idea away. 'I've signed the non-disclosure agreement now. I can't do anything that will harm Robert Carlson or he'll sue me.'

'I've risked everything to get this far,' Lewis said. 'I'm not going to stop now.'

A black taxi neared. Irina held up her hand to stop it.

'Let this drop,' she said. 'You've won.'

'I've not won anything. Only Robert Carlson has. He's played everyone for his own ends. Don't let him get away with this.'

Irina opened the door of the taxi and climbed inside. The driver pulled out into the afternoon traffic. She turned and glanced back through the window as the cab disappeared. Lewis could see her face, wracked with guilt.

55

CHARLIE KING WAS at his desk when Lewis returned to his office. The copies of the non-disclosure agreement were still laid out before him. He was examining Irina's signature, making sure everything was in order. He seemed pleased with the way events had concluded.

'Good work, Lewis,' he said. 'It took a little longer than I'd hoped, but you got there in the end. I have to say I'm impressed with your diligence.'

So much had happened since they had last spoken in the taxi out at Docklands. That first meeting felt like it had taken place in a different age. Since then there had been a whirl of chases and fights and attempts on Lewis's life. He thought about keeping his doubts to himself but the facts were too damning.

'I hate to ruin the party,' Lewis said, 'but I don't think an NDA is going to end this. Not by a long way.'

King pointed to the seat in front of his desk. 'You look shattered, Lewis,' he said. 'Sit down and tell me what's on your mind.'

Lewis tried to work out where to start. There were too many factors to spell everything out delicately, piece by piece. He decided to be blunt. 'I think Maria Brennan was murdered,' he said. 'I resisted the idea at first. But all the evidence points to it. There's no other explanation.'

King took a moment to let the words sink in. He appeared unsettled at what he was hearing. 'Are you sure?' he asked gravely.

'Maria definitely didn't die by suicide. That much is certain.'

'And you think Robert Carlson killed her?'

'He's a suspect. One of many.'

'Who else is in the frame?'

'It's a long list. Four or five different people have questions to answer.'

King frowned. 'Do you have any proof?'

'Nothing conclusive. Just lots of fragments. I need to find a way to put them all together.'

'But you're suspicious of Carlson's involvement?'

'He's hiding something. That much I'm sure of. But so are many others.'

'Do you have anything you can show me?'

Lewis took out his phone and opened the photograph of Emilia Carlson and Maria together in her car. King adjusted his reading glasses and squinted at the screen.

'Where did you get this?' he asked.

'It was sent to me anonymously,' Lewis said. 'I don't know its significance yet but I have to find out who sent it. I've tried calling the number but they just hang up on me.'

'So at least we know it's still active,' King said. 'I'll ask the techies to try and trace the account. You have the number so it won't be too difficult to find out who owns the phone.'

Lewis nodded. 'I think whoever sent this photo knows exactly what happened to Maria. She was fired because of an argument she had with Carlson's daughter at a charity gala. This photo has to be connected with that event.'

King stood and walked to the cabinet in the corner of his office. He took out a bottle of cognac from the collection of liquor he kept inside. He poured two glasses and handed one to Lewis. 'You deserve this,' he said. 'It's a rare vintage. A gift from an old friend.'

Lewis accepted it gratefully. It was hot and rich and burned the back of his throat as he drank.

King swirled the amber liquid in his glass. He peered into it thoughtfully. 'Robert Carlson is one of our most high-profile clients,' he said, 'but he's not above the law. If there's any suggestion of wrongdoing, by him or anyone in his family, we have to uncover it. This company has a long and hallowed reputation to protect. We must be on the right side of justice. It's our first duty.'

'That's my instinct exactly,' Lewis said, relief running through him.

'Good. Keep probing and looking for evidence. You've done an admirable job so far. Don't let up now. Report back to me, whatever you find. We can decide together how to proceed.'

Lewis sipped his cognac. 'Thank you, I will. I'm so close I can feel it.'

King smiled paternally. 'I'm proud of you, Lewis. I can see you have a bright future here. This company has always produced men of substance. It appears you're going to be one of the finest.'

'I won't let you down,' Lewis said.

King rested a hand on his shoulder. 'I've arranged a dinner for the Commercial team tonight. It's supposed to be for senior staff only but I'd like you to join us. Consider it a mark of my gratitude for all your hard work. You deserve it.'

Lewis flushed with pride. 'Of course,' he said. 'I'll be there.'

56

THE FLAT WAS full of ghosts. Every shadow seemed to hold another terrible memory. Irina let the tears fall from her eyes as she came through the door. She stood for a while in the hallway and sobbed. Her life had been one of unrelenting hardship: a husband who had deserted her; a tearaway son; a murdered daughter. And now the man who had killed Maria was going to walk away unpunished. The sense of defeat was crushing.

She went into the kitchen and took a seat at the table. It felt like everything had changed in the flat. The quiet emptiness filled her with despair. She thought of the cheque she had received from Charlie King. It was only a piece of paper but it had taken away the last scrap of hope she had clung to. Irina wished she could tear it into pieces and toss it away but that was impossible now. The money was going to save Drew's life. Despite all the mistakes he'd made in the past, she couldn't face losing another child.

Irina thought of her husband, long gone for many years now. Pat Brennan had been a brawler and a thief, just like his son. The apple hadn't fallen far from the tree in Drew's case. He was his father's double, in character as well as appearance. He had the same chiselled face and deep-set eyes, the same hard-nosed manner. That was why Irina had been so tough on Drew all of his life, she thought to herself. It was her only way of reclaiming some pride after she had been abandoned by her husband. Pat Brennan hadn't called or left a note before walking out on her all those years ago. She remembered the shame she had felt overhearing all the hushed gossip in the street, the neighbours whispering to each other that Pat had run off in the night. He'd had enough of the foreign wife who could barely speak English, they had said. He had gone to find one of his own kind. The neighbours had cold-shouldered her after that. They had acted like it was Irina's fault that she couldn't keep a man. That she didn't deserve to be happy. Watching Drew grow up and slowly turn into his father meant the wound could never heal. He was a constant reminder to Irina of her own failings, no matter how hard she tried to suppress them.

Sitting at the kitchen table, she felt like a failure all over again. A piece of trash blown wherever the wind took her. But Irina knew these feelings would gain her nothing. She asked herself what Maria would have done in her place. Maria would have been stronger, Irina thought. She wouldn't have just sat there, crying and feeling sorry for herself.

Drying her tears, Irina went out to the hallway and pushed open the door to Maria's room. She looked along the rows of books on the shelves. Cheap paperbacks and scientific journals. On the highest shelf was a thick dusty dictionary. Irina reached up and took it down. She opened the heavy cover. Inside, the pages had been cut away to create a deep hollow.

This, Irina had long known, was Maria's hiding place for her secret things. Among the letters and photographs, the teenage keepsakes Maria had placed there, Irina saw the matchbook, embossed with the crest of the Carlingford Hotel.

She took it out and flipped open the thin cardboard cover. Inside, a phone number was scrawled in a drunken hand. Below it was a name. The ink was smudged, but it was still legible. Irina thought of the privacy agreement she had signed. If she broke it, she could lose everything. Robert Carlson was a vengeful man. He wouldn't hesitate to ruin her just to protect his reputation. Standing there, looking at the matchbook, Irina made her decision. Carlson had already taken her daughter from her. What else did she still have to lose? With a calm, steady hand she took out her phone and made a call.

'Hello?'

'Lewis,' Irina said, 'it's me. I've found the name you're looking for.'

57

THE MERCEDES GLIDED through the city. In the back seat, Robert Carlson was checking his emails. Work was his only refuge lately. His last consolation in a sea of troubles. He tried to let it occupy his mind fully, allowing himself to be submerged in the minutiae of the tasks at hand. Beyond these concerns only danger lay waiting. When his phone rang, he hesitated. Looking at the screen, he saw it was Susannah. Carlson relaxed visibly as he answered.

'Are you coming home?' his wife asked.

'I'm in the car now.'

Susannah sighed down the line. 'I'm worried about Emilia.'

'Why?'

'She's been acting strangely. Some things she's said are terrifying me.'

Carlson frowned. 'How?'

'She keeps talking about Maria Brennan. About that night at the Carlingford.'

The memory made Carlson gnash his teeth in despair. 'That damned gala,' he said. 'I wish it had never happened.'

'Look, there's something I've never told you,' Susannah said. 'I thought it was best to keep it to myself. I'm not sure I can any longer.'

The skin on Carlson's neck prickled. 'Go on.'

'I . . . I saw Emilia arguing with Maria Brennan on the day she died. They were parked in a car outside the house. I'd just arrived back from shopping and I saw them together. I hid behind the park railings so they didn't spot me while they were arguing. After ten minutes, they drove away together. I was suspicious so I hailed a taxi and followed them.'

'Where did they go?'

'To a bar in Soho. A horrible little dive. From the back of the taxi, I could see into the place so I waited to see what would happen. They met a man in there. A nasty-looking piece of work. He made me shudder just looking at him. Emilia seemed to know him well. As soon as Maria laid eyes on this man, she turned away and left.'

'And Emilia?'

'She stayed inside the bar with the man. They went to the back where I couldn't see them. I started to worry, so after a few minutes I went in to look for her. I searched the place but she was gone. The barman told me she'd left with the man by a back door.'

'Did you ever ask Emilia about this?'

'I was afraid. In a way, I didn't want to know what was going on.'

Carlson sighed but understood his wife's reluctance to rock

the boat. Emilia was too unpredictable and self-destructive as it was. He heard Susannah take a deep breath down the phone line.

'I think we should tell Emilia what happened that night at the Carlingford,' she said.

From the gravity in her voice, Carlson knew his wife was serious. 'No, Susannah, we've discussed this. Emilia is too fragile to know the truth.'

His wife's voice grew strident. 'She needs to know what happened. It will only make matters worse if we keep it from her.'

'I don't want her to know. It might just cause more grief for everyone.'

Susannah sounded pained at his reticence. 'Then this will never heal,' she said. 'The pain will just keep going on.'

The phone beeped in Carlson's ear. A call was waiting. 'Someone else is ringing me,' he said. 'Let me get rid of them. I'll be right back.' He switched over to the second line. 'I can't talk,' he said brusquely.

The reply was cold and clinical.

'Tell me about Viktor Zhirkov.'

The name hit Carlson like a hammer blow. 'Who . . . who is this?' he stuttered.

'Lewis Miller.'

Carlson took his head in his hands. The night was drawing tighter around him, closing in from all sides. The mounting pressure was unbearable.

'How did you find out about Viktor?'

'That's not important,' Lewis said. 'What's important is how long he's been your business partner.'

'That information is very sensitive, Lewis. I can't state that clearly enough. It's essential that you don't make his name public. For both our sakes.'

'At least admit that Zhirkov is Andrei's father.'

Carlson saw no point in denying it. 'He is.'

'I've researched the Zhirkov family,' Lewis said. 'Their bio makes horrifying reading.'

'I admit they have made some questionable decisions over the years.'

'Questionable?' Lewis snapped. 'Viktor Zhirkov is a war criminal. A man wanted for human rights abuses in Eastern Ukraine. He's a puppet of the Kremlin. Why on earth would you want a man like that as a business partner?'

Carlson felt his world slipping away from him. The walls he had created to protect himself were tumbling down and there was nothing he could do to stop it. He had nowhere left to hide.

'My company is on the rocks,' he said. 'I've been trying to hold everything together for some time now. I needed money and Viktor Zhirkov was my only chance. I had nowhere else to turn.'

'The Zhirkov family are banned from doing business by international sanctions. They're unable to trade in the UK. It's totally illegal to accept money from them.'

'It was the only way I had to stay afloat. There was no other option. I had to accept their offer of investment.'

'Maria Brennan found out about your deal, didn't she? That's why you killed her.'

Carlson's tone was absolute. 'No,' he said. 'I meant it when I said I would never have done anything to hurt Maria.'

'I read her transcript. She was frightened of you. She knew

how dangerous it was to expose what you were doing out at Coldharbour Marshes. But Maria was brave enough to do it anyway. You can't expect me to believe that her death wasn't linked to that?'

'It's not how it appears,' Carlson said. 'This is only part of the story.'

Lewis was undeterred. 'I thought you were different. A man of integrity. Turns out you're just another selfish capitalist. People have died because of you. I can't allow this to stay secret.'

Carlson was thinking on his feet. He could still see a way out. 'Come to my house. Let me explain myself face to face.'

'When?'

'Tonight. I'll text you my address.'

There was an interminable moment of silence as Lewis deliberated. 'I don't know,' he said. 'I'm supposed to have dinner with the Commercial team tonight. Anyway, I'm not sure it's wise for us to speak in private again.'

'Please,' Carlson pleaded. 'If you want to know why I was trying so desperately to speak to Maria before she died, you'll come.'

He was dangling the revelation like bait. Finally Lewis relented.

'OK. Give me thirty minutes,' Lewis said.

Carlson was relieved. 'Fine. I'll be waiting.'

When he hung up, Carlson returned to the other line. It was dead. Susannah was gone.

58

THE MERCEDES PULLED into Lowndes Square and stopped in front of Carlson's house. He stepped out on to the pavement and wished the driver goodnight. He needed time to think so he crossed the street to the small private park at the centre of the square. He opened the heavy gate and took a seat on an empty bench. Tall ash trees were grouped neatly around the perimeter, their branches hanging low over the wrought-iron railings. There was a sinister quality to the shapes they cast in the moonlight. His empire was bleeding to death before him. Everything he had worked for was ebbing away. If Lewis Miller wanted to be mixed up in this affair, then so be it. He should be careful what he wished for, Carlson thought.

He took out his phone and made another call.

'Robert? How nice to hear from you again so soon. What can I do for you now?'

Andrei's voice was always so patronizing, so supercilious. Carlson hated hearing it. At least the news he was about to deliver would knock the smirk off that Russian face once and for all.

'Your father's name is about to be made public, Andrei,' he said. 'Lewis Miller managed to track him down. There's nothing I can do to keep our deal secret any more.'

The line crackled with static in his ear.

'This is a major problem,' Andrei growled. 'There will be implications.'

'Such as?'

'Miller will have to go.'

There was a long stretch of ominous silence. Andrei's meaning was plain.

'I want out,' Carlson said. 'This has all gone too far.'

Andrei's voice began to grow desperate. 'You're not thinking straight, Robert.'

'I can't carry on. Too many people have been hurt.'

'And that number will only increase if you do anything rash. Ours is a dirty business. If you can't accept this, perhaps you should find another line of work.'

'Don't patronize me, Andrei.'

'Desperate times are moments of great opportunity. You told me that. We can use this to our advantage if we're smart.'

'How?'

'Go to the Minister for Energy. Inform him that my father and I are going to be publicly revealed as your partners. Use this as leverage to have my family taken off the Magnitsky sanctions list. It's within the Minister's power. God knows we've got enough dirt on the man to force his hand.'

Carlson shook his head. 'If you try that, it will end our

project at Coldharbour Marshes. The government can't be publicly connected to your father. You know that, Andrei.'

'My father has invested a substantial amount of money in this deal. Hundreds of millions. I can't allow a nobody like Miller to jeopardize it.'

'He's coming to my house tonight. I intend to tell him everything.'

'That would be very foolish,' Andrei said.

'It's over now. I've accepted it, Andrei. I suggest you do the same.'

Carlson hung up. A flood of relief washed over him. He could sense salvation close at hand. It was time to face his family, he thought. It was important for Emilia to know the truth. He gathered his belongings, left the park and mounted the steps to his front door. Searching for his keys, he found them in his coat pocket and turned the lock.

Stepping into the dark hallway, Carlson stopped suddenly, all his senses on full alert. Standing before him was a stranger, holding a knife to his wife's throat. He was rough and menacing, his build like that of a boxer. The sight was bizarre enough that, for a split second, Carlson wondered if he was in the wrong house.

'Close the door,' the man said flatly.

Susannah Carlson whimpered as the blade was pressed against her throat.

Carlson did as he was ordered. 'Where's my daughter?' he asked.

'Come with me,' the man said. 'I'll show you.'

59

ANDREI ZHIRKOV WAS alone in his hotel suite. London sparkled beyond the darkened window, a sea of twinkling lights
far below. A black line twisted through the vast plain, the
Thames snaking east through the city. Out there, far down-
stream, lay the Coldharbour Marshes. Andrei had only visited
the place once. It had meant nothing to him when he saw the
landscape with his own eyes. It was just a desolate expanse of
scrubland and reed beds. Some sad-looking birds nesting in
the scrawny, leafless trees. Andrei didn't understand why anyone would object to tearing up that pitiful scrap of ground
and starting again. He couldn't believe such a worthless place
had caused so much trouble.

The simple ruse had been to latch on to Carlson's plan to
build a hydrogen fuel plant. It was a deluded fairy tale, Andrei
had thought, listening to Carlson's desperate pitch for money
to save his business. Why generate a new source of energy
when it was possible to drill the stuff out of the ground? It was
all part of Carlson's misguided saviour complex. Andrei treated

such illusions with scorn. Behind Carlson's back, Andrei had obeyed his father when he had demanded that not one molecule of hydrogen be produced at the facility. It would be a conduit for their methane business and nothing more. Like a dutiful son, Andrei had done all in his power to fulfil his father's request.

Now Carlson was threatening to pull down the whole house of cards. His reasons made little sense to Andrei. Was he truly so squeamish over the killing out at the marshes? Andrei had seen so many deaths that one more made little difference to him. But Carlson was too easily swayed. He had proved an unreliable partner in many respects over the past months. Andrei knew it was up to him to stop Carlson's weakness causing any more damage.

He rose from the armchair and walked over to the telephone on the nightstand. He picked up the receiver and dialled a number.

'Mr Egan,' he said as the call was connected.

'Andrei.'

'How is progress out at the marshes?'

'Good. Two more days and the lower lake will be drained.'

Frank Egan's Irish brogue was hard for Andrei to understand. He had to listen intently, the handset pressed to his ear.

'Two more days?' he barked. 'You need to work faster. I told you to have the lower levels ready by tomorrow.'

Egan tutted disapprovingly. 'Why don't you do your job and let me do mine?'

'That's precisely the problem, Frank. You and too many others are willing to let me down. I can't allow this to continue.'

'I was promised more money,' Frank Egan said. 'If you want me to build your power station any faster, I need more funds.'

'Only Robert Carlson can pay you. My father and I have transferred our investment to him. We have to operate in the background. You know this.'

Frank Egan snarled down the line. 'I don't care about your financial trickery. Get me the money I need.'

'Why should I when you fail in the tasks I give you?'

'You mean taking care of Miller?'

'I wanted him gone. You told me you'd handle it.'

Frank Egan sighed in disappointment. 'I sent someone to finish him in the Tube station. I chose badly. The plan was bungled. He got away.'

'That mistake could be costly.'

'If you don't like it, maybe you should consider doing your own dirty work,' Frank hissed.

Andrei nodded sagely. 'From now on, that's exactly what I plan to do.'

He hung up and walked over to the wardrobe. Opening the door, he entered the security code on the safe and the heavy steel lock clicked open. From inside, he took out a folder of paperwork. Sitting on the edge of the bed, Andrei flicked through his copy of the joint partnership agreement for the Coldharbour Marshes project. He turned the pages, scanning the clauses until he found the one he was looking for. It was well hidden, placed innocuously along with instructions for allocating board seats and asserting voting rights. In the event of Robert Carlson's death, the clause stated, complete owner-ship of the new facility would pass to the Zhirkov family, via their offshore shell companies. The clause was ironclad. Andrei guessed Carlson hadn't been informed of its existence. If he had, there was no way he'd be behaving so recklessly.

In the margins of each page, Andrei had written copious notes. He prided himself on his attention to detail in meetings. His father had taught him to be thorough as a child. He passed a curious eye over his writing. His penmanship verged on the obsessive, the result of his expensive education in Zurich. There was no trace of his native language when he wrote in English. He'd been outraged when he'd heard of the note left on Maria Brennan's car. Such a basic error. Not one he would have made if he'd been there the night she'd been killed. That's what happened when amateurs were sent to do a professional's job. So far the only killing that hadn't been mishandled was the one he had done himself. The lawyer Martin Sobel had been dispatched with a minimum of fuss. Why were the other people he employed incapable of matching his ruthlessness? They were incompetent clowns, Andrei thought. From now on, he was going to have to take care of all such tasks himself.

Closing the folder, Andrei stood and returned it to the safe. Stretching his arm, he reached a hand into its furthest recesses. He smiled to himself when his fingers touched the object he was looking for. The reassuring touch of cold gunmetal. He gripped the pistol and took it out of the safe, feeling its weight and heft. He checked it was loaded and then tucked the gun inside the waistband of his trousers. Buttoning up his jacket, Andrei looked at himself in the mirror and smiled with satisfaction. Tonight he was going to really make his father proud.

60

ROBERT CARLSON MADE his way down the winding staircase that led to the basement. Behind him, he could hear his wife's breathing. The small whimpers of pain she gave with each step.

'Please let her go,' Carlson said without looking back.

'Shut up and keep moving.'

The edge of menace in the stranger's voice was clear. Carlson did as he was told. He had taken a hostage course earlier that year. Complete compliance was the key to survival. Whatever was demanded – money, valuables, jewellery – it was better to hand them over than to try anything heroic. Preserving life was paramount and that was exactly what Carlson intended to do. His family was too precious to take any risks. When he reached the bottom step, he stopped. To his left was the wine cellar. To his right, the swimming pool complex.

'Which way now?' he asked.

'Go right.'

He followed the instruction and pushed open the door to

the pool. The intruder followed, shoving Susannah before him. The room was unnaturally warm. It hit Carlson in a giddy wave. Their footsteps echoed as they walked along the edge of the pool. Light reflecting from the surface of the water cast crazy patterns on the ceiling. Carlson could see glass scattered on the floor where the access window had been smashed, the security grille over the wooden frame twisted back with a crowbar.

'Straight on,' the voice commanded.

That meant the door to the spa room. Carlson headed for it and pushed the door open. In the corner stood the glass-walled steam room. Inside he could see Emilia crouched on the floor. She was bound and gagged, her hands tied to the pipework inside the cubicle. Mercifully the temperature had been turned down. A bucket had been placed next to her. Bottles and containers of household chemicals and cleaning fluids were stacked nearby.

Carlson rushed towards his daughter in a burst of pure parental instinct.

'Stay where you are!' came the urgent shout behind him.

Susannah squealed in pain as the knife was pressed to her neck. Carlson stopped short. He could see Emilia was in a state of panic. Above the length of fabric gagging her mouth, her eyes were wild with terror. But they were all together now and they were alive, and Carlson planned to keep it that way. Slowly he turned to face the intruder.

'Tell me what you want,' he said. 'Just don't hurt my family.'

'The way you hurt mine?'

Carlson was confused. 'Who are you?'

'Guess?'

The man was young and solidly built, with a tough battle-scarred face. Carlson felt a wave of fear as he studied his features, only now seeing the similarities to the young woman who had worked for him.

'You're Drew Brennan,' Carlson said, his voice full of trepidation.

'How do you know my name?'

'Maria used to talk about you.'

Drew dug the knife into Susannah's neck. It was on the verge of drawing blood. She held herself still, her eyes squeezed tight shut. Any movement and the knife would puncture her skin.

'You killed my sister,' Drew said. 'Now you're going to pay for it.'

Carlson was growing frantic. His famous charisma had crumbled to dust. 'I have money in the house,' he said. 'A lot. I can get it for you.'

'I don't want your money. I want revenge. You took Maria's life. Now you can watch your daughter die.'

Emilia gave a cry of anguish. Carlson began to understand why the containers of cleaning products were inside the steam room. He took a step towards his daughter. Drew grasped Susannah closer to him, forcing her head back. A vein was pulsing blue beneath her skin. She squealed in fright and Carlson stopped.

'I know how Maria was killed,' Drew said. 'It was in all the newspapers. She suffocated, breathing in toxic fumes. A nasty way to go. When I add bleach to the mix in that bucket, your daughter's going to die just like Maria. You and your wife get to watch.'

'Please,' Carlson said, 'don't do it.'

'There's just one way to save her.'

'How?'

'Tell the truth. Admit that you killed Maria. You were having an affair. She rejected you and you wanted her dead.'

'No,' Carlson pleaded. 'Maria and I were colleagues. Nothing more.'

'So why did you come to our home the night before she died?'

Carlson looked at Susannah. She was trembling with fear.

'I was trying to warn her.'

'Of what?'

'Of the damage she was doing.'

'To you?'

'To my daughter. Maria was going to accuse Emilia of planting cocaine on her. My daughter has a drug problem. I couldn't allow it to become public. It would ruin her reputation.'

Emilia was wracked by sobs as she listened to her father's confession. Drew looked at her in disgust.

'So you tossed Maria aside to protect that spoiled brat?' he said.

Carlson held his hands up in surrender. 'I'm guilty,' he said. 'I sacked Maria to protect my daughter. I've hated myself for doing it ever since.'

Drew hesitated. He shook his head as if he refused to believe what he was hearing. 'Even if you're telling the truth, your daughter wrecked Maria's life. She needs to pay for that if nothing else.'

Susannah tried to speak. The knife was tight to her windpipe and the words came out in a hoarse whisper. 'It wasn't

Emilia,' she said. 'She didn't plant drugs on Maria. I know she didn't.'

Drew frowned at her. 'How?'

Tears flowed from Susannah's eyes. She was trembling with fear as she spoke, her words coming out in gasps.

'Because it was me,' she said.

61

THE TAXI STOPPED on the west side of Lowndes Square. The park was quiet, the grand houses dark. Lewis paid the fare and stepped out on to the street. He'd never been to Belgravia before. It wasn't a part of the city that welcomed people like him. He looked up at the huge stone mansion, bathed in the cold moonlight, and stood for a moment, taking it in. The pillared entranceway, mullioned windows and the flawless white stucco. It was no surprise to find that a man like Robert Carlson lived in such a place.

He gathered his courage as he mounted the steps to the front door. He remembered how frantic Carlson had sounded on the phone, the burden of guilt becoming too much for him. Under the portico, Lewis pressed the intercom and waited. There was no answer so he pressed again. After a minute of silence he stepped back and looked up at the façade. The windows were quiet and still.

Lewis felt uneasy. Carlson had definitely wanted him to come to the house that evening. He had insisted on it. Now he wasn't answering his door. Searching for clues, Lewis's eyes were drawn down the steep stone steps that led to the basement. He could see an open security grille over a sash window, a smattering of smashed glass spread out beneath it. From the opening, the smell of swimming pool chlorine drifted out into the night.

Lewis took out his phone and called Carlson's number. As it rang in his ear, he walked back down the steps and out on to the pavement, staring up at the house, searching for signs of movement. The ringing of the phone line consumed all of his concentration.

Suddenly, out of the gloom, the twin beams of a car's headlights flashed brightly. Lewis was blinded by the glare. He threw up an arm to cover his eyes and spun away instinctively. Behind him, he could hear the roar of an engine and the squeal of tyres as the car sped forward. The headlights bounced wildly as the car mounted the pavement, heading straight for him.

Muscle memory took over as Lewis regained his senses. He sprinted out on to the road. The car swerved towards him, tracking his path. As he reached the iron railings surrounding the park, Lewis vaulted over. The wing of the car struck the line of metal posts and cast a shower of sparks like a match running across sandpaper. Tumbling on to the wet grass, Lewis looked back. The car was wrenched sideways and buckled against the fence, smoke billowing from a smashed bonnet. The driver's door opened and a tall man got out. He looked unsteady on his feet, stunned by the impact. He reached into his waistband and pulled out something metallic. It glinted in the moonlight.

Lewis scrambled to his feet and ran for the shrubbery on the opposite side of the park, diving for the safety of the undergrowth where the darkness was heaviest. Lying flat on the sodden ground, dead leaves piled around him, he waited, trying to quieten his breathing as he figured out what to do.

From across the park, a squeal of rusty metal rang out as the gate was opened. Lewis could see the man begin to search the undergrowth slowly and methodically, pausing from time to time to kick a patch of shrubbery or pull back the leaves of a laurel bush.

Lewis pressed himself into the earth. The footsteps were nearing. There was nowhere he could run without being seen. He was trapped.

With his pursuer almost on top of him, Lewis prepared himself to stand and fight. It was futile but he had no other option.

A footstep landed inches away and he tensed, ready to spring up, his fists clenched.

'Hey!' a voice called out in the darkness.

It was a woman's voice, high and clear.

Startled, the man spun around.

There was a *swoosh* as a heavy branch was swung. A *crack* as it connected with the side of the man's head. He fell in a heap, his body landing in the mud next to Lewis.

A hand reached down to pull Lewis up.

'Hurry! Follow me.'

Instantly Lewis was on his feet, running, stumbling on the wet grass as he was dragged towards the open gate. In the moonlight he saw the face of his rescuer. Rachael was pulling him along, a broken length of fallen timber in her hand.

'What are you doing here?' Lewis gasped as they sprinted along together.

'I followed you,' Rachael said. 'Luckily for you.'

They raced across the lawn. At the gate, Rachael began to turn left towards the junction at the end of the square. Glancing behind him, Lewis could see the fallen man start to clamber to his feet.

He spun to the right. 'This way,' he said, taking Rachael with him. 'It's closer.'

62

'I DID IT,' Susannah Carlson sobbed. 'I planted the drugs in Maria's coat. I knew Emilia had taken cocaine at the gala that night. I knew she kept it in her handbag. When she wasn't looking, I stole it from her bag and went to the cloakroom. I found Maria's coat and stashed the drugs in her pocket. It was a moment of madness.'

Drew pressed the knife to her throat. 'You found out about your husband's affair, didn't you? That's why you wanted to hurt Maria.'

'I never believed those rumours,' Susannah gasped. 'I always knew why Robert treated Maria so well. It had nothing to do with an affair. Maria was the daughter he never had. Robert wanted her to succeed him at the company. She was going to be the new CEO when Robert retired.'

Carlson took a step towards his wife, his face pale with anguish. 'I'm so sorry,' he said. 'I never meant for any of this to hurt you.'

From the steam room, Emilia began to weep. It was too

painful to hear how much of a failure she was in her father's eyes. How Maria was the daughter he'd really wished for. She was his anointed successor, Emilia only a constant disappointment. Susannah grew more tearful as she heard her daughter's distress.

'How could Emilia compete?' she cried at her husband. 'She had to watch you give all your attention to Maria while you ignored her. It broke my heart. That's why Emilia turned to drugs. It's her only escape from the shame she feels for letting you down.'

Carlson looked distraught. He had known this was the truth for a long time but it was painful to hear it spoken aloud.

Drew was listening intently. He clutched Susannah by the neck, the knife digging into her flesh. 'So you tried to destroy my sister in revenge for your husband's mistakes,' he hissed.

'I didn't know what else to do,' Susannah sobbed. 'I'm so sorry. I didn't think how destructive it would be. I had no idea that Maria had found out about Robert's business dealings. His project out at Coldharbour Marshes. I couldn't have foreseen how the threat of taking Robert to court would be so dangerous.'

Carlson held his head in his hands. 'This is all my fault. I should have been honest from the start. I thought I was protecting my family but I was only hurting them.'

Drew looked from one to the other. They had the intense, manic energy of people unburdening themselves. He could feel his anger ebbing away. From what he could see, there was no way Robert Carlson could be a murderer. He wasn't ruthless enough. Drew had broken into the house to find out the truth.

Now he was certain – whoever had killed Maria, it wasn't anyone in that room.

Suddenly a scuffling came from beyond the door to the swimming pool. The crash of furniture being upended. The slap of running footsteps on wet tiles. Drew instinctively stepped back behind the door where he couldn't be seen.

The door flew open and a couple burst in. Drew instantly recognized the lawyer Lewis Miller. He was with a young woman with dark hair, holding her by the hand. They looked like they were running from danger, Drew didn't know what exactly. He was about to say something when a second figure entered. A tall man, staggering slightly as if groggy. In his hand, Drew saw a gun. The man raised it at Lewis and prepared to shoot.

Lunging forward, Drew sank his knife into the man's thigh, burying the blade up to the hilt. With a yell of shock and pain, the man squeezed the trigger and a shot struck the wall over Lewis's head. Drew pulled the knife out. It tore against soft flesh as it came free, blood pulsing from the wound. Howling, the man began to turn around, the gun still gripped in his hand. Drew swung a fist into his jaw, knocking the man to the floor. The gun skittered off against the hard tiles.

Drew bent low, ready to swing another punch if necessary. There was no need. The man was knocked out cold.

'Don't move,' a low voice said.

Drew looked up. Robert Carlson was holding the pistol, pointing it straight at him.

63

CARLSON HAD TO resist the temptation to kill Drew on the spot. His finger twitched eagerly on the trigger. If he shot an intruder in his own home, it would be self-defence, he reasoned. He could kill Drew and walk away, unpunished by the law. But he knew the emotional consequences for his family would be devastating. They'd experienced enough trauma for one night. Taking a breath, Carlson allowed his better nature to take over. He lowered the gun to the floor.

'You've got some explaining to do,' he said.

Drew breathed out heavily. 'You should be thanking me. I just saved your lawyer from taking a bullet.'

'Who is that?' Lewis asked, pointing to the man lying unconscious before him.

Carlson looked down at the prostrate figure. 'That is Andrei Zhirkov.'

Lewis nodded. 'He was waiting outside when I arrived,' he said. 'He tried to run me down with his car. Luckily I had someone watching out for me.'

Rachael was breathless, unsure exactly of who these people were or what was going on. Emilia continued sobbing loudly in the small steam room where she had been trussed up. Susannah rushed in to untie her. Rachael followed to help. Together they got the distraught girl on her feet.

'You could have killed my daughter,' Carlson said to Drew. 'Mixing those chemicals in an enclosed space is dangerous.'

Drew shook his head. 'The containers are all empty,' he said calmly. 'I only wanted to scare you so I could make you talk. It worked.'

Carlson didn't look like he appreciated the ploy. 'I should shoot you anyway for putting a knife to my wife's neck,' he said.

Drew smiled derisively. 'You haven't got the guts.'

Carlson stepped closer, his teeth gritted in determination. 'Is that what you think?'

Lewis waved a pacifying hand in the air. He pointed to Andrei's prone figure. Blood was oozing from the wound in his thigh, seeping out steadily on to the tiles.

'Whoever this is, he's in a bad way,' Lewis said. 'He needs help.'

'I'm going to stop the bleeding,' Rachael said. She found a towel and began to twist it into a tourniquet. Carlson bent down to help her. They worked quickly, binding the wound.

Lewis took out his phone and opened the photograph of Emilia arguing with Maria Brennan. He showed the screen to Carlson.

'I need your daughter to explain this,' he said. 'I've been trying all day to find out who sent it. I'm sure she knows.'

Carlson was hesitant. It was clear he had never seen the image before.

'Emilia, what do you know about this?' he asked his daughter gently.

She gave a weak sniffle. 'I don't know who took the photo but I can explain why I was with Maria.'

'Go on,' Carlson encouraged her.

'I was told to meet Maria on the day she died,' she said. 'To tell her I had information she'd want to hear.'

'What information?' Lewis asked.

'About the disappearance of her father.'

Drew's ears pricked up. 'What do you know about that?'

'Nothing,' Emilia sobbed. 'I only passed on the message. I was told to take her to a bar in Soho. The man who paid me was waiting there. Maria seemed to know him. When she saw who he was, she refused to sit down and talk to him. He tried to stop her but she walked out. That's all I know.'

Lewis was concentrating hard, trying to piece the information together. 'Who was the man you met there?' he asked.

Emilia looked embarrassed. 'My dealer. He was paying me in heroin. I was desperate.'

Carlson stood and hugged his daughter close. 'Don't you worry,' he said. 'Everything is going to be fine.'

Lewis spoke softly. 'Tell me the name of your dealer,' he asked.

Emilia looked up with tear-soaked eyes. 'Glenn,' she said.

A low moaning growl came from the body on the floor. Lewis looked round quickly. Andrei Zhirkov was beginning to stir. He tried to lift his body from the floor, but lacked the strength and collapsed back to the ground with a cry of pain. Rachael tried to pull the tourniquet tighter but it was no use. Blood was now pouring on to the tiles from his leg, the pool widening by the second.

'He needs an ambulance,' Rachael said.

Carlson shook his head. 'No. It's quicker to drive him to the hospital. Take my wife's car.'

'Fine,' Lewis said. 'Let's get him out of here. We need to hurry.'

They took Andrei by the shoulders. His face was ashen, his lips pale. Together with Carlson, Lewis lifted him up and Drew took his feet. Andrei was heavy but they managed to manoeuvre him past the swimming pool and up the stairs to the ground floor of the house. Carlson put the gun down on the hallway table as he looked for his wife's key fob. Finding it, he opened the front door and they carried Andrei to a black Range Rover parked at the kerb. Carlson bleeped the door open and they hoisted Andrei inside.

Carlson stood back. 'I have to stay with my family,' he said. 'I'm sorry but they need me.'

'Fine,' Lewis said. 'Rachael and I will take him.'

Rachael took the keys from Carlson. 'I'll drive,' she said.

'We might need some muscle with us,' Lewis said, 'for protection.'

'What about Drew?' Carlson asked.

They looked around, expecting to see Drew standing behind them. The street was eerily deserted. Drew Brennan was nowhere to be seen.

64

RACHAEL RAN RED lights and cornered wildly, hammering the Range Rover through the night-time traffic. Andrei was groaning on the back seat, clutching his leg and writhing in pain. He was drifting in and out of consciousness.

'Hang on,' Lewis said to him. 'Stay awake.'

It was a strange sensation, he thought. Trying to save the life of a man who had been intent on killing him only moments before.

'Don't want to die . . .' Andrei moaned.

Lewis was leaning over him, pressing a folded towel to the wound on his thigh. 'We're almost there,' he said. 'Just hang on.'

His voice seemed to make Andrei drop his guard.

'Not my fault,' he babbled.

'What's not your fault?' Lewis said.

'Coldharbour Marshes. The girl.'

'You're talking about Maria Brennan?'

'Not my fault.'

'Who did it, Andrei?' Lewis asked. 'Who killed her?'

Rachael swerved around a slow-moving bus. The car hit a pot-hole and Andrei gave a howl of pain as the car was jolted. Lewis was cradling the man's head, trying to make him comfortable.

'Can't tell you,' Andrei groaned. 'They'll kill me next.'

'We won't let that happen to you. You're safe here.'

Andrei shook his head. 'No one is safe. They'll get you too.'

Lewis stared into Andrei's half-closed eyes. 'Who killed Maria Brennan?' he demanded. 'If it wasn't you, who did it?'

Andrei gasped in pain. 'You know,' he said. 'You've known all along.'

The lights of the hospital came into view. Rachael took the corner at speed and screeched into the forecourt of the emergency department. Ambulances were stacked up, waiting at the kerbside to unload their patients. She stopped next to them and left the engine running as Lewis opened the rear door and pulled Andrei out. Together, they dragged him by the armpits and staggered towards the hospital entrance, the automatic doors opening as they neared. In the brightly lit lobby, they stumbled and Andrei's body fell from their grasp. He collapsed to the floor with a cry. Hearing this, nurses in green scrubs swarmed towards them. They saw the blood flooding from Andrei's leg and began shouting instructions, demanding a stretcher trolley be brought up in haste. Lewis seized Rachael's hand and they inched back from the crowd. In the melee, they turned and slipped back to the Range Rover.

'Let's get out of here,' Lewis said. 'We don't have time to answer questions.'

Rachael nodded in agreement. She jumped into the driver's seat and they sped out of the car park, turning back towards the main road heading north. The rear seat of the Range Rover was a mess of blood, sweat and grime. Lewis leaned back to examine it. Smeared with crimson, a crumpled greetings card lay on the upholstery where Andrei had been. There was a photo on the cover, a studio portrait of a red-headed woman. Lewis recognized her. It was Olivia Ward. He picked up the card and opened it.

Dear Susannah,

Thank you for inviting me to an unforgettable gala at the Carlingford. I had a wonderful night. Looking forward to seeing you again soon.

Yours,
Olivia x

Lewis stopped dead. He read the scrawled message once more to make sure he wasn't mistaken. Some of the letters were out of shape, strange and curiously formed. They were like those of another language, he thought – one that used the Cyrillic alphabet. Lewis was certain of it. The handwriting was identical to that on the note found on Maria Brennan's car windscreen.

65

DREW PICKED THE lock with ease. Closing the door behind him, he stood in the dark hallway, allowing his eyes to adjust to the gloom. He listened intently for any sound or movement. Hearing nothing he began to check from room to room. Gripping the gun he'd taken from Carlson's house, he pointed the barrel forward as he moved, ready to fire. The house was pitch-black. He moved through the rooms slowly, scanning for danger as he went. Pushing open the door to the living room, he stopped dead. Slumped in an armchair beneath the eerie glow of neon from an oversized fish tank was Glenn. There was a rubber tourniquet tied around his arm. A syringe had dropped to the carpet beneath his fingers.

Drew approached slowly. Glenn didn't move. He was taking soft, quiet breaths, his eyelids flickering. He was stoned to oblivion, Drew thought. He lifted his foot and pushed him with the sole of his shoe. 'Wake up!' he barked.

Slowly Glenn began to stir. At first, he was confused by his surroundings. A string of spit hung from one corner of his

293

mouth. It was heart-breaking for Drew to see his friend so wasted.

'Damn,' Glenn wheezed as he recognized him. 'You ruined my high.'

'I don't care,' Drew hissed. 'Sort yourself out.'

Glenn unstrapped the tourniquet from his arm and laid it on the table. He wiped his runny nose with the back of his hand.

'How long have you been using that crap?' Drew asked. 'I thought you only sold it.'

Glenn gave a hazy smile. 'I couldn't resist trying a taste. That was a few months back.'

'Why didn't you tell me?'

'Because I knew what you'd say.'

'At least it explains why you've been acting so strangely.'

Glenn looked up. He saw the gun pointed at his head and seemed to register it for the first time. His expression hardened. 'What's that for?'

'To make you tell the truth.'

'About what?'

'About why you wanted to meet my sister at a bar in Soho.'

Glenn's eyes widened. Drew could see his mind working. He wanted to talk his way out of this but was in no fit state to spin a convincing story.

'Don't lie to me,' Drew said. 'I know you too well.'

'It . . . it wasn't my idea,' Glenn stammered. 'Frank had information about your dad. He thought Maria wouldn't be able to resist hearing it. I knew your sister hated me so I sent one of my customers to speak to her first. A rich girl who said she knew Maria. As soon as she came to the bar, your sister saw me and stormed out. I never got to arrange another meeting. Maria died before I could set it up.'

'What was the information?'

Glenn looked nervous. 'Leave it alone, Drew. Take my word for it. You don't want to know.'

'Why?'

'Because Frank will kill both of us if I talk.'

Drew levelled the gun at his friend's head. 'I'll kill you first if you don't.'

Glenn swallowed hard. 'It was a long time ago. Leave it in the past.'

Drew pulled back the hammer with a deafening click.

'Start talking,' he said.

66

Twenty years earlier

THEY PARKED THE JAGUAR *outside the off-licence. The sign over the door read* Marsh & Sons, Wines and Liquors for All Occasions. *Frank had been keeping an eye on the place for a while now. The shop was open late every night. There was only one woman who worked there, left to mind the place all on her own in this rough part of Stepney. It was almost too easy.*

'I'll go in first,' Frank said. 'Make sure the place is empty. You follow me in when I give you the signal.'

'Let's just go home,' Pat said. 'This dump isn't worth it.'

'Why?' Frank taunted. 'You scared?'

Pat Brennan didn't answer. He talked a good game but he was all mouth. That was Frank's opinion. Now it was time to see if he could deliver when the chips were down.

'It's late, Frank. You're drunk.'

'We'll be in and out in two minutes. I'll grab the blonde and

296

give her a slap. That'll keep her quiet. You empty the till while I take care of her.'

Frank opened the glove compartment and took out two black balaclavas. 'Put this on,' he said, tossing one of the masks to Pat.

Before Pat could argue, Frank was out of the car and crossing the street, turning his collar up as he approached the door. The road was dark, most of the street lights out of order. The shop doorway was propped open by a newspaper stand. Unsold copies of the Evening Standard. The usual headlines of chaos and destruction in far-off places.

Pat Brennan had a sinister feeling right down in the pit of his stomach. He wanted to run but he couldn't summon the strength. To leave Frank Egan to rob the place alone would be a death sentence for the poor woman behind the counter. He'd slice her up for fun.

Frank appeared in the shop doorway and nodded slowly. That meant the place was clear. Pat watched as Frank slipped his ski mask on. He swallowed hard. There was no backing out now. He opened the car door and crossed the street, pulling on his own balaclava as he walked. It was too small, the fabric too tight as he pulled it over his head. He could barely breathe through the material. Checking no one was watching, he jogged up to the door and stepped inside.

Music was playing in the dingy shop. An oldies station on the radio. A soul tune. The place stank of stale beer and desperation. The racks were full of bottles of cheap gut-rot vodka and cans of strong cider. It was a low-class street-drinker's paradise. The woman behind the counter had her back turned to the door as she straightened the dusty whisky bottles on a high shelf behind the till. She was blonde and petite, standing on a stepladder, dancing along to the radio, bouncing from foot to foot without a care in the world. She turned to look as she heard Pat enter.

She was startled to see the black masked faces staring back at her. 'What the . . .?'

'Don't move!' Frank Egan shouted.

She didn't listen. She jumped down from the ladder and started to run for the end of the counter. There had to be an alarm down there, Pat realized. Frank reached a hand over the counter and seized the woman by the hair. She screamed, more in fright than in pain, but loud enough to wake the whole neighbourhood. Pat felt the danger level ratchet up.

'Let me go!' she shrieked.

Frank swung a fist at her. He connected with the side of her face with a heavy crunch and she slumped to the floor.

He looked at Pat, his eyes blazing through the slit in his balaclava.

'Open the till. Get the money.'

'Let's just go,' Pat said.

'Do what I tell you, man,' Frank snarled.

The easiest way out of this was to follow Frank's instructions. Pat threw up the hatch, slid behind the counter and hurried to the till. The cash drawer was almost full, a solid day's takings neatly arranged in the separate compartments. Snatching up a plastic carrier bag, Pat began to grab notes by the fistful. As he did so, he looked down at the woman's hunched body. She had fallen on her side, her face pointed straight up at him, her eyes closed. Pat recognized her instantly.

It was Ron Miller's wife, he realized. He'd seen her at the

boxing gym a few times. What was her name? June. That was it. June Miller. She came in sometimes to drop off Ron's lunch and help him out around the place. Everyone liked her. She was fun, bubbly. A constant talker. What was Ron doing, letting his wife work in a late night off-licence like this? It was asking for trouble leaving her alone here. Pat remembered the sign Ron had put up over the ring. We are what we repeatedly do. Ron loved to shout it at the fighters as they sparred together. It was his motto and he used it constantly, saying it over and over, urging his boxers on as they trained.

A wave of regret hit Pat hard. We are what we repeatedly do, he thought. What Pat did most days was hurt people on Frank Egan's orders. Beat men to a pulp for a handful of dirty money. And what good did he do with the cash once he had it? Stayed out all night drinking and chasing women and wasting his earnings at the dog track. Neglected his wife and kids while he ran around with a psycho like Frank Egan. Now he'd sunk so low he was stealing the takings from an off-licence, staring down at the bruised face of a friend's wife. Pat felt about as worthless as he had ever done.

'Hurry up!' Frank shouted. 'I haven't got all night.'

'We need to make sure she's not hurt,' Pat said.

'What are you, soft? Just get the cash. Let's go!'

Pat grabbed the last of the banknotes and stuffed them into the carrier bag. He turned to leave. As he reached the hatch and took a step down on to the shop floor, he felt a stinging blow to the back of his head. Suddenly he was face down on the soiled linoleum, surrounded by broken glass and a pool of white rum. The world seemed to move in a woozy kaleidoscope before his eyes.

299

'You scumbag . . . you thieving low-life . . .'

A woman's voice was raging above him.

Pat looked round. It was June Miller. She must have regained consciousness while he wasn't looking. She had the remains of a Bacardi bottle in her hand, the jagged edge of broken glass pointed straight at him. Pat's head was pounding. The tight material of the balaclava was making him feel sick. It was like his brain was being squeezed. He reached up and pulled the mask off. June's eyes widened at the sight of his face.

'I know you,' she said. 'You go to my husband's gym.'

Pat raised a hand to his neck. Blood was pouring out. His fingers were slick with the stuff. The bottle had sliced a deep gouge into his flesh. June's face tightened in concern as she realized what had happened.

'Stay there,' she said. 'I'll get help.'

'Don't . . .' Pat croaked.

June turned to go into the back room. As she moved, a stunned look came to her face. Her mouth fell open as her gaze dropped to her chest. Pat followed her eyeline. Frank Egan was beside her, gripping the handle of the knife sticking out of her ribs. She grasped his arm as if to push him away but she lacked the strength.

'Serves you right,' Frank Egan spat. 'Nasty bitch.'

Pat got to his feet. He shoved Frank aside. Taking June in his arms, he laid her down on the grimy floor. Frank had buried the knife in her heart with all his strength. She was trying to speak but no words were coming. All around them, blood was pooling among the spilled booze and broken glass.

'Get moving!' Frank shouted.

He seized the back of Pat's coat and dragged him to the

door. Pat took one last look behind him. June was fading away, her eyes rolling back into her skull. There was nothing anyone could do for her now. The cold night hit him as they ran out and stumbled across the street. Frank opened the passenger door of the car and pushed Pat inside. He ran around and jumped behind the wheel and they set off in a squeal of tyres. Pat could feel the blood flowing from his neck, running down into the fabric of his shirt. He was awash with the stuff. We are what we repeatedly do. He looked at Frank and tried to speak.

'We are what we . . .' he whispered, his voice trailing off.

Frank scowled at him. 'What the hell did you say?'

Pat tried to finish the sentence but the words wouldn't come.

67

LEWIS READ THE greetings card once again. The writing was unmistakable. It must have been Ward who placed the warning sign on Maria Brennan's car. So she was the one he'd been searching for all this time. Ward had skilfully kept herself out of the spotlight, but now her distinctive handwriting had given her away. It was a mistake she'd regret. Lewis checked the time. It was nearly nine p.m. From what he had gathered about her, Lewis guessed that Olivia Ward would still be at the office.

'Turn around,' he said to Rachael. 'We're going to the Ever Sine building. I'll give you the address.'

Rachael threw a wild U-turn. Angry car horns sounded all around them as she accelerated back towards the south bank of the Thames. Lewis took out his phone and called Robert Carlson.

'Lewis. Are you OK?'

'I'm fine. I'm going to the Ever Sine building.'

'Why?'

'I don't have time to explain. I need you to call ahead and tell the security guards to let me in.'

Carlson hesitated for a moment. He could hear the urgency in Lewis's voice. 'I'll do it,' he said, 'but I'm coming too. I'll meet you there.'

'Fine. Be quick.'

Lewis hung up.

Rachael raced through the night-time traffic. When they reached the Ever Sine building, she parked on the windswept plaza before the entrance and they hurried into the lobby together. The guards saw them and opened the gates without challenge. The vast brick and iron atrium was completely deserted. The huge blackened steel casings of the old iron foundry loomed over the echoing space. Lewis led Rachael to the lift and they rode up to the top floor.

The lights were on in Olivia Ward's office. Lewis held a finger to his lips. Rachael nodded. They crept along the silent corridor towards the open door. Peering inside, they could see Ward deep in conversation, talking in halting sentences, her voice panicked. She was on speakerphone, the long-distance line crackling.

'I can't do that, Viktor,' she said forcefully. 'The money is untraceable. There's no way to get it back. I can't return any funds to Moscow. Andrei wanted the banking pathway destroyed to cover our tracks and I did exactly what he asked. The shell companies were shut down one by one as I moved the money around the globe.'

'I want my money back,' a voice shouted down the line. 'Otherwise I'll make you sorry.'

Ward hesitated. 'I don't like your tone, Viktor,' she said.

'My tone is the least of your worries.'

Lewis could hear the fear in Ward's voice. So this was the famous Viktor Zhirkov he was hearing via the speaker. He sounded desperate.

'You need to speak to Andrei about this,' Ward said. 'It was all his doing.'

'My son called me earlier. He was taken to hospital tonight. He was stabbed and underwent emergency surgery. I need you to go and collect him from the hospital and drive him to the airport. A plane will be waiting to fly you both back to Moscow tonight.'

Ward swallowed hard. 'You want me to fly to Moscow with Andrei?'

'Yes. I want you to come and explain yourself to me in person. I've paid you lavishly for the work you've done behind Carlson's back. Now I want you to show your loyalty.'

'And if I don't?'

'Then I suggest you find a very dark corner of the world to hide in. Because I will come looking for you. You can trust me on that.'

The line went dead as the call was disconnected. Lewis watched as Ward scratched nervously at the side of her neck. She was evidently unsettled. So it was Ward who had masterminded the financing for the power plant deal, he thought. She had betrayed Robert Carlson and plotted with his Russian partners. Now it looked like she'd been too clever for her own good. Lewis decided it was time to announce his presence.

'You've got a lot to answer for,' he said, walking into the office. Rachael followed on behind.

Olivia Ward swung round in her chair. She looked aghast as he approached her desk. 'Miller? What are you doing here?'

'I've come to ask you about this.'

He tossed the greetings card at her and Ward picked it up. She scanned the handwritten message.

'Where did you get this?' she asked.

'Never mind,' Lewis said. 'All that's important is the handwriting. It's identical to the note found on Maria Brennan's car.'

Ward flinched as she understood what he was implying. 'You're accusing me of killing Maria?' she said.

'If you didn't do it, you were there when it happened.' Lewis took out his phone. He showed Ward the photo of Emilia Carlson and Maria Brennan arguing with each other. 'You sent this picture to me, didn't you?'

Ward shook her head. 'You're clutching at straws, Miller.'

'I'll prove it,' Lewis said.

He rang the number that had sent him the photo earlier that day. All eyes in the room looked down at Ward's mobile, lying on her desktop. It remained silent.

From outside the office, the sound of a telephone began to ring out. Lewis turned towards the door. It was coming from the desk of Ward's assistant.

He walked out of the room and looked around. The desk was unoccupied. A mobile was ringing next to the computer keyboard, juddering across the surface of the desk as it vibrated. It was a cheap, disposable handset. A burner phone, Lewis thought. It was probably unregistered and untraceable. He rang off and the phone fell silent.

Ward walked from her office door and stood next to him. She tossed the greetings card on to her assistant's desk.

'Do you really think I have time to write my own thank-you cards?' she said triumphantly.

68

'SO WHAT HAPPENS now?' Glenn asked.

Drew stood over him. He lowered the gun until it was pointed at his friend's leg. 'Now I put a bullet in your knee.'

'Come on, Drew,' Glenn pleaded. 'Don't do it.'

'Why not? Would you have shown my sister any mercy?'

'You know what Maria was like. She was a troublemaker. She was causing problems for a lot of powerful people. Maria didn't know when to keep her mouth shut.'

'You're supposed to be my friend,' Drew said. 'You should've come to me and told me what was going on. I would have got Maria to calm down.'

'No one could calm Maria down. Especially not you.'

Drew shook his head dismissively. 'Maria was a civilian. Civilians are off limits. You know that. You didn't have to kill her.'

'I didn't kill her,' Glenn begged. 'I promise. She was dead before I could set up the meeting.'

'Did Frank do it?'

Glenn shook his head. 'No. He would have told me if he had. Anyway, mixing chemicals is too complicated. That isn't his style.'

'Why don't we call him? Get him to come over so I can ask him myself. While we're at it, I can see if Frank remembers a rainy night in Stepney all those years ago.'

Glenn cowered. His hands were shaking. 'Don't call him, Drew. He'll kill us both.'

'Not if I don't give him the chance.'

Glenn was thinking fast. His eyes were darting around wildly as his brain tried to find a way out of the fix he was in. 'How much would it cost to get you to forget about this?' he asked.

Drew frowned. 'What do you mean?'

'I can pay you. Enough to get away from here. Enough to leave London for good.'

Drew looked at his friend with a mixture of curiosity and scorn. 'You don't have that kind of money,' he said.

'I'll show you.'

Glenn stood slowly and walked over to the fish tank while Drew kept the gun trained on him. Drew watched as Glenn lifted the lid from the tank, rolled his sleeves up and dipped his hands down into the bubbling water. In among the gravel at the bottom of the tank, he uncovered a plastic box. Fan-tailed guppies and Siamese fighting fish swam lazily around his arms as he shook it free. Streams of water ran down on to the living-room carpet as he lifted the box out and laid it on the floor.

Glenn opened the waterproof case. It was full of bundles of twenty-pound notes, strapped together with elastic bands. 'There's almost fifty grand there,' Glenn said, wide-eyed. 'Take it. It's yours.'

Drew could see his friend's naked desperation. 'Where did you get so much cash?' he asked.

'I sold a kilo of heroin.'

'No way. You're putting that stuff in your arm, not making a profit from it.'

'OK, I won it,' Glenn said. 'At the races.'

'Stop bullshitting me.'

Glenn was trembling. 'Just take it. Who cares where it came from?'

Drew thought for a moment. 'Pass me one of those bundles,' he said.

Glenn took a stack of banknotes and tossed them over. Drew unstrapped the elastic band and held a crisp, new twenty-pound note up to the light.

'You dirty scumbag!' he said, throwing the money at Glenn. The notes fluttered to the ground around him. 'You can keep your blood money.'

'Why?'

Drew raised the gun, ready to shoot. 'Because it's fake.'

'You're lying,' Glenn said and picked up a note. He studied it in disbelief.

'It's worthless,' Drew said. 'And what's worse – I know how you got it.'

69

LEWIS PICKED UP a notepad from the assistant's desktop. It was covered in messages and scribbles in cheap blue biro. Hurriedly written names and addresses. Long lunch orders and random shopping lists. Lewis looked closely at the pad. The handwriting was identical to the message in the greetings card. His mind was racing. He remembered his last visit to the Ever Sine building. How Ward's assistant had whispered a warning to him out on the street as she escorted him outside. The hushed way she had given Emilia Carlson's name as a suspect. It had been a ruse to throw him off the scent, Lewis realized. He kicked himself for falling for it.

'Where's your assistant now?' he asked.

Ward shrugged. 'Around here somewhere. If I work late, so does she.'

'When will she be back?'

'Not long. She knows I don't like her straying too far.'

With a chime, the lift arrived at the executive floor and the doors opened at the far end of the corridor. Rachael and Lewis turned towards the sound. Ward's assistant stepped out, seemingly lost in thought. After a few paces, she stopped as she noticed the people standing around her desk. The significance of it seemed to hit her immediately and her face dropped in shock. The coffee cup slipped from her hand and hit the floor with a steaming splash as she turned and ran.

Lewis set off after her. The assistant pushed through a door at the end of the corridor and he followed her. It led into a darkened research lab lined with benches full of equipment. She was sprinting through the room, shoving microscopes and glass vials and containers of liquid on to the floor behind her. Lewis lost his footing as he ran through the debris, grabbing the countertop to keep his balance. Regaining his composure, he had lost sight of her. An exit door at the back of the laboratory was standing open. Lewis ran to it and stepped through cautiously. The door led on to an old fire escape that twisted upwards towards the high industrial ceiling of the Victorian building. Lewis craned his neck to peer up the black ironwork of the staircase. The assistant was on the highest level, standing by an emergency door that led out on to the roof. She shoved the handle with all her strength. It was locked.

Slowly Lewis began to ascend the steps. As the assistant realized she was cornered, she grew increasingly frantic. She began to climb over the railings at the edge of the fire escape in her desperation.

Lewis called to her. 'Stop! I won't come any closer. I promise.'

The assistant ignored him and hauled herself over the barrier. Standing on the outside of the fire escape platform, balanced precariously on her toes, she gripped the railings tightly in her fists. Lewis looked down the eight storeys to the

311

hard stone floor of the atrium far below. His knees weakened at the sight.

The assistant was wild with fear. 'Get away or I'll jump!' she called out to him.

Lewis backed off, his body language calm and reassuring. 'It's OK,' he said. 'I'm not going to hurt you.'

The young woman was half crazed with terror, her face drained of all colour. 'I didn't kill Maria, I swear,' she wailed.

'I believe you,' Lewis said gently. 'Now climb back over the railings and we can talk it through.'

'Maria was my friend. Andrei knew she trusted me. He begged me to take her out to the marshes that night. I did what he asked. I persuaded her to go out there with me but I thought they were only going to scare her.'

'Why would they want to scare her?'

'To make her drop her wrongful dismissal claim. Andrei told me the court case was going to expose him. He had to find a way to stop Maria speaking out.'

'Did Andrei kill Maria?' Lewis asked.

The assistant looked distraught at the notion. 'No. Andrei would never do something like that. He's a good man. He only does what's best for us.'

Lewis's brow furrowed. 'Us?'

'Andrei loves me,' the assistant said defiantly. 'When this is all over, he's going to take me away with him. Just the two of us. We can be together then. He promised me.'

She was still balancing on the edge of the platform on the tips of her shoes, holding on to the railings for dear life. The long drop down to the atrium floor yawned beneath her. Lewis tried not to look. The idea that a man like Andrei Zhirkov was going to start a life with this mousey young woman was a fantasy, Lewis thought. Andrei had lied to her to persuade her to do his bidding. It was a cynical move. The assistant's voice was deranged with emotion as she hung on to the fire escape railings. Lewis knew he had to distract her to make her calm down.

'Tell me your name,' he said.

'Anya.'

There was a slight East European accent as she answered. It was so soft Lewis hadn't noticed it the first time they'd met.

'You're Ukrainian?' he asked.

'I came here when I was a young girl. That's how Maria and I first became friends. We found out we came from similar backgrounds. We knew the same Ukrainian people here in London. We even went to the same church.'

'You wrote the note that was left on Maria's windscreen? You were there when she died.'

Anya began to sob. 'When I saw what happened to Maria, I didn't want anyone else to get hurt. It was horrible. I couldn't stand for that to happen to someone else.'

'Did you send me the photo of Maria and Emilia Carlson arguing?'

She nodded.

'Did Emilia have anything to do with Maria's death?'

'No. I was told to make it look like she had, that's all. I became friends with her when she worked here. We both had miserable jobs so it wasn't hard. After Maria died, I stayed in touch with Emilia and went to her stupid pool parties. Andrei told me to spread rumours about her. I did it to protect him.'

'Tell me who killed Maria.'

'I don't know,' Anya said.

'But you were there?'

'Yes, but I'd never met the man before. He was waiting out at the marshes when we arrived. Maria seemed to know him. She wanted to speak with him alone in her car. That's how he was able to kill her.'

'What was his name?' Lewis demanded.

Anya shook her head. 'I don't know.'

'Then tell me what he looked like?'

She was about to answer when there was a commotion in the atrium far below. Lewis looked down. Robert Carlson rushed in through the entrance doors, followed by a squad of police officers. They saw the scene unfolding high on the wrought-iron fire escape and stopped in their tracks. Robert Carlson stared up, his face filled with horror.

Panicked at the sound of the police sirens, Anya twisted her body to look down at the distant gathering. One foot slipped and she grabbed at the railings to steady herself.

'Why are they here?' she screamed at Lewis. 'What's going on?'

'Just keep looking at me,' Lewis said calmly. He began to inch towards her, ready to make a grab for her hands.

Anya turned to Lewis, her eyes filled with despair. 'I don't want to go to prison,' she said.

'You won't. I promise.'

'I'm sorry for what happened to Maria,' Anya sobbed. 'I really am.'

A stillness came to her face, a sense of resolution. A flicker of regret passed behind her eyes as she released her grip from the iron railings and her body began to slide backwards. Lewis lunged towards her, grasping at her fingers and the sleeves of her jacket but he was too late. Gravity took hold and Anya fell, her wide brown eyes locked with his. Horrified, Lewis watched as she plummeted down, landing hard on the grey flagstones far below.

70

FRANK EGAN DROVE at speed to his nephew's house. The text he had received from Glenn had rattled him. *Bad news on the Coldharbour Marshes job. Come to my place asap.* Glenn had been a liability recently. The screw-up with the bookie had been his last chance. Glenn had better have a good reason for dragging him over there at this hour, or he was out of the business. Frank couldn't afford to carry him any longer. He was getting older now, slower, and he needed someone to take the strain. A successor he could trust. Frank had wanted Glenn to replace him but now he wasn't so sure. He didn't need his nephew going around the city creating more problems than he solved. That was no way to run a business.

Frank pulled up at the kerb. The lights in the house were off. He walked down the garden path and saw that the front door was ajar. Stepping inside the hallway, he called out Glenn's name. There was no answer. Through the open living-room door he could see the tropical fish tank bubbling away, the walls lit up by its soft neon glow. Beside it a figure was slumped on the sofa, money showered all around him like fallen leaves. A thick scattering of twenty-pound notes. Frank pushed the door open and rushed inside.

Glenn was barely breathing. A syringe and a packet of brown powder lay on the table beside him. Glenn had promised him his drug-dealing days were over. Now he was injecting the stuff. Frank raised his hand to slap his nephew hard.

There was a movement behind him and Frank spun around instinctively. A figure was standing in the doorway, his features in shadow. Frank could see the gun in his hand, pointed straight at him. If he was going to shoot, he would have done so already, Frank reasoned. He weighed up his options. He was too old and slow to make a lunge for it. He would just have to talk his way out of trouble. Frank watched as the figure stepped forward into the greenish glow from the fish tank. He squinted, his eyes struggling to focus in the semi-darkness. For a moment, it looked like someone from his deep past, as young as the last time Frank had laid eyes on him. But that couldn't be true, Frank told himself. Pat Brennan had been dead for twenty years. He had dug the pit and thrown in the body himself. Watched as the corpse was covered in cement.

Frank breathed out as the figure stepped closer. It was Drew Brennan. 'Jesus. You're the spitting image of your father,' he said, sighing in relief. 'For a moment it was like seeing a ghost.'

'Do you believe in ghosts?' Drew asked.

'Not really.'

'Well, now's a good time to start. You'll be seeing some very soon.'

Frank bristled at the hostile tone. He'd assumed Drew was

317

only protecting his wasted nephew. 'You'd best remember who you're talking to, son.'

'Only if you start giving me some answers.'

'What kind of answers?'

'Was Pat still alive when you buried him?'

Frank's pulse quickened at the mention of Pat's name. 'What's got into you, son?' he barked. 'Have you lost it completely?'

Drew raised the gun. 'Just answer the question, Frank. Did you kill him before you threw him in the hole you dug?'

'Who told you that?'

'Who do you think?'

Frank looked at his nephew in disgust. 'Glenn's out of his mind. The drugs have ruined him. You can't believe a word he says.'

'Tell me what really happened, Frank. I want to hear it from you.'

Frank could see there was no point in denying it. Glenn must have spilled the whole story. His voice was hoarse and cracked as he spoke. 'Pat was dead minutes after we left that off-licence,' he said. 'The crazy bitch who worked there had cut through an artery in his neck. There was nothing I could do to help him.'

'Was he still breathing when you poured the cement on him?'

Frank shook his head gravely. 'He was dead and cold.'

'So you covered him in concrete and walked away?'

'Your father knew the score, son. What did you want me to do? Pay for a funeral cortège and two white horses?'

'Why didn't you take him to hospital?'

'It was too late. He'd lost too much blood.'

'Bullshit,' Drew said. 'He'd seen you commit murder. You didn't want any witnesses.'

Frank wagged a finger before him. 'Listen to yourself, son. You're not so different from me. You know the rules. It's survival of the fittest out there. That's why I need men like you. Winners. Glenn can't cut it. I've given him his final chance and he's blown it. You wanted a job? Well, I'm offering you one. Forget about all this and come and work for me. No more torching cars. I'll send you straight to the top where the big money is. I guarantee it.'

Drew shook his head. 'Not a chance. I've got a plan of my own worked out.'

Frank looked over at Glenn. He was still comatose, the money littered around his slumped form. 'You're going to take this drug money? How long will that last you? A few months at most? I'm offering you the chance to earn cash like you've never seen before.'

'I'm not taking any of this money,' Drew said. 'Not a penny.'

What he was hearing didn't make sense to a man like Frank Egan. Money was his only motivation in life. 'Why would you leave it?' he asked.

'Because it's worthless,' Drew said. 'It's all counterfeit.'

Frank picked up a note and rubbed it between his fingers. The paper was harsh and sticky to the touch. He tried another and it was the same. It was all fake. There were thousands of pounds in counterfeit bills scattered around the room.

'Where did Glenn get so much fake cash?' he asked.

'Adem the bookie.'

Frank took a moment to think this through. Why would Adem pass a load of dodgy money to his nephew? When the

319

realization hit him, Frank slammed one heavy fist into the other in disgust. 'So Glenn was scamming me?' he spat. 'My own nephew.'

'Adem and Glenn were working together. When I went down to the car wash, Adem gave me a bag of fake money. The gun was a distraction. They knew I'd have to throw the bag away when the police chased me. Then they could blame me for losing your money and keep the real winnings for themselves. But Glenn messed up as usual. He took his cut from Adem without bothering to check it first. Adem gave him fifty grand of fake twenties. You and I both got scammed, but Glenn got double-crossed too.'

Frank looked at his wayward nephew in despair. 'So that's where family loyalty gets you,' he said. 'I never should have trusted him.'

'You should never trust anyone, Frank. I thought you knew that?'

Frank Egan looked old and tired in the eerie light of the room. He was aware that his power was waning, his authority almost gone. 'I need people like you, Drew,' he pleaded. 'My business can't survive without new blood. You wanted a chance? Come and work for me. Forget anything else that might have happened. It's ancient history. You've got to put the past behind you.'

'Behind me?' Drew hissed incredulously. 'None of this can ever be behind me. It's not even the past. I live with it every day. My sister and I had to grow up without a dad. My mum had to spend her life not knowing if her husband was alive or dead. She couldn't grieve. It messed with her mind and she took her frustrations out on me – still does. Guess who I'm going to take mine out on?'

320

'Kill me and you'll go back to prison,' Frank said. 'Work for me and I'll make you rich.'

Drew lifted his chin in defiance. 'This is for my mother,' he said.

Frank saw Drew's expression harden. He tried to lunge for the gun but Drew didn't hesitate. He fired, pulling the trigger twice in quick succession. Frank stumbled and grasped his chest where the bullets had struck, pulling at his clothes, falling as his legs buckled beneath him. He lay there gasping, his lips moving, blood bubbling from his mouth and nostrils. Drew watched until his body became still.

Good riddance, Drew thought.

A haze of gun smoke hung in the room. The sour scent of cordite. He didn't have much time. Drew went into the kitchen, found a towel and wiped the gun clean. He returned to the living room and walked over to Glenn, still out cold on the sofa. Drew checked his pulse. It was stable. The bruise on his temple was livid where Drew had struck him with the butt of the pistol. Glenn would have a headache when he finally woke up, but he'd have a lot more important problems to worry about by then. Drew thought of all the years they'd been friends. The good times they'd spent together. How they'd been inseparable since they were kids. Then he remembered collecting the money from Adem. The police chase across Tower Bridge. The deadly meeting with Frank in the underground car park. Glenn had set him up without a second thought. Risked his life for a few thousand pounds. Now Drew was going to pay him back. It was only fair.

Drew lifted Glenn's hand and gently placed the gun into it, putting his finger on the trigger. He aimed at Frank's body and fired a shot, making sure forensic deposits were left on Glenn's clothing.

Leaving the chaos behind him, Drew slipped out of the back door and jogged through the garden. He climbed over the back wall and crept along the alleyway until he reached the main road. He kept his head down, walking briskly until he found a phone box. He went inside and dialled 999.

'I need the police,' he said. 'I think I just heard shots being fired.'

71

LEWIS AND RACHAEL watched as a team of paramedics loaded Anya's body on to a gurney, covered her in a blanket and wheeled her out to the waiting ambulance. The police had cordoned off the Ever Sine building with criss-crossing lines of plastic tape. A small crowd had gathered outside to rubber-neck at the emergency vehicles in the plaza, blue lights flashing in the darkness. Lewis was seated in the cavernous lobby, his head in his hands, looking crushed. Rachael touched his face tenderly. She could tell how hard he'd taken Anya's death.

'It was my fault,' Lewis said. 'I should never have chased her out on to the fire escape. As soon as I saw how crazy she was acting, I should have backed off.'

Rachael shook her head gently. 'You had no way of know-ing what would happen, Lewis. It was an accident.'

Robert Carlson approached. 'The police want to speak to you, Lewis,' he said solemnly. 'They're interviewing Olivia now. Taking her statement. We only have a few minutes until they take over the investigation.'

Lewis looked across the lobby. Two plain-clothes female detectives were speaking to Ward, taking notes on clipboards. She looked like she was trying to fend off their questions, squirming as if she was hiding secrets. Ward had known all along that Andrei Zhirkov had sent Anya to do his dirty work out at Coldharbour Marshes, Lewis thought. The more she had to explain herself, the more she would inevitably dig herself into the mire. Lewis doubted even an accomplished liar like Ward could dodge her way out of this one.

'What's wrong with Olivia?' Carlson asked. He had noticed her odd behaviour too.

'She's scared,' Lewis said. 'She's in league with the Zhirkovs. Anya would still be alive if Olivia hadn't played a part in manipulating her.'

Carlson looked quizzical. 'You think she's been scheming behind my back?'

'We heard Olivia arguing with Viktor Zhirkov on the phone when we arrived here earlier. It sounded like he was issuing orders to recover the money he's paid you for the Coldharbour Marshes project.'

Carlson nodded sagely. 'I always suspected Olivia was serving two masters.'

'I was so close,' Lewis said despondently. 'Anya was about to describe Maria's killer to me. I could have identified him if we'd kept talking a little longer. Once the police take over the case, they'll go back to square one. Everything will slow down to a snail's pace. Maria's killer will never be found now.'

Carlson wrung his hands. He knew his arrival had only escalated tensions. 'When you called me and said you were coming here tonight, I felt I had no choice but to alert the police. I thought you were in danger, Lewis. I had to bring police backup, if only as a precaution.'

'I'm not blaming you, Robert. You did the right thing.'

'So it was Anya who enticed Maria out to the marshes,' Carlson said. 'I never even knew they were friends.'

Lewis tried to remember all the details of the conversation out on the fire escape. He had been searching for clues for days now and the key to the mystery still eluded him. He tried to focus on the cold, logical facts but his mind was racing. The turmoil of the evening had drained him but he had to find the answers he was looking for. It was the only way he would find any peace.

'Anya said that a man was waiting out at the marshes when she went there with Maria,' Lewis said. 'I'm certain Maria wouldn't have spoken alone with a stranger at night. She must have known him. She'd dressed smartly as if she was going out to a business meeting, as if she knew this person professionally somehow. Anya said that Maria was alone in the car with him while they talked. It must have been someone Maria was comfortable with, someone she trusted. We know Maria died by inhaling poisonous gas. There couldn't be any violence or signs of a struggle because that would blow the suicide cover story. Maria had to allow this person to sit with her voluntarily.'

Carlson could see how tired and frustrated Lewis was. It had been an epic night of action.

'Let the police take over now,' Carlson said. 'Tell them everything you know and put this behind you. That's all you can do. Then you should go home to rest.'

Lewis was adamant. 'I'm fine. I need to think, that's all.'

Carlson took a silver hip flask from his jacket. He unscrewed the cap and handed it to Lewis.

'Have a drink,' he said. 'You look like you need it.'

Lewis accepted gratefully. He tipped the flask back and took a long hit. It was sharp and strong on the back of his throat. Carlson rested a paternal hand on his shoulder.

'You should be proud of your efforts, Lewis,' he said. 'You've shown real determination to get this far.'

Lewis brushed off the compliment. 'That's not good enough,' he said. 'I have to solve the case or I've failed.'

'Don't be so hard on yourself.'

'I have no choice now. I owe it to Maria to find her killer.'

Lewis took another sip from the flask. He rolled the liquid in his mouth. The bitter, peppery flavour was familiar.

He looked at Carlson inquisitively. 'Is this cognac?' he asked.

'One of the finest,' Carlson said. 'A rare vintage.'

'I've already had a glass of this today.'

'Impossible,' Carlson said. 'That flask is filled with one of the most valuable cognacs in the world. There are only five bottles in existence.'

Lewis took another sip. 'I'm sure it's the same.'

'You must be mistaken. It was a gift. A very special one.'

Lewis felt the hairs rise on the back of his neck. He jumped to his feet and faced Carlson, his eyes lit with astonishment.

'Who gave it to you?' he demanded excitedly.

72

THE CAR WASH was deserted when Drew walked on to the forecourt. The place was dark, the Portakabin silent. He remembered his last visit. If the money Adem had given him was fake, then the real cash had to be stashed somewhere.

He walked to the rear of the hut and pressed his ear to the window. It was silent. From his bag, he took out a small crowbar and forced open the window frame. Carefully he began to climb inside.

The interior of the cabin was full of the stale stench of mildew. The previous piles of counterfeit designer clothes and handbags now lay scattered around. Drew pulled himself in through the broken window, crouching low as he hit the floor. He went to the door he had seen Adem enter on his last visit and pushed it open. Inside was a dank, foul-smelling toilet. The stink made Drew retch.

Holding his breath, he stood in front of the toilet bowl and began to feel with the palms of his hands along the wall panels. They all felt secure. Lifting the lid, he peered inside the cistern. Nothing. There had to be a hiding place in here some-where. He could feel it in his bones. Looking up, he saw that the edge of one ceiling tile was scuffed, with grimy fingerprints smeared on one corner. Drew stood on the rim of the toilet, pressed on the surface of the tile and it pushed up easily. He stood on tiptoe, peering up into the roof cavity of the hut. The edge of a cardboard box was visible in the darkness. Drew reached in and lifted it out.

Setting the box on the floor, he ripped open the tape that sealed it shut and looked inside. The box was full of brick-sized stacks of twenty-pound notes. Drew took one out and lifted a note up to his flashlight. It was real, the foil strip and water-mark all genuine. He looked at the bundles filling the box. There must be two hundred and fifty grand inside, he reckoned. And it was all his now.

73

ANDREI LOOKED UP from the hospital bed as the curtain surrounding his cubicle was pushed back. Olivia Ward peered in
through the gap. Recognizing Andrei, she hurried inside and
pulled the curtain closed so they were hidden from the sharp-
eyed nurses patrolling the recovery room.

'We have to be quick,' Ward whispered.

'My father sent you?' Andrei asked hopefully.

'He's arranged for a private jet to fly you back to Moscow
tonight.'

Andrei was still groggy from the strong painkillers he had
been given, his thigh swathed in a thick dressing beneath the
hem of a surgical gown. A heady smell of sweat and disinfect-
ant filled the cubicle. Olivia Ward slid an arm around Andrei's
shoulders to help him sit up, then began to gather his clothes
from the chair where they had been folded.

'Is my father angry?' Andrei asked, pulling out the saline
drip that fed into his arm with a pained grimace.

Ward nodded. 'You know what Viktor's like. He doesn't

appreciate complications. He's unhappy at the way the Maria Brennan situation was handled.'

Andrei gave a low growl of frustration through gritted teeth. That night out at Coldharbour Marshes had been the source of so much trouble, he thought. If only it had been handled properly in the first place, none of this chaos would be happening now. He smacked an angry fist into his open palm.

'I should have killed that damn Brennan girl myself,' he said. 'It was a mistake to send amateurs to do the job.'

Ward looked at him with a dark expression full of reproach. 'But you did send them, Andrei. You organized the killing. You arranged the whole thing. That's what your father is upset about. He holds you fully responsible.'

Andrei knew she was right. He was going to have to face the consequences. Too weak to pull on his own clothes, he perched on the edge of the bed as Ward helped him into his suit trousers. He looked at her indignantly.

'I know my father will blame me,' he said, 'but I played my part to perfection. I mixed the container of chemicals. I arranged for Maria's phone to be hacked so it looked like she'd visited suicide sites. I forced Anya to convince Maria to drive out there with her. I set up all those arrangements without a glitch. But I had to send someone else to do the actual deed – that's where the plan failed. If I could have killed her myself, I would have.'

Ward stood back and looked him in the eye. 'You, Andrei Zhirkov, would have killed Maria Brennan?'

She posed the question the way a prosecution lawyer would ask a defendant in court. The formal tone of the question made Andrei pause.

'Yes,' he answered. 'Just like I killed that lawyer Sobel.'

Ward breathed out. A tension seemed to leave her. From her pocket, she took out her phone and held it up. Andrei could see the voice recorder running.

Outside the cubicle, footsteps slapped on the hard linoleum and the sound of radios crackled. The curtain was flung open and Andrei was confronted with the satisfied faces of half a dozen uniformed police, handcuffs at the ready.

'What is this?' Andrei asked, his voice full of trepidation. Inside, he already knew the answer. Ward had made a deal to save herself and he had blundered into the trap.

Ward gave a sigh of relief. 'This?' she said. 'This is the end of the road.'

74

IL SORRENTO WAS an Establishment haunt. All the legal firms in the City spent fortunes there, wining and dining their high-profile clients in an effort to drum up business. Standing at the restaurant door, one foot on the threshold, Lewis felt like he had made it. This was the moment he had been striving for all these years. The reward for the relentless hours at the office. The sacrifices he'd made. It was the finishing line. He had arrived.

He stepped inside the restaurant and was greeted by the manager. The party from Renfrew and Hall was in a back room, the manager informed him. A waitress was summoned to lead him through the long dining room. Lewis could feel the heat from the open kitchen as he passed. Smell the garlic and rosemary and the pungent aroma of roasting lamb.

In the private room, the meal had already been served. The lawyers from Renfrew and Hall were seated at a long table. Expensive bottles of claret and burgundy were lined up, the starched white tablecloth already stained red with spillages.

The lawyers were purple-cheeked, their eyes glassy. They looked appreciatively at Lewis as he entered the room and raised their glasses in greeting.

Charlie King beamed at him from the head of the table, his silver hair combed back from his statesman-like face. His navy lounge suit and silk club tie were immaculate.

'So glad you finally made it, Lewis,' he said. 'I've saved a place for you next to me. There's still time to order something before the kitchen closes.'

Lewis accepted the seat that King offered him. He held himself still for a moment, taking it all in. Savouring the feeling of success before he tore it all down.

'Why did you kill Maria Brennan?' he asked flatly.

King's face twitched. 'I don't know what you're talking about,' he said.

'I've been all over London,' Lewis said. 'Searching everywhere, when it was you I was looking for all along.'

King glanced uneasily along the table. The other lawyers were too busy gorging themselves on dessert to pay any attention to their private conversation.

'You're tired, Lewis,' King said, trying to change the subject. 'You've been working too hard. But I forgive you. Now you must order. You look famished.'

'I don't want your hospitality. I want the truth. Why did you kill Maria Brennan? Did Andrei Zhirkov order you to do it?'

King was restraining himself, trying not to let his emotions show. The harder he tried, the more the muscles in his face twitched and spasmed. 'What makes you think I could have anything to do with such a terrible crime?' he asked.

Lewis fixed him with an icy stare. 'Because I know it was you,

Charlie. I was at a complete loss until a sip of cognac betrayed you. Robert Carlson was given the same brand by Viktor Zhirkov. That cognac is one of the rarest in existence. There are only a handful of bottles in the world. Zhirkov gives them as gifts to people who do his dirty work. People like you and Carlson. As soon as I tasted it, I made the connection with you.'

King looked unconvinced. 'That isn't proof,' he said. 'It won't stand up in court.'

'But I've got something else. Something much more damning.'

'Such as?'

'The contract you left in Maria Brennan's car.'

King's face flushed crimson.

'I was looking in the wrong place all the time,' Lewis continued. 'I was scouring the contents of the paperwork, trying to find something incriminating in the clauses. I was concentrating on how the contract had been drafted – the legal terminology and the financial structure. But all along, I should have been focusing on the document itself. The actual pages. Where the physical copy had come from. Who it belonged to. The contract found in Maria Brennan's car is yours, Charlie. You can't deny it. It's got your fingerprints all over it.'

King's eyes were darkening rapidly. 'Maria Brennan could have got that contract from any number of places.'

Lewis jabbed a finger at his superior. 'But she didn't. It came from you. You left it in her car when you killed her. Maria was persuaded to go out to the marshes by her friend Anya. She thought she was going to a business meeting, so she dressed formally. My guess is that you told her there was a chance she could stop the hydrogen plant from being built. You knew how much she wanted to save that nature reserve. You insinuated that as Carlson's legal representative you could make him see sense. That way Maria agreed to sit in the car with you alone so you could talk privately. Andrei had already given you the chemicals mixed up in a sealed container. You only needed to open it at the right moment, step out of the car and watch as she suffocated. But you forgot to take the contract, didn't you? You left it behind in the car. You couldn't open the car door because the gas would escape. You had to leave the folder behind. There was no other choice. If you opened the door, it would ruin the scheme to make Maria's death appear as a suicide. She couldn't have opened the door to let the gas out herself, could she? You prayed that no one would ever trace the contract back to you, didn't you, Charlie? Well, guess what? Your prayers have failed.'

King took a moment before speaking. He wiped his mouth with the corner of his napkin. 'I can see you're a smart young man, Lewis,' he said, his voice full of authority. 'You've got a bright future ahead of you. The brightest I've ever seen. Don't jeopardize it all for a woman who wouldn't listen to reason. Don't make the same mistake she made.'

'What mistake, Charlie?'

'Biting off more than you can chew. You're smarter than that. You can go right to the very top if you show loyalty.'

Lewis laughed derisively. 'Are you going to make me an offer now?'

'Why not? Offers and acceptances make the world go round.'

'You think you can buy me off?'

'I'm not buying you, Lewis. I'm rewarding you.'

'What will you give me?'

'Anything,' King hissed, seizing his hand desperately. 'Name your price.'

Lewis shook him away. He looked at his exalted superior with disgust, repulsed at the sight of an old man desperate not to lose his privileges. 'I've been chased and beaten and almost killed,' he said, 'all because I wanted to do my job. To do what I was trained for. I've dreamed of being a lawyer all my life, but not like this.'

Lewis stood, pushed his chair back into place and picked up a wine glass. He tapped it with a knife and the table turned to him as if he were about to raise a toast. The voices of the feasting lawyers dropped to silence.

'I suggest you drink up,' Lewis said, a note of satisfaction in his voice. 'In about five seconds, a squad of police officers are coming through that door. They only want to arrest Charlie King, but I'm sure they'll handcuff any smart-mouthed lawyers who get in their way.'

With that, the doors burst open on cue. A gang of excited police piled into the room, heading straight towards the startled figure of Charlie King. None of his colleagues attempted to help him. Lewis turned to the two female detectives as they entered side by side. They nodded to him in solemn gratitude for his efforts.

Lewis left the restaurant and strode out on to the night-time streets, his hands shoved deep in his pockets. The night drew close around him as he walked down to the Thames in the pouring rain. On the banks of the river, looking down into the dark water, he took out his phone and made a call.

75

IRINA KOVAL WAS alone. The newspaper clippings of Maria's suicide were spread on the coffee table before her. She had always known the reports about her daughter's death were lies. She felt no sense of triumph now the truth was known. When the front door opened and she heard Drew come home, she was simply glad not to be alone any more.

'I know who killed Maria,' she told him bitterly. 'Lewis Miller called me. It was Lewis's boss at the law firm. Charlie King. The police arrested him tonight. He met Maria out at the marshes and—'

Drew held up a hand to interrupt her. He was breathless, fizzing with energy. 'You'll have to tell me the rest while we drive,' he said. 'We have to leave here right now.'

Irina was confused. 'Leave? Where are we going?'

'Anywhere. We're getting out of London.'

'Why?'

He dropped a bag at her feet. It landed with a solid thump on the threadbare carpet. 'Open it,' Drew said.

Irina slid the zip back apprehensively and peered inside. The bag was stacked full of pristine twenty-pound notes, bundles of them piled up to the brim.

Her eyes widened at the sight. 'Where did you get all this money?' she asked.

Drew tried to act cool. 'Don't worry about that.'

'But I am worried, Drew.'

He shrugged. 'I got it from a man who doesn't need it any more.'

'Why doesn't he need it?'

'Because he's dead,' Drew said flatly. 'Anyway, it's rightfully ours. This money is owed to us for all the years of misery and heartache we've had together.'

Irina looked up at her son. She was fearful at the manic look in his eye.

'Sit down, Drew,' she said. 'Tell me what's going on. Otherwise I'm not going anywhere.'

Drew did as he was asked. He thought about everything that had happened that night. Everything he'd heard from Glenn. From Frank. The secret of his father's fate that had remained hidden for so many years. He didn't know quite where to start.

76

IT WAS A clear, bright morning. London was bathed in sunshine. The streets were busy, the pavements crowded now the weather had improved. Rachael drove Lewis to Whitechapel to return the photos and cards they had found at Coldharbour Marshes. It seemed fitting to give them back to Irina now Maria's killer had been arrested.

Lewis flicked through the pictures as they drove. The photographs were faded and water-stained but still intact. Maria's hopeful, innocent face stared back at him. Lewis knew he had done all he could to find justice for her.

'The police called this morning,' he said to Rachael. 'They told me that Charlie King has confessed to Maria's murder. He's asking for leniency in return for giving evidence against the Zhirkovs.'

'Will the police agree?' Rachael asked.

'I hope not. King deserves to rot in prison for a long time for what he did to Maria. Apparently he's been working secretly for Viktor Zhirkov for years. Maria's wrongful dismissal case threatened to expose him. King was in so deep that it was easy for the Zhirkovs to blackmail him into killing her. He's a lawyer so Maria never suspected she was in danger. When they were alone together that night, her guard was completely down.'

'If it wasn't for you, he'd have got away with it,' Rachael said.

Lewis gave a short shrug. 'Maria's still dead. There's nothing I can do about that.'

She smiled at him affectionately. 'You're not a miracle worker, Lewis. Only a lawyer.'

'I'm not even that any more.'

'Why?'

'I've quit. I can't stay at the firm now. I've just had one of the senior partners arrested. My reputation in the City is destroyed.'

Rachael was outraged. 'They should be giving you a promotion. What you've done is remarkable.'

Lewis smiled wryly at her earnestness. 'You've never worked for a City law firm,' he said. 'It's only profit they reward, not virtue.'

When they arrived at Crowmoor House, Lewis gathered the cards and photos and they took the lift together up to the fourteenth floor. Walking along the landing, Lewis knocked on Irina's front door. There was no answer so he knocked again.

After a few minutes, Rachael pressed her face to the kitchen window and peered through. 'The place looks half empty,' she said.

Lewis stood beside her. He cupped his hands against the glass. Most of the furniture was still in place but the pictures and family photographs had been taken down from the walls. Only faded patches of paintwork remained.

'Did Irina tell you she was moving out?' Rachael asked.

Lewis shook his head. 'She didn't say a word to me.'

'It looks like she left in a hurry.'

Lewis stood back, unsure of what to do. He looked down at the doormat on the landing. The corner of an envelope was sticking out from beneath it. He bent down and took it out. The envelope was addressed to him. Lewis tore it open and pulled out the letter folded inside.

Dear Lewis,

I hope this reaches you safely. I wanted to thank you for everything you've done for me. Maria would have been proud to have you fighting on her behalf over these past days.

Drew and I have decided to move on. I can't tell you where we're going. We don't really know ourselves at the moment. After everything that's happened, it's not safe to stay in London any more.

My son came home last night and told me a story about an incident that took place a long time ago. I often think that the past should be left alone, but in this case I think it's only fair that I share the story with you. I hope you can find some peace once you read it . . .

77

ANGELA MILLER LISTENED in rapt silence, standing at her kitchen counter as Lewis read the letter to her. As the story unfolded, her face alternated between grief and horror, her eyes glistening with tears. Rachael waited outside in the car, not wanting to intrude on a private moment. Lewis's voice faltered as he reached the end of the final page.

> *. . . I know that nothing will ever take away the pain of losing your mother, but I want you to know that justice has been served on the man responsible for her death. I hope that alone can give you a little comfort.*
>
> > *Take care of yourself,*
> > *Irina Koval*

Lewis put the letter down on the table. Silence hung in the room. The clock ticked loudly on the kitchen wall. A tear trickled down Angela's cheek. Lewis stood and wiped his sister's face gently. Their adult lives had been forged on the night described in Irina's letter. The death of their mother. The breakdown of their father. It had been a crime that had remained unpunished for nearly two decades. Now they knew that Frank Egan was responsible. He was the man who had destroyed their family in a single moment.

'We need to go to the police,' Lewis said. 'If what Irina has told us is true, then Frank Egan has to be held accountable.'

'What do you think she meant about "justice being served"?'

'I don't know.'

'All these years he's been walking the same streets as us,' Angela said bitterly. 'Living his life as if nothing had happened.'

Lewis was resentful at the thought. 'If I'd known he was so close to us, I would have murdered him myself.'

'What would that have solved?'

'At least I wouldn't have spent years blaming myself.'

'None of it was your fault, Lewis. Sometimes bad things happen to good people. There's nothing anyone can do to change that.'

'I can't live that way, Angie,' Lewis said. 'I have to try to make the world a better place, even if I never succeed.'

Angela lifted the blind over the kitchen window.

'Why don't you ask your girlfriend to come in?' she said. 'It's too cold to wait out there in the car. Anyway, I'd like to meet her finally.'

'Rachael thought we should be alone. She wanted to give us some space while I read you the letter.'

Angela shrugged. 'Well, it's done now. No amount of letters can alter the past. Ask her in. I'll put the kettle on.'

343

Lewis went to the front door and opened it. He waved at Rachael and she waved tentatively back. She was in the driver's seat, listening to the radio.

'Come in!' he shouted. 'Angela wants to meet you.'

Rachael opened the car door and got out. Her face was pale as she entered the kitchen. She tried to smile but her distress was plain to see.

'What's wrong?' Lewis asked.

Rachael looked at him with concern. 'I . . . I just heard a news report on the radio,' she said.

'What's happened?'

Rachael shifted uneasily on her feet. She glanced at Angela.

'Frank Egan was shot and killed by his nephew last night.'

78

THE SOUND OF rumbling engines filled the air. Wheels turning and gears grinding. The land was quaking underfoot, the bedrock shaking. In a slow-moving column, the heavy trucks were leaving Coldharbour Marshes.

Robert Carlson watched from the back seat of the Mercedes as the vehicles filed past on the gravel track, heading for the highway back into London. On the perimeter, workmen were pulling the fencing down, tossing away the signs bearing the Egan Construction logo.

There was a knock on the misted window. Carlson pressed the button to lower the glass. A face loomed in, cheeks flushed with cold. It was the American who had attended the sales conference, asking endless awkward questions about his plans for the hydrogen facility. The American was different now. He'd dropped the arrogant persona he used as a professional disguise. Resumed the earnest, forthright manner Carlson had first known when they were climate activists together, so many years before.

Carlson opened the door. 'Get in. You'll freeze out there.'

The American slid in beside him. He blew on his hands to warm them up. Tucked under his arm was a copy of that morning's *Metro*. He tossed it on to Carlson's lap.

Egan Construction Boss Slain by Nephew

Carlson read the headline and handed the newspaper back. He remembered how Drew Brennan had left his house with a loaded gun the previous night. He was sure that fact was connected with the headline, but it wasn't necessary for him to intervene, he thought. Whoever had shot Frank Egan had done the world a favour.

'Everything went as you predicted, Robert,' the American said. 'Apart from a few minor hiccups, you called this one right from the start.'

Carlson shook his head ruefully. 'Good people have died. I feel far from triumphant.'

'You played the long game. Took risks. Nothing runs smoothly when you gamble like that. There's always going to be a few hitches. I have to admit, when you first targeted the Zhirkovs, I thought you were crazy, but you outsmarted them all the way.'

The American was buoyed with a sense of victory. Carlson shot him a steely look to disavow him of any such notion.

'I don't regard decent people losing their lives as hitches,' he said starkly.

Maybe he was growing soft, Carlson thought to himself. His natural ruthlessness was diminishing with age. This was probably the last time he would be able to pull off such an audacious plan. The last few weeks had been an ordeal. Pretending his business was weak to attract beady-eyed vultures like the Zhirkovs. Enticing them to invest in the Coldharbour Marshes deal by convincing them that his company was going under. Making them believe they could hijack his hydrogen plans with their own ambitions to build a gas-burning power station. Acting as if he was blind to Olivia Ward's double-dealing. Carlson had always known that Andrei Zhirkov's youthful arrogance would bring him down in the end. That the labyrinthine structure of the deal would leave his father unable to retrieve the funds Ward had illegally transferred. With the injection of the Zhirkov money, Carlson now had all the funding he needed to make his hydrogen dreams a reality.

It had taken supreme effort to maintain the illusion that his business was bankrupt. Carlson had played his part like an actor inhabiting a role. Like bait on a hook, he had thrashed and writhed, attracting the bigger, greedier fish to the line. Making them take the fatal bite they were powerless to resist. But it wasn't a ploy he had enjoyed. If he had seemed devious to outside observers like Lewis Miller, it was for a higher cause, he told himself. His one true regret was that Maria hadn't trusted him. If only she could have had more faith, he thought. So much heartache could have been avoided.

He had tortured himself night after sleepless night over her fate. Why couldn't Maria have followed his instructions? If she had, she would still be alive now and he could finally reveal his ruse to her. They would be able to enjoy the moment together, safe in the knowledge that the marshes would remain untouched. It was a loss he knew he was going to regret for a long time. He was infinitely weaker without Maria at his side.

It had been a knee-jerk reaction to fire her that night at the Carlingford. The combination of her discovery of the Cold-harbour Marshes project and her accusation against Emilia had provoked him into making a rash decision. But Carlson had seen it as a temporary measure. Once he had wrapped up the scam he was playing on the Zhirkovs, he had intended to explain himself and then Maria would come back to work for him. He had made sure that Maria was off limits to any competitors who might be eager to employ her. What Carlson hadn't factored into his plan was her dogged persistence. Maria simply wouldn't let go of her legal action against him, no matter how hard he tried to persuade her. She had refused to listen to his warnings of the danger she was creating. Once Maria had perceived him as an enemy, she had mistrusted his motives entirely. Still, Carlson berated himself. He should have found a way to save her. He'd let Maria down and her death would linger long on his conscience.

The American pointed at the vehicles noisily departing the nature reserve, the workmen waving them through the exit in an orderly procession. 'Do you think they ever knew this was a scam?' he asked.

Carlson shook his head. 'I doubt it. It's troubling how many people are willing to destroy a place of such beauty.'

'What's going to happen to these workers now?'

'I'm sending the construction crews to a more suitable location. A brown-field site north of London. Now that Frank Egan is gone, with the Zhirkov money I can buy out his business and put these resources to good use for a change.'

'You won't be forced by the authorities to pay the Zhirkov funds back?'

Carlson shrugged. 'It's untraceable. Olivia was a magician at hiding money. She covered her tracks completely, just as Viktor Zhirkov ordered. He never thought his chicanery would work against him. Now that she's made a deal with the police to help convict his son of murder, she won't admit to any illegal financing. That would only make matters worse for her.'

'You're not worried about Viktor coming after you?'

'I doubt he'll survive long once his partners in Moscow discover how much money he's lost.'

'So your hydrogen plans can still go ahead?'

'Of course. The country needs clean energy. It's our sacred duty to provide it, even if we have to plot and scheme our way to a greener future. We can't afford to fail. The stakes are too high. It's a truth so simple that anyone can see it. The ends justify the means, no matter how twisted.'

The American raised an imaginary glass. 'You've won, Robert,' he said. 'To the victor the spoils.'

Carlson gave a wistful smile. 'All I did was see a few moves further ahead than most, that's all,' he said.

'And now the game is yours.'

'It appears that way.'

'Here's to better times.'

Carlson looked out at the wide expanse of marshland. The empty wilds, shimmering in the winter sunlight. 'I prefer desperate times,' he said sagely.

'Why?' the American asked.

Carlson looked at him as if the answer should be obvious. 'Desperate times are moments of great opportunity,' he said.

79

One week later

THE TAXI DROPPED Lewis off on the corner of Cable Street. He paid the fare and stood for a while, taking in his surroundings. The streets were strewn with litter, the air heavy with smog. He could taste the grime in the neighbourhood as he breathed. It was familiar and comforting in a strange kind of way. Standing there, absorbing the spirit of the place, he felt like he was coming home.

It had been a relief not to travel into the City every morning for the past week. Not to arrive at the offices of Renfrew and Hall and force a smile on to his face for the benefit of the high-handed lawyers he worked with. It felt good to be free of them at last. Lewis realized now how much of a disguise he had adopted to survive the ordeal of each working day. To leave that life behind was reward enough for solving Maria Brennan's murder.

That was why he had turned down the offer of a job from

Robert Carlson. After everything that had happened, he felt it best to put the matter behind him. Close the book and move on. Lewis had wondered whether to report what he had discovered about Robert Carlson's business dealings – the dodgy Russian finance that Lewis doubted Carlson would be in any hurry to pay back. But ultimately he had decided against it. Carlson had seemed genuinely distraught at Maria's death. The rest of his dealings were none of Lewis's concern.

He walked up to the entrance and looked at the faded sign. *The Whitechapel Law Centre*. Gazing at his reflection in the window, Lewis checked that his hair was combed, his collar straight. Happy with his appearance, he opened the door and walked into the lobby.

The receptionist recognized him as he entered. She gave him a cool, distant look. 'You're the lawyer from Renfrew and Hall,' she said. 'You were working on the Brennan case.'

Lewis shook his head. 'Not any more. I've left that firm.'

'Then what can I help you with?'

'I'm here for an interview,' he said. 'I'm hoping to take over from Martin Sobel.'

The receptionist's attitude softened. She looked at the screen of her computer to check the interview schedule. Satisfied, she stepped out from behind the desk and led him through the maze of worn corridors to the back of the office. Lawyers' voices rang out from behind closed doors. Heated arguments were underway, legal points being forcefully made, people's lives hanging in the balance. The atmosphere in the office was urgent and efficient. This was where real people came to solve real problems, Lewis thought. He felt instantly as if he fitted in. *We are what we repeatedly do*, he told himself. This, he knew, was what he wanted to do. To spend his working life helping others. To find justice for people in need.

Walking into the interview room, Lewis felt a heavy burden leave him. A smile broadened his face. He knew this was the place for him.

Epilogue

OUT ON THE flat expanse of Coldharbour Marshes, the rain fell steadily. A north wind rippled over the reed beds as the light faded at the end of another day. Tall blades of marsh sedge rustled as banks of massed clouds drifted darkly over-head, their cold shadows passing over the land like unmoored ships broken free from their anchors. Spectral formations of gulls whirled in the evening sky, stark against the pale sun sinking beneath the grey horizon.

In the sodden earth of the lane, the tyre tracks were steadily being washed away, shower by shower, squall by squall. An abandoned bouquet withered slowly in a lonely hedgerow. All human traces seemed to fade from the land as the Thames flowed east, perpetual and dependable, carrying the last rem-nants of their presence out towards the sea.

Acknowledgements

Thanks to Jonathan Caplan, Jane Lord, Nicki Phillips and Tony Phillips for their invaluable insight and feedback. To my agent, Jane Finigan, and all at Lutyens & Rubinstein. Special thanks to Tash Barsby, Imogen Nelson, Finn Cotton, Kate Samano, Monica Byles and all at Transworld.

All my love to my wife, Isabel, whose trust and support made the writing of this novel possible.

James Buckler lives in London. He has worked in film and TV for many years, most notably for MTV and BBC Films. His first thriller, *Last Stop Tokyo*, was published to critical acclaim in 2017. *The Simple Truth* is his second novel.